Whisper

of Darkness

Banshee's Curse Book I

Kristen Braddock

Front Cover Design by Justin Heinen

Full Cover Wrap Design by Mibl Art

Book Interior by Kristen Braddock and Maven Books Co.

ISBN: 978-1-7371027-0-0

For those who continue to fight their darkness.
You are not alone.

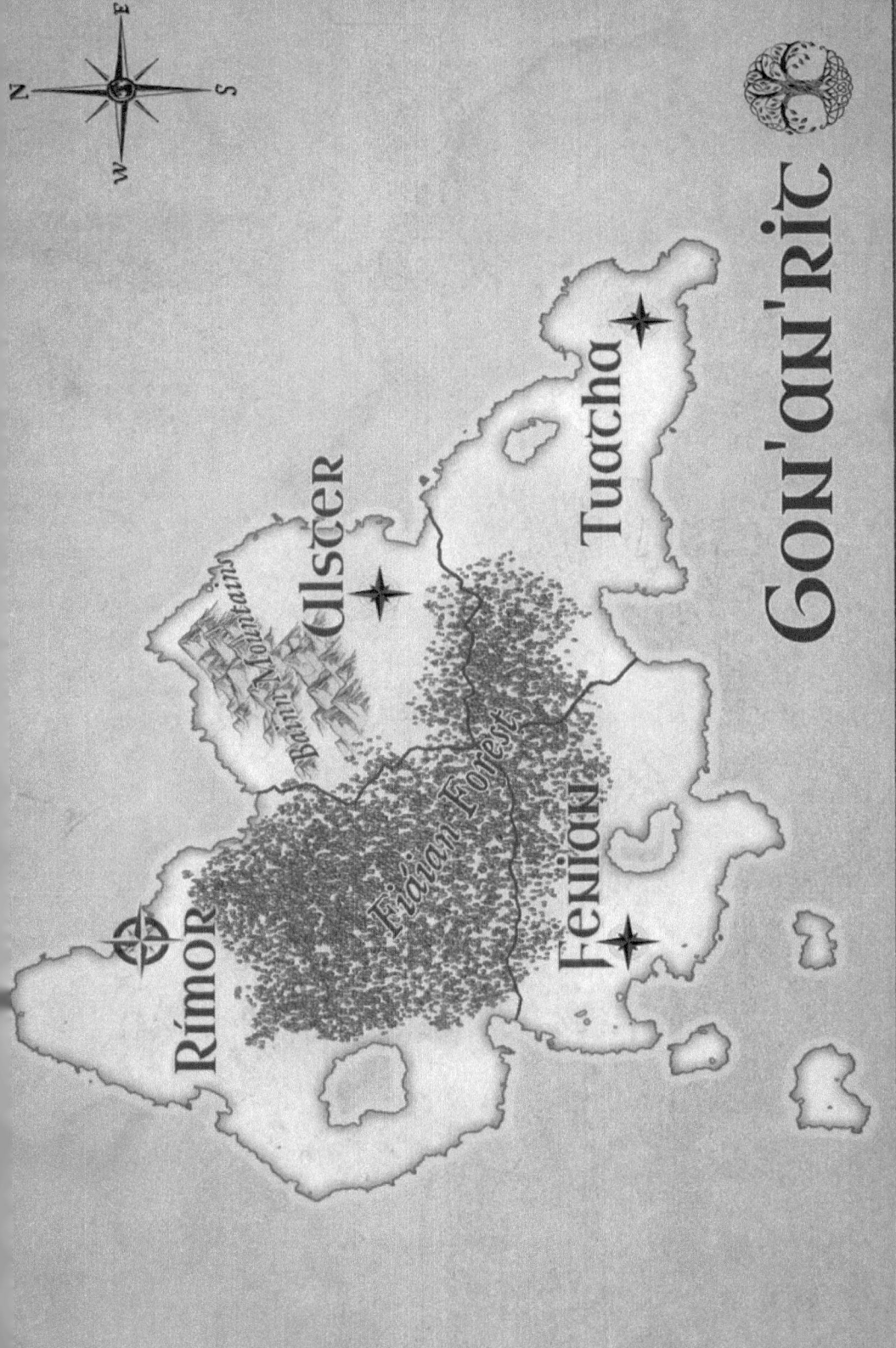

ONE

"You're a lifesaver." I praise my sister as I curl my hand around the mug she hands me, inhaling the earthy aroma of coffee.

"I don't know how you drink it like that, Cara." Shauna grimaces as I pour my fourth container of half and half into the mug.

No sugar, all cream, and one hundred percent bliss.

"I don't know how you expect me to function when you wake me up at six in the morning to work out... without coffee," I grumble before taking a sip of the liquid gold.

She rolls her piercing green eyes, a shade lighter than my own, and a match to our mother's. "You mean the *workout* that lasted five minutes because you were too busy whining about how hard it was? Or do you mean the *workout* of walking to your favorite coffee place after you gave up?"

I glare at her as she air quotes "workout."

"You wanted me to run... two miles! Run! Do you think I changed into another person overnight?" I huff as I settle into the velvet armchair in the back corner of the quaint coffee shop.

Comfortable reading chairs fill the room. Books line the walls, and the bottom half of the tables have shelves to hold more options. Plants glow in the windowsills and hang from the ceiling, morphing the area into an inside garden. The morning light drifts through the large windows, casting leafy shadows across my blue leggings.

"Woah, woah, woah. I gave you options." She takes a sip of her caramel frappuccino, and I gag at the sugar content.

"You said I could either go out tonight with you or do a workout. I don't know if those were fair options." I pout when I bring my cup to my lips only to find it empty.

Shauna rubs her right temple as she leans back into her seat. "You were the one complaining how frail you are and how you have no life. I was trying to help."

"Can't a girl complain anymore without someone trying to solve her problems?" My eye snags on a waitress as she walks through the cafe with a coffeepot in hand.

Spotting my pleading look, the goddess that she is waltzes over to top me off.

"Keep it coming, but room for extra cream, please," I smile at her.

"Need anything else?" She asks my sister as she fills my cup to the brim.

I hold my breath as I take a couple gulps of the bitter substance, ignoring the scorch on the roof of my mouth. Three more creamers later, the coffee is back to the rim of the cup.

"Is there anything you suggest?" Shauna runs her hands through her pixie cut brown hair with a smirk.

"We have fresh chocolate croissants. I made them myself," the waitress smiles as she places the pot down on the small table between us, transfixed by my sister.

"Oh, sounds delicious. I'd love one of your treats to go," Shauna winks.

The server blushes before nodding and turning away, forgetting her coffee pot.

"Keep it in your pants," I say. I top off my cup again with coffee and another container of half and half.

"Don't hate the game." She leans back with a smug look.

"Whatever." I stew at my sister's confidence because when I manage to speak to someone remotely attractive my words twist into gibberish.

"Since you didn't complete the workout, I guess that means you are coming out with me tonight." A devilish grin forms across her face, causing my stomach to instantly drop.

I cough as I choke on my coffee. "What? No! That's not fair."

"It's one hundred percent fair, Cara. You had a choice, and you didn't complete the workout, so going out it is."

"Shaun," I revert to her nickname, "I'm twenty." Heaven forbid I am at a bar past ten at night, but I can give my life to serve my country. Welcome to the United States.

"So?" She casually inspects her nails.

"Are we going to an eighteen and over club?" I raise an eyebrow.

My sister looks at me in abject horror. "Absolutely not! Talk about predators galore. I'd rather sleep with a man than go to an eighteen and over club."

I snort, "I guess I'm off the hook."

"Don't you worry about that. What time are your classes over today?" Her attention drifts over my shoulder as she talks to me. No doubt appreciating our server again. The corner of her lip quirks up. Hypothesis confirmed.

"My Intro to Animal Physiology ends at six p.m." I'm in my third year of a local state university thanks to Shauna's willingness to support me while I attend school full time.

My sister shakes her head, "I still don't understand why you chose to take a Saturday class."

"It's the best local college for veterinary medicine, of course they have these kinds of classes. Plus, Saturday classes help open up time during the week for work-study programs."

"Have I told you recently how proud I am of you?" She smiles.

I wave her off. I haven't found the courage to tell her about my C on my most recent exam. "I'm barely hanging on with the scholarships as it is. I have no idea how I'll pay for graduate school," I grumble.

"That's what student loans are for!" She sticks her tongue out at me.

I turn my head, biting my inside cheek. I love animals, and after our parents died when I was eight, I dived into academics.

My sister is six years older and fought to keep us together while we bounced between foster homes, but once she turned eighteen, she adopted me. With all the inconsistencies and moving, let's just say that school became the stability I desperately needed in life. I hadn't been planning on going to university due to finances. I saw how hard my sister worked to raise me, and I wanted to get a job immediately out of high school to help out, but she wouldn't let me. Since she was busy raising me, she never got the chance to go to college due to raising me, so her guilt trips easily swayed me. She claimed with my grades compared to hers, I was the better choice for higher education.

Today is the first day in months she's only working one of her three jobs. She is an assistant during the day, bartender at night, and drives for a ride share company in her spare moments. She has been the one constant in my life, and I hope to return the favor one day.

"Speaking of," she drawls before slamming an envelope onto the table. "When were you going to tell me about this?" Her hand peels away to reveal a letter addressed to me, the top ripped open like it's been through a lawn mower accident.

"You know it's illegal to open other people's mail." I glare at her. I drag the contents out of the white sleeve, and my eyes widen at the words written on the page.

Dear Cara Winters,

Congratulations, you have been accepted to the Atlanta Veterinary Internship Program.

I read the first line five times until the words sink in.

"I didn't think I'd get in," I whisper. This is one of the most prestigious internships in the area. They receive thousands upon thousands of applicants every year and only accept five.

"I'm so proud of you!" Shauna bounces in her seat like a kid on Christmas. "But still a little vexed you didn't tell me you applied."

"Vexed? Have you been binging British TV shows again?"

"What? Have you heard their accents?" She fans her face. "One day I'm going to find myself a sexy woman from the UK."

I continue to stare at the paper as my sister prattles on about her obsessions with the Brits. I can't believe I actually got in. This is almost a guarantee I will get into a graduate program; no one who has done this internship has been denied.

"Yup, definitely going out tonight to celebrate. Will your boyfriend be joining us?" Shauna waggles her eyebrows, eliciting an eye roll from me.

"How many times do I have to tell you Marcus is not my boyfriend?"

"Why aren't you two official yet? You've been dating for, like, six months! And he's a total cutie."

I shrug. "You know how it is with college boys." Shauna raises an eyebrow, and I chuckle. "Okay, well maybe *you* don't. But it's casual, nothing serious."

"Just keep it to when I'm working so I don't have to hear you're 'casual' through the walls."

"Whatever." I shake my head. "You of all people shouldn't act so innocent."

"What do you mean? I'm pure innocence." She bats her eyes and holds her hands above her head in a circle to symbolize a halo.

"I think your horns are making it a little crooked," I retort.

"Damn, I really need to do something about those things." A wide smile breaks out, and we both fall apart laughing. "Okay, well, I'm off. Since our workout ended early, I'm hoping to do a couple rides before my shift starts at the office. Be home by six-thirty to get ready. Feel free to invite your man." Shauna packs her things and throws a twenty on the table as the waitress walks over.

Okay, apparently she will be working one of her other jobs.

"Leaving already?" The server hands a white paper bag to my sister. "Here's your croissant."

"Thanks." She grabs it with a sly smile. "I'm sure I'll be back."

Again, my eyes roll. Of course she'll be back, I drag her here every other Saturday.

"Well, I guess I'll see you soon," the waitress hesitates, searching for something more to say, but a customer waves for her attention across the restaurant. "Have a wonderful rest of your day," she says.

As she walks away, my sister unabashedly checks her out.

"Excuse you!" I gape. "What if she doesn't swing that way?"

My sister grins as she tilts the side of the bag towards me. Written in black sharpie is the name Rose with a phone number underneath.

With a shake of my head, I stand and give her a hug. "See you tonight. Although six-thirty seems awfully early to get ready."

"We've got to eat and pregame, girl!" Pulling away, Shauna chuckles at my stricken face before turning to saunter out the door.

"Stupid bus," I mutter to myself. "How can anyone plan their day if buses range anywhere from being ten minutes early to twenty minutes late?"

Even though I wasn't talking to him, Marcus still decides to answer. "Walking not only reduces our carbon footprint, but will increase our cardio and pulmonary fitness, reduce the risk of heart disease, improve management of hypertension, and improve balance."

"I don't have hypertension I need to manage," I say.

He laughs. "And thank goodness for that. Taking the bus will help keep it that way."

I glance sideways at Marcus. He walks casually beside me, a satchel slung over his shoulders containing all of his pre-med texts and hands shoved in his pockets. His short chestnut hair catches the sun, while his pale skin is covered in jeans and a jacket. He is the epitome of health, which makes sense with his determination to become a doctor. When he's not studying for his classes, he's often working out or making meals with fresh produce. He's a good looking guy, and I have no doubt I'm not the only girl he makes breakfast for in the morning. But he does a good job of not making it obvious. Not that I care, we never made what we have official.

I mull over the conversation with my sister this morning. He is a nice guy, can cook, determined, and not terrible in bed. Maybe I should try to make him my boyfriend. "Hey, Marcus?"

"What's up?" He peers down at me, a smile of perfect teeth crossing his face.

Losing my moxie, I change my question last minute. "Do you want to come out with Shauna and me tonight?"

"Oh." He massages the back of his neck while giving me an apologetic smile. "I have plans."

"Oh, yeah, no worries. It's no big deal."

"Maybe next week?"

"Yeah, sure. Sounds good."

Marcus whistles a random tune to fill the silence.

A brown leaf crunches under my foot, causing a shallow smile to creep onto my face. Despite our crisp pace, I veer under the maple trees whose autumn leaves litter the ground. I tuck my hands into my grey sweater as the leaves continue to crackle beneath my shoes.

My feet slow when I notice a jet black dog beside a tree ahead of me. No other person is nearby to claim him. Despite being an avid lover of all animals, I have always been most fond of dogs.

A sharp breeze blows, causing my dark hair to drift into my face, carrying with it the scent of autumn, chimney smoke, and sandalwood.

The dog lifts his head and sniffs the air, turning his head to stare directly at me. My mouth drops as his amber eyes seem to darken.

"Hey bud." I reach my hand tentatively towards it. "Where's your owner?" I ask as I eye his collarless neck. His thick fur shimmers in the afternoon light, and his body is lithe with muscles without showing any bones. I doubt he is a stray.

"I don't think you should do that," Marcus says from behind me.

I ignore him, and continue to coo at the dog.

He inches towards me with his head down and ears back. I know that a barking dog with perked ears may seem more aggressive, but a timid dog is more likely to attack.

I gulp as I crouch, nerves knotting my stomach.

Shauna and I got evicted from multiple homes due to my need to rescue strays I found in the streets. At times, it seemed like they found me. Never has an animal not warmed in my presence and learned to trust me. I ignore my rolling stomach.

He is large for a dog, bigger than a German Shepherd, but smaller than a Bernese Mountain Dog. His specific breed is unknown to me.

At two feet away, he stiffens, looking over my shoulder at Marcus. He drops lower to the ground, a small snarl rippling from the side of his mouth.

I pause with my hand hovering in front of me.

His eyes narrow, and he bolts to the left. Straight into the street.

I gasp, standing to chase after him, as a pit forms in my stomach at all the cars. Before I take a step, a screeching sound fills my head. My hands grasp my temples, fingers digging into my scalp, as the sound grows. Through blurry vision, I watch the dog race between cars as the drivers slam on their breaks. My knees strike the concrete sidewalk as a crash echoes in the background.

Not again. Not again. Not again. Tears burn my eyes as pain ricochets through my skull. It has been two years since my last episode. Two years since I heard this sound, since my curse has reared its ugly head. Breathing shakily, I will myself not to lose my breakfast in public.

Within minutes, I hear sirens, but I have yet to uncurl from the ground. A thudding in my brain replaces the high-pitched scream. The stench of burnt tires assaults my nose. I look up, unveiling the commotion.

A three car pile-up blocks the road. Smoke rises from the car in the back, a fender bender for the truck in the front. But the sedan in the middle, if you could even call it one, now resembles an accordion. Nothing more than a twisted piece of metal with the windows blown out. The car is angled so I can't see anything, but there is no way the passenger, or passengers, could've survived.

"Are you okay?" Marcus's large hand holds my shoulder while he helps me into a sitting position.

I nod, unable to form words.

Marcus's focus jumps between me and the crash. The worry in his eyes makes it apparent he's unsure which to choose.

"Go," I croak.

His forehead crinkles. "Are you sure?"

"Yes, go help them."

He doesn't hesitate to walk away, already directing people to call 911 and explaining he's an emergency responder.

Heaving to my feet, I turn away from the commotion and my college campus. While I walk away, my teeth grind together to stifle the pain from my throbbing head.

TWO

Shauna barges into my room. "What're you doing in bed?"

I wince at the sound. My sister has always been a bull in a china shop, but the dull pound in my head makes it worse.

She pauses when she sees my face. "Are you okay? Are you sick?" Sitting on the side of my bed, she rubs my shoulder as she stares at me with worried eyes.

"It happened again," I mumble.

"What happened again? Did you get food poisoning? I told you all the coffee you consume was bound to hurt your stomach."

"No. It happened again." I frown as her eyes grow big in realization.

"What? But the doctor said you'd grow out of it. It's been years." Shauna brings her fingers to her mouth, chewing on her thumbnail. A bad habit she hasn't done in years.

"You mean I'd grow out of the thing the doctors couldn't diagnose?" Tears spring to my eyes. "I'm cursed," I whimper, throwing my arm over my eyes to hide my pain.

"Cara Maeve Winters, you are not cursed."

"But… it happened again." I say into the crook of my arm, muffling my words.

Shauna pulls at my wrist until my arm slides across to free my face. "Oh hush, you're overreacting. Does your head still hurt?"

My lip juts out. "Not as much. I took migraine pills and fell asleep. I woke an hour ago, and the pain is better."

"Then what're you still doing in bed?" She folds her arms across her chest. Her determination and goal-oriented self would've been a much better choice to pursue a college degree.

"What?" I shoot her a wide-eyed stare. Why was my sister being so cruel? Granted, she's never fully believed in my curse, but it's unlike her to be this cold.

"We're going out tonight. I already told you this." She stands and quirks an eyebrow at me as though she's waiting for me to bound out of bed after her.

"I'm not in the mood." I deflate further into my bed. If only I can sink in far enough I'll never have to leave it again. I can stay where it's safe, away from the world.

"Stop being a drama queen." Shauna's green eyes flash in determination.

"Shaun… someone died. Again," I utter. I thought I was finally free of this, but death was determined to follow me everywhere.

Her arms drop, her mouth opening a hair, before shaking her head to refocus. "Nope. It's a coincidence. Get up." She reaches forward and grabs my arm to drag me.

My brows furrow. "Coincidence?" I pry myself from her grasp. "Seriously, Shauna, this isn't a joke."

She's being unapologetically harsh. My sister has had to toe the line between friend, sister, and parent throughout our lives, and morphing between the roles can muddy our relationship at times. She will always be my favorite person in the world, but now was not the time to take an annoying, big-sister approach.

This isn't a coincidence. It wasn't in the past, and it isn't now. It's a curse. One which caused me to stop socializing and become distant from everyone until my only companions left were animals and my sister.

Her face drops, and her body crumples onto the mattress until she wraps me in her arms. "I'm sorry, okay? I'm surprised. It's been so long since this has happened. I forgot how to act." She pulls away. "But you should not let this define your life. It already has, and just last night you were complaining about needing a life. Don't let this control you. You are in charge of your life."

I am in charge of my own life.

Unease coils through my stomach. This doesn't feel true, and yet, a sliver of hope glistens in the back of my mind, making me want to believe it.

With a nod, I swing my legs over the side and leave the comfort of my warm bed. The cool floor against my bare feet refreshes me.

Shauna beams at me. "Okay, first, food. I brought home tacos. As your sister, I'll teach you to drink responsibly, and you should never drink on an empty stomach." She nods as though agreeing with herself.

"Aye-aye, captain." I salute her, putting on a fake persona which we both ignore as light laughter falls from us.

Fake it until you make it, right? I can do this. I can be like any young adult, go out and have fun without fearing the world. I have to do this.

"Come on. Let's hop to it!"

⚓

"Hold still for one more second," Shauna says as she prods at my eyelid with a brush.

"I told you to go with a natural look. This doesn't feel like it's natural," I whine.

"Just drink."

I stare at the fruity concoction Shauna made me, something she begrudgingly did after mocking me for gagging when I took a sip of a vodka shot. The drink is dangerously delicious, and I'm already halfway done with a small buzz. I need to eat another taco before leaving the house.

My eyes snag on the dark green bustier my sister wrangled me into earlier. The tight black pants and heeled boots were easier to convince me of, but the top hinges on lingerie and the nerves slosh the liquid in my stomach.

"Why'd you make me wear this top?" I groan, bringing the straw of my drink to my lips. The liquid courage should be kicking in soon.

"Because it brings out your eyes," she mumbles over the tip of the blush brush sticking between her teeth.

"My poop green eyes? Great…"

Shauna steps back and glares at me, ripping the brush from her mouth. "They're marsh green, not poop green. Stop being self-deprecating, and own what the world gave you."

"I wish it'd given me your eyes," I grumble to myself.

My sister ignores my comment and leans down with an eyebrow pencil in hand. After a few seconds, she snaps back up. "Okay, all done!"

I rise from our dining room chair and waltz into my bedroom, where a full-length mirror hangs beside the door. With the smokey eyeshadow, light wings of eyeliner, and mascara, my eyes pop. The brown tints I hate about my green eyes are lighter. My jet black hair, which is flat as a board, hangs loosely to my belly button. No hair product or technology could bring volume to my straight hair, but at least it's got length. Despite cutting my hair to right below my shoulder each year, it reaches the top of my butt within months.

I don't recognize the petite body before me. The outfit gives the illusion of curves I don't have. For once I don't completely look like a twelve-year-old before puberty.

I spent most of my life underweight and sick. The smallest kid in every class. I was tested for anemia and various diseases multiple times, but everything would come back negative. Only in the last two years I have put on weight, thank you nutrition drinks meant for children, and eliminated my sickly look. However, I still desire to put on more muscle to turn my slight frame into something leaner, thus my failed attempt at exercise this morning.

"You outdid yourself, Shaun," I beam.

"You like it?" She squeals as she pops her head into my room. Her eyes sparkle as she takes in my full wardrobe. "You're a bombshell."

"Bombshell?" I chuckle. "I don't think people say that anymore." I shake my head, my hair falling across my face to cover the smirk on my lips.

"Doesn't matter what people say, it's still true."

I follow Shauna towards the front door of our shared apartment and reach for a taco sitting on the kitchen counter.

She slaps my hand away. "No way! You'll ruin my makeup." She ignores my pout and pulls me with one hand while using her other to order a ride share. "Don't drink and drive kids." She winks at me over her shoulder.

I roll my eyes. "This was your idea."

"I know, and I told you I would teach you how to have fun safely. That's rule number one." She closes the front door, and we cross the short, drabby hallway to the stairs.

"Shouldn't 'you must be of legal drinking age' be rule number one?"

"Don't be such a Debbie Downer. You drink the least out of anyone your age. You had one drink and I see you wobbling."

I glare at the back of her head before looking at my white-knuckled grip on the handrail as we climb down from the third story. I sway a little from the mixture of the heels, alcohol, and tiny steps. I bristle over the fact my sister took notice before I did. Damn, alcohol. "Well, you made the single drink strong. It was more like three drinks in one."

"I, also, made it delicious." A wolfish grin spreads across her face as she turns at the landing to the last flight of stairs. "I guess it's a good thing you ate." At the bottom, she waltzes to the front door, which has zero security, and throws the glass door open.

I scurry after her, ignoring the flip-flop of my gut as I step outside our building into the real world. I'm more of a jeans and t-shirt from secondhand shops kind of girl. This legitimately might be the fanciest I've ever looked in public. The exposure of the top half of my body doesn't help either.

Shauna strides over to a hybrid car waiting for us at the curb.

I follow with my eyes trained on the ground, ignoring the curious glances of strangers as they walk by. I pretend I'm in my normal clothes. Nothing weird here, everyone. People have worn crazier outfits in public. Although, they are probably wondering if they should call the cops because I look like a thirteen year old. With the makeup and outfit, maybe I could get away with fifteen.

Ducking my head, I slip into the backseat beside Shauna.

"Thanks," I call to the driver before shutting the door.

Shauna walks straight to the bouncer, ignoring the line in the alley. Without any signs hanging, this is the only clue there is an entrance to a club.

I raise my eyebrow at her. This girl oozes confidence. I wonder if this is a trait passed onto her from our parents, but managed to skip me. Or, maybe, it was something she had to learn from growing up way too fast and way too young.

The bouncer gives my sister a nod before unlocking the barricade to let us through. He doesn't give me a second glance. Clasping the rope back in place, I hear his gruff voice ask for an ID from the next person in line.

Bass reverberates through my body as we step through the black door. The air is humid and smells of sweat and alcohol. Flashing lights draw our path down a short hallway until it opens to a large dance floor. A churning mass of bodies dances while laser lights pierce the space. The disjunction makes the smooth dancing choppy.

"I need a drink," Shauna shouts into my ear over the music.

I nod to her and mouth *I'll follow.* There is no way I am leaving her side.

My body shakes with adrenaline, and not the good kind. Is there a way butterflies can metamorphose into something bigger? Like bats? Because these are not gentle little bugs flapping around in my stomach and making me want to dissolve into a dark corner. How did Shauna convince me to do this again?

Shauna leans on the bar to give the male bartender her drink order. He flashes her a smile, giving her a once over with his eyes. She ignores his obvious interest. Poor guy doesn't realize he has no chance.

As I watch my sister evade the bartender's charm, a hand grips my waist and pulls me back. I freeze. Slowly, I turn my head to peer over my right shoulder.

A guy with dark blonde hair and five o'clock shadow gives me a lazy smile. His droopy eyes show his inebriation, which is confirmed when his whiskey breath fumes across my face.

"Hey, wanna dance?" He leans forward, using me to support his weight.

My ankle wobbles from the strain. I shake my head.

He ignores my unease and rejection, grinding against my backside to the beat of the music.

I blanche and my mind blanks. How do I get out of this situation?

"Watch it, buddy. She's with me."

THREE

My sister shoves the man away, causing his hand to slip off my waist. Shauna flings her arm over my shoulders as she puts a drink in my hand.

I fumble, grasping it with both hands, as the syrupy liquid spills on my knuckles.

"Drink up, darling. We gotta hit the dance floor soon." Shauna smirks.

The guy takes a step towards us but stops in his tracks when my sister whips her head towards him with a glare. "Beat it."

With a huff, the guy turns and stalks off into the crowd. As soon as he is out of sight, Shauna drops her arm. "Seems there are creeps no matter where you go."

I attempt to hand her drink back, but she shakes her head and grabs a second one off the bar. She raises it in a toast to me before knocking it back. The light pink liquid in my glass ripples from the bass of the song. I'm unsure what it was, but before I can second guess myself, I toss back the liquor. It burns down my throat and settles in my belly. My face screws tight at the sharp taste; I don't understand how people like this stuff.

Shauna snatches the empty glass from my hand, drops it on the edge of the bar, and turns towards the dance floor.

I hustle after her, like a baby duck following its mother, fearful another guy will bother me without her there.

We shove our way through the sweating bodies moving to the beat. Once in the center of the crowd, my sister turns and starts swaying her hips. I eye her warily, standing stock still amongst everyone.

Shauna tilts her head back and laughs, but I can't hear her. She grabs my hands and pulls them one at a time to help loosen me up. All I need to do is step on her feet and I'd seem like a five year old dancing with an adult.

I burst into a fit of giggles at how ridiculous we look.

A wide grin forms across her face as I start to move on my own. Releasing my hands once more, she throws her own above her head as the beat drops.

I lean my head back, swaying it from side to side. My hair swishes against my shoulder blades, and I close my eyes, allowing the music to encompass my senses. The bass beats through my body. Tingles course through me from the mixture of alcohol and music. I smile to myself from the feel.

The DJ transitions into the next song, and everyone cheers as they jump. Lyrics I don't know mix in, and everyone in the crowd sings along, including Shauna.

Her eyes hook onto the female performer on stage, and a smile tugs at her lips.

My eyes flutter shut as the beat continues to rock through me. This isn't my usual music, but in person I can see the appeal. I move in time with those around me— jumping, grinding, and swaying to the variations within the melodies.

Soon I hold my hair in a ponytail off my neck as sweat beads down my skin. I should have brought a hair tie. With my sister's short hair, it's not something she would've thought of and my hair feels like a shield against my barely-there top.

Both of us lose ourselves to our own worlds. This time no one bothers me, thankfully. From the heat on my back, multiple bodies have stepped close to me, but within seconds they move away. I assume Shauna is the reason for this. If looks could kill, she'd be an assassin.

The music switches to top hits, no longer having the same lull of electronic music being mixed live for us, but it still has the perfect beat to dance to.

"I'm going to go say hi to my friend," Shauna leans to shout to me. Her eyes catch on the DJ as she leaves the stage.

I give her a thumbs up in encouragement.

"I won't be far. I promise." Her face scrunches in worry.

I wave her off as I continue to dance. No one has tried to dance with me in a while. I'm certain everyone understands not to bother me by this point. Plus, the alcohol and music has loosened me enough to where, for once, my mind feels free.

With a nod, she walks into the crowd and disappears.

My body continues to move as though it has a mind of its own. Five songs later, despite my momentary confidence, my stomach squirms. Perhaps it's the alcohol, or the heat. There's a good chance it's dehydration.

The hairs on the back of my neck stand on end. I turn to see if someone is behind me.

People grinding against each other assault my eyes. No one is there, but I can't rid the feeling of someone watching me. The need for space and fresh air consumes my mind. I push my way through the crowd towards a side exit. I'll find Shauna after I take a breather.

Shoving open the door, crisp air hits my face, the droplets of sweat turning cool against my skin. An overhead light brightens half the alley, which is the opposite side of the building from the entrance. Here trash cans loiter around the space instead of people.

I lean against the brick wall and close my eyes, allowing a deep breath to calm my body. A slight buzz rings in the back of my mind. I'm unsure if it is leftover effects from earlier today, the booze, or the loud music. My lungs fill with the cool air, but it's cut short when a glass bottle skimming across the ground echoes in the depths of the alleyway.

My body stiffens.

I turn my head toward the sound and lean away from the wall to peer into the shadows. "Is anyone there?"

Silence greets me.

The hair on my arms stand on end as goosebumps sweep across my skin. I listen, holding my breath, but the only penetrating sound is my racing heart.

I think it's time I find Shauna.

A small whimper escapes the darkness.

I startle at the sound of an animal in pain. I take hesitant steps further into the alley, and reach into my back pocket to pull out my cell phone. I press a button on the screen and the flashlight feature helps guide me.

A discarded fast food bag, empty soda cans, piled cardboard boxes, and endless beer bottles litter the ground.

Another whine slips to my ears.

It's coming from behind a large trash bin to my right.

I tiptoe forward, avoiding the broken glass, and when I wind around the corner, I'm met with black fur curled in a ball.

A large head lifts, its pink tongue slipping back into its mouth from where it had been licking its back hind leg. Its muzzle sneers and it greets me with a growl.

It's the same dog from earlier today.

The wounded animal emits another grizzly sound, a warning sign I ignore as I push my phone forward to brighten the hind leg. A thick liquid matts the coat and based on the red paw prints I see on the ground, I assume it's blood.

"Hey, bud, I'm here to help." I take a tentative step, but halt when the dog rumbles. I lower myself toward the ground. "I promise I won't hurt you."

His eyes dart over my shoulder, and with a show of fangs, he snarls.

A hand lands on my shoulder, causing me to jolt. There's a moment where I wonder if it's my sister before the scent of a distillery wafts over me.

"Need help?" A gruff voice asks.

I huff in relief as I turn. "Actually, yes, this dog is hurt and—" I take in the man's face from the bar, the same one who had gotten a little too friendly.

He drops his hand as I stand to face him, but he doesn't step away.

A leering smirk fills his dark face. "I meant do *you* need help," he says as he takes a step closer.

The dog growls, causing the man to stop, but cuts off with a small whine.

My eyes flit over my shoulder to see the dog has attempted to stand.

The guy glares down at the dog. "Get out of here, mutt." He raises the beer bottle, and lobs it to the right of me. It smashes against the brick wall, causing shards of glass to rain down over the helpless animal.

"Back off!" I say as I shove him away.

The man scoffs. "You're going to protect some rabies-infected stray?" He throws his head back and cackles. Without any grace, he barrels forward, and my small stature isn't enough to stop him as he knocks me aside. He bends over the snarling dog. "Damn cock-blocking flea bag," he spits before standing and lodging his boot into the dog's side.

The dog yelps as it crashes against the wall, landing onto the broken glass.

Rage fills my mind, blocking all reason.

Who does this man think he is, hurting an innocent animal?

Before I can think twice, I am off the ground and leap onto the man's back. I grab his dark blonde hair, giving it a yank back until he howls in pain, stumbling backwards from my forceful pull. His heel catches, and the ground rushes towards me as we both fall backwards.

A sharp crack hits my elbow. The air escapes my lungs with a wheeze when the guy lands on top of me. I suck in gasps of air. My head rings. I wrap my legs around the man's waist and hold his hair firm in my grasp. I blink away the tears from my eyes.

To my left, the dog stands a couple of feet away. Its dark golden eyes are torn as they look between me, the man I hold in a death grip, and the opening to the alley. It takes another step towards me.

"Go! Get out of here!" I yell.

The dog hesitates.

"Go!" A shrill sound escapes my throat.

The dog jumps before tucking its tail and half limping, half running away. At the end of the alley, it looks back once before rounding the corner.

The man reaches up and pries my hand off.

A gasp escapes my lips from the pain in my fingers.

He drops my hand, and uses the freedom to push himself off the ground.

My legs lose their grip and I slip off his back, landing back on the ground with my black hair lying across my face and skewing my vision.

"If you want to lock those legs around me, baby, I have a much more fun way." The man grips my hair and pulls me to my feet.

I have no choice but to follow to help lessen the pain in my scalp. I bite back a cry.

He backs me up until my shoulders press against the chilled brick wall. He leans towards me, licking his lips with malicious intent in his eyes.

My heart pounds as my arms cross in front of me. I brace them against his chest to keep a few inches of distance between us.

He presses himself further against me and I grit my teeth as weakness tugs at my muscles.

Damnit, I really need to start working out.

The tugging on my hair intensifies. My head tilts back with a whimper.

His gaze locks onto mine. His blue eyes are predatory. He glances at my shaking arms trying to block him. Excitement flashes across his wretched features at my distress. His sour breath fumes over my face.

My stomach churns. I won't be able to hold on much longer. Tears sting the back of my eyes as my heartbeat quickens. A ringing sounds through my head. With no options, I take in a deep breath and scream at the top of my lungs.

The man drops me.

I slump onto the ground. My abdomen contracts while I continue to scream.

He covers his ears as he doubles over in pain. His face is red, and eyes squeeze shut.

Please let someone hear me.

The man lands on his knees.

By the time my air runs out, a third figure stands in the alley.

FOUR

Leather clings to his large, muscular frame. He turns my way. A hood covers a majority of his face with only a frown peeking from the bottom.

I stare wide-eyed at him.

The man from the bar pulls his hands from his ears and looks at his blood coated fingers. A trickle of blood dribbles from his ear to his chin.

The man in black faces my assailant. His right hand reaches over his shoulder, and metal rings through the air as he unsheathes a sword.

Who the hell casually carries a sword on their back? Is there a convention in town? I pale at the high-pitched wail in my head.

With sudden awareness, my attacker lifts his face to check his surroundings. Upon seeing the new addition to the alley, he jumps, fumbling onto his back before scuttling backwards like a crab.

Frozen in place, my fingers dig into my thighs as the man with the sword takes a swing towards him. I cover my mouth in horror as blood spills from the man's neck. His body goes limp and there's a small thud as his back hits the tarmac.

The ringing in my head stops.

Did... did he just kill him? Without warning or anything? Was I roofied in the club?

The hooded man wipes his blade along his black leather pants, swings the sword back into place, and turns to me. His head cocks sideways as he studies me.

With fewer shadows, I can see light stubble along his chiseled jawline. The hood connects to a leather vest which cuts off at his shoulders where bulging biceps escape. Swirling black symbols cover his upper right arm. In a flash, he looms above me, holding his hand out.

I swallow the tennis ball lodged in my throat, waiting for it to clear to scream for help. Again. Ignoring his hand, I push myself from the ground.

His head tilts, taking in my shaking legs, and a set of white teeth flash in a taunting smile. "You'd think you'd be better at this," his baritone voice rumbles.

I shiver at the behemoth before me. He is at least six and a half feet tall, so my neck cranes back to stare up at him from my five foot three height.

"I'll accept the usual," he says as he takes a step closer.

The scent of cloves stings my nose. "Huh?" Despite my stupor, I mentally berate myself for not being more articulate.

"A thank you should suffice." He crosses his dark, sepia-toned arms across his broad chest.

"Thank...you?" I whisper. I have no idea what I'm thanking him for, aside from the hours of therapy I will need from seeing someone murdered in front of me. My limbs refuse to respond while I gape at him in stunned silence.

Running, running and screaming is definitely what I should be doing right now.

A devilish smile crosses his face as he places an enormous hand on my shoulder. "We should get going, before someone comes."

"Wait, what?" I snap out of my shock and step away from under his weight. "I'm… I'm not going anywhere with you." My words fumble with my shaking voice. "You j-just killed someone!"

"Yes, you screamed," he states.

"For help," I gasp. Not for the man to be killed. The indifference in his tone has my head reeling. He murdered someone without a single thought simply because I screamed? There are a million other things to do before murder!

"And that's what I gave you," he sounds bored. "And now you owe me a life debt. I'll collect when we get back."

"Life debt? Collect when we get back?" I shake my head to try and clear it. I've gone from one crazy person to another. I need to get away from here. My eyes dart down the alley to the side door of the club. Maybe I can outrun him. There are stories of humans getting super strength in times of need. I need to at least try. I need to get to Shauna.

"I wouldn't if I were you," he warns. "I have no idea what you are doing here, but we will figure this out back home."

"I'm here with my sister," I explain. If he knows someone is looking for me, then perhaps it'll deter him. "And I'm not going to any home of yours." I stand straighter, trying to make myself larger than I am, which feels like a mockery in this moment.

With an annoyed huff, he reaches forward. "Enough of this." As his hand lands on my shoulder, the world melts away.

The walls drip with color, the light blending as though someone is smearing an oil-painted world. Vertigo clashes against my vision, dipping my stomach to the point of sickness. I shut my eyes tight, fighting the urge to vomit. Colors dance behind my eyes, until a faint red is seen through my eyelids. The rush of nausea wears off.

I need to get away from this man. The muscles in my legs tense. My fist clenches at my sides. I'll kick him hard in the groin and make a run for it.

I will have one shot. God, why didn't I work out?

I take a deep breath.

Three...two...one.

I open my eyes and swing my right leg.

In my mind, I hear my self-defense teacher's voice from when I was twelve years old. Swing through like your target is the head.

The man crumples beneath me, gripping himself. A groan escapes his lips.

I turn and sprint. Straight into a forest.

I stumble to a stop. Green trees surround me. Trees I can see because of daylight. The sky is overcast, but the sun is up, silhouetting birds that flit between the branches.

Male cursing joins the leaves rustling in the breeze. Over my shoulder, the man rises to his feet.

I need to get away. I need to get away. I'll figure out whatever fever dream this is after I get away from the sword-happy stranger.

I run on my tiptoes to prevent the heels on my boots from sinking into the rich soil. I jump over roots and zigzag through the trees. I hope my random running pattern will throw him off in a way my speed can't. Apparently, that only helps with bullets and not an angered male you've kicked in the balls.

My breath pitches from me as I'm tackled around the waist. I throw my arms in front of me to protect my face, which it does, but my arms slide along sticks, rocks, and roots which tear through my skin. I wince at the pain, but have no time to check my injuries before I am hauled around to face a burning gaze.

His hood has fallen off in the tussle. Smooth, brown skin shines with sweat as he pants through parted full lips. The nostrils of his strong nose flare in anger as his dark brown eyes bore into mine. Juxtaposing his skin, a crop of copper hair curls at the top of his head, and pointed ear tips brush the small ringlets. Strength mingling with beauty radiates off of him.

"It's rude to stare," he growls, his palms pressing my shoulder deeper into the damp ground.

I open my mouth to retort, but words escape me. My face heats from being caught.

"Out with it," he demands as he purses his lips.

"Is…" I falter. "Isn't red hair recessive?"

Seriously? I went from an alley in the middle of the night pressed to the ground of a forest during the day, and that's what I decided to ask? No wonder I got a C on my last exam with this level of idiocy coming from me. Also, I went with the hair? Not, you know, freaking pointy ears?!

"Asking about my heritage is not your place, *Beansidhe*." His grip tightens on my forearm.

"S-sorry," I stammer as my eyes fall to the left.

Please don't kill me, sword man. I'm unsure what a *Beansidhe* is, but there is no way I'm going to ask now.

"Red hair is dominant for my lineage," he mutters before hoisting us both to our feet. He still holds me under my arm, his fingers encircling my bicep.

I raise a quizzical eyebrow, but say nothing. I think through the different countries of the United Kingdom and don't think redheads are a dominant feature for any of them. However, my biology class in college focused more on proteins than genetics, so who am I to question someone's knowledge on their own identity?

"Let's go." He gives my arm a yank until I stumble after him as my heels catch on a root. I shove my feet into the ground to stop him, but my weak frame makes no impact on his brute strength. I pitch forward, slamming onto his back, which does cause him to stop.

He turns, mouth pinching in annoyance.

I cover my cower with a glare. "I'm not going anywhere with you." My voice comes out a squeak.

He drops my upper arm to throw his hands in the air. "You agreed to our terms! Why are you being so difficult?"

"I don't understand what's happening!" I burst. Exhaustion, fear, and confusion penetrate me like a stake in a vampire's heart. Instead of turning to dust, the frustration pricks tears in my eyes.

I don't know if I'm dreaming, dead, or if someone did something to my drink. I want to believe this isn't real, but the pain searing along my bleeding arms and the cool breeze across my face makes it hard to do. I witnessed someone get murdered, and now I am in the middle of a forest. It makes no sense. An overwhelming pressure builds in my chest until tears finally escape.

The man takes a step back with shock covering his face. "What do you mean, *Beansidhe*? I brought you back to *Gon'an'rit*."

"I don't understand what you are saying. Those words mean nothing to me," I say, barely controlling myself from screaming it in his arrogant face. I cross my arms over my chest. Trembles move through my body as the adrenaline wears off and it takes everything in me not to collapse onto the ground.

His brown eyes roam over my body before capturing my attention. He focuses for a couple heartbeats before closing his eyes. He leans forward, and breathes deeply through his nose. "You are a *Beansidhe*. I have no doubt about that." He exhales.

"What is a *Beansidhe*?" I slur through the pronunciation. My three years of high school Spanish is not helping me.

"You are a banshee, are you not?"

"What?" I scoff. Laughter bubbles at my lips but I clamp it down. "Oh, yes, I'm a banshee." I roll my eyes. "Clearly not. I am human. Hu. Man."

"You are definitely not human." Again, he assesses me.

A shiver runs up my spine.

"You really don't know?" He raises a sharp eyebrow, his thumb and forefinger tracing his chin.

I shake my head.

A smirk crosses his face. "Let's make a deal."

I bite my lip. The last time I did what he said, he swept me away to what can only be explained as another land. "What kind of deal?" My eyes narrow in his direction as I balance my hand on my cocked hip.

"For every question I answer, you owe me."

I already owe him a life debt, whatever that means, what more could he want from me?

"No more life debts."

The corner of his lip quirks. "Fine, no more life debts."

My stomach drops at how easily he gave in, but he agreed nonetheless. "And you have to return me home!"

He stares at me a moment before nodding. "I will take you to where you belong."

"Fine, it's a deal." As soon as the last word slips from my mouth, a zap races through my insides like a shock of static electricity.

"Well?" A smile spreads across his face, and dread fills my core.

I swallow my unease. "Who are you?"

"My name is Shay." He begins to walk away. "For the first question, I'll make it easy. Follow me," he calls over his shoulder.

I hold still, watching in stunned silence, but a tingle in my limbs forms and the further away he gets, the more painful it becomes. A grunt forces its way out when I double over.

"What is it?" he asks.

It's hard to concentrate on his words, but with every crunch of his boots towards me the pain lessens.

"What the hell." I straighten still clutching my abdomen. "This can't be real." I squeeze my eyes shut, willing myself to be back in the comfort of my bed when I open them. Nothing, but a bad dream. Cliché, but clichés exist for a reason, right?

"What're you doing?" His stern voice ruins my concentration.

"Shh," I say. "I'm trying to wake up from this nightmare."

He snorts. "This is no dream."

My eyes snap open. "Prove it, because so far there's nothing to prove this is reality."

His hand lashes out, grabbing my scraped arm, squeezing into the open gashes with the dirt grinding in deeper.

I cry out and yank my hand away.

He releases it, and walks backwards away from me. "If this was a dream? Would you feel that? Would you feel this?" The further he gets, the pain in my stomach ratchets up until I expect to see an open wound there.

"Stop," I gurgle out.

He acquiesces. "You are tied by magic to our deal. I told you to follow and when you do not the magic will suck at your life force. This is not a dream," he repeats.

I narrow my eyes at him.

He takes another step away, and the shooting pain stabs my gut.

"Okay! Okay! It's not a dream! Please, stop!" I holler.

"I will answer your questions, but the faster you believe your situation, the better it will be for all of us. If you try to leave before completing your part of the life debt, you will die."

You. Will. Die. It definitely felt to be true.

"Okay, I get it. Not drugs. Not a dream," I grumble. Even as I say it, I still have a hard time believing it. "If there's some weird voodoo magic, show me. Prove it."

"Was the pain you felt not enough?" He sighs, smoothing his face with his hand. "First, it's not voodoo. Second, I'm not a dog to do your bidding." He turns around to continue his way through the woods.

I jog after him until I walk beside him, the magic melting away until my body feels normal again.

He slows his pace so I can keep up without winding myself.

"Where are we going?"

"The castle." He gives me a sideways glance. "Piece of free advice, I would ask better questions or else you'll owe me a lot more than you're getting."

I ball my fists in annoyance because he's right. He technically is answering my questions, but I'm not getting very much information, and I now have debt he has yet to collect. If this truly isn't a dream, which definitely seems to be the case, I need to know as much as I can. Unlucky for him, I'm a curious person.

"How do you know I'm a *Beansidhe*," the word still feels strange, "or banshee?" I correct in case I butchered the words.

"Your song called to me. Plus, your magic smells of rain."

I trip when he mentions me having magic. "My song? Rain?" I mumble to myself. It's official, I've lost my mind. No, he's lost his mind because there's no way he can be talking about me.

"Yes, when you screamed of his death." He *tsks*, "Now you owe me three favors."

"The last one wasn't a question! And he died because you killed him!"

"Ah, but it was, and I did answer," he titters. "And yes, I killed him, just as you predicted."

I predicted nothing; I was trying to get help. I glower at the mossy ground in front of me.

"When will you take me home?"

"I said I would take you where you belong, and we are here. You are fae, which means you belong in *Gon'an'rit*, the fae realm."

I stop and after two steps, so does Shay. He turns to me with pure annoyance flashing on his face.

"I'm… not on Earth?" I ask, blinking slowly in disbelief.

He opens his mouth to answer, but I can feel in my bones that I'm not home. I hold up a hand to stop him from answering. "Don't answer that!"

He smirks. "Ah, you're learning."

"Fae realm," I scoff. "At least that explains the ears."

"Not all fae have pointed ears. Another trait unique to *Druids* and other higher fae. You are fae and you do not have pointed ears. It would be hard to blend in with humans."

My jaw drops. All I want to do is ask about the casual pretending to be humans bit, but I don't want to owe him anymore favors. I bite the inside of my cheek as a sinking feeling washes through me while I take in the forest surrounding me in the middle of the day. The one person who knows where I am, where we are going, and how to get out of here, stands before me. Well, *if* this is real. I wave my hand forward. "Well, go on then."

"No more questions?" He raises an eyebrow.

"No," I say between clenched teeth.

FIVE

Rain dribbles off the leaves, slapping against my scalp and shoulders. I twirl my wet hair around my finger as I continue to follow Shay. My mind wanders to my sister and a pit forms in my stomach. She must be worried sick about me. Unless she found me passed out in the alley because this is all absolutely nuts. Earlier, I had checked my pockets for my cell phone, but I must've lost it in the scuffle. Anyway, chances were I wouldn't get a signal in the 'fae realm'.

Yes, using mental air quotes for that piece of information.

I need to focus on a way to get home, my actual home, or get out of this hallucination. I frown at my bloody arms which still sting. Shay did have a point about the pain I've felt thus far, and I've never heard of any psychedelic that could create such a potent delusion.

I hate how I have to trust a stranger, but there's nothing else for me to do. The one solution I can think of is to play along until I convince him to take me back to Earth or the drugs wear off. I agree, I'm not dreaming. But I'm still not half convinced I haven't been roofied or something.

We step out of the trees into rolling fields. They're a luscious green, from all the rain, and off in the distance a castle sits on a cliff's edge. Its sandy-colored exterior contrasts with the grey cliff side and overcast skies. It's a type of structure that deserves to be on a sunny beachside, not a dreary landscape. There's at least ten levels of rooms and the towers on the corners reach up to pierce into the cloudy sky.

"It's beautiful," I whisper.

Shay frowns as his gaze traces it. "I can't say I agree with you."

Another half hour passes as we cross the hills and approach an iron gate that separates us from the palace. My shoes hit solid pavement, and a sigh escapes my lips. My feet ache from the hours of trekking, most of it spent on my toes to limit how much my heels sank into the moist soil. Traversing the hills is more difficult than the woods, surprisingly, and without the trees blocking part of the pattering rain, my clothes are completely soaked through. A shiver runs through my body when the sea wind whips around the side of the wall encircling the perimeter of the castle.

Two men incline their heads at Shay before opening the gate to let us through. This is the first time I've seen anyone else wherever we are. Neither of them have pointed ears. They are both tall, but not as tall as Shay. Swords sit on their hips, and a golden chest plate sits atop a green leather-like material. Their pants are black, made of the same material as the shirt, and similar to what Shay wears. I would normally expect them to be dying of heat, but it's probably a lot better than wearing soggy clothes.

I reach up and feel the top of my rounded ears. Perfectly round, human ears, right?

"For my next debt payment, you cannot speak until I give you permission." Shay doesn't look at me as he speaks.

I open my mouth to retort, but a zip of electricity causes my throat to tighten to where it cuts off my breath. The moment I abandon attempting to speak, my airway reopens and I take in a shuddering breath. What the heck? To feel pain is one thing, but to immobilize my speaking at someone else's command. There's no way that's possible. Unless... nope, no way, this can't be actually happening. Pushing aside my internal freak out, I embody my sister and shoot daggers at Shay, who ignores me.

We walk through an open area filled with more hills and dotted with trees. The barrier surrounding the castle continues so far in the distance to my right it disappears over a hill before I see the end of it. As we move closer to the palace, its walls loom over us until I feel like an ant. I crane my head to stare at the expansive building, using my hand to block the droplets from getting into my eyes. Windows speckle the side, and at five-stories-high begins a smattering of balconies. There's not many doorways from what I've seen, and by not many I mean I see only one so far.

Shay clears his throat in front of me, but doesn't stop walking, so I'm left scrambling to catch him.

Upon entering through the large set of wooden doors, I follow Shay through the empty halls. He walks with confidence, as though he could find his way through this maze of passages with his eyes closed. We end at another set of dark wood doors where two more guards stand. Again, with an incline of their head they open the entry for us.

The other side is anything but silent. Hundreds of people... uh, I mean fae, loiter in what can only be described as an expansive throne room. No one turns to us when we enter, but it's clear we're late to the event. Unlike the outer walls and the hall, this room is made of grey stone. There are no windows, but lights hang from the ceiling which is supported by massive pillars.

Shay squeezes through the crowd with me right on his tail until we reach a side wall. I silently stand beside him like a good little puppy, eyeing her master for any kind of explanation.

He ignores my existence, which has a huff of annoyance leaving my lips.

Another shiver wracks through my body as I stare longing at all the dry bodies around me. It's warmer without the wind. Plus, the humidity from the mass of bodies and moisture in the air, but the water plastered to my body is still cold.

A hush falls across the crowd as a man steps onto the dais at the front of the room. His red hair lies in a low ponytail at the nape of his neck, pointy ears on full display, and a large cape with gold brooches clasps on his broad shoulders. He sits on the throne, crosses his legs, and stares out across the crowd. His eyes fall onto Shay, lingering for a moment, before they snap to me.

I'm half hidden behind Shay's large frame, but his commanding stare makes me shrink into myself. I wonder if Shay has magic to make me disappear, or maybe I have that magic. Anything would be great right about now.

He holds my gaze before grimacing and continuing to sweep the room with his hard eyes. With a snap of his fingers, a desk appears before him.

I jolt in place as my mouth drops, which has those beside us giving me a questioning look. Nerves from the attention wrestle in my gut until I'm giving a tight lipped smile to them, praying they look away soon. A relieved exhale leaves me when they finally do. I stare at the desk mesmerized by the object. Really, really strong drugs, or I'm traumatized by the night. Lots and lots of therapy in my future.

Next, papers materialize on the table the man magics out of thin air. A quill inside a bottle of ink appears next to the stack.

I don't jump in surprise this time, but my eyes are wide in fascination. Shay said I have magic, or in my weird hallucination I do; I wonder if I can do that too. Part of me wants to snap my fingers to try. My lip curls at the corner when I imagine having a feather boa drape across Shay's stiff shoulders. The only thing stopping me is the dead silence. There's no way I can snap my fingers without drawing attention to myself. Guess I'll have to try it later.

With another snap of his fingers, a thin crown forms on his head. Nothing to dominate his powerful aura, but distinct enough to prove his position.

Everyone bows.

My head moves side to side. Do I follow along? Is this like a Catholic thing where I participate if I follow a certain religion? I look to Shay for instruction.

He hesitates a moment before following suit with everyone else, so I mimic those around me. I peer sideways to gauge when to rise, but no one has yet.

"May the blessing of light be on you," a booming voice says.

"Light without and light within," the crowd, minus Shay and myself, chorus back.

As everyone stands straight, I press my lips into a hard line to hide my amusement at the light they all speak of considering the hours of drizzle I recently walked through.

A tingle rises in my chest, pulling my attention to my left.

A strikingly handsome man stares at me. A blush forms on my cheeks and my eyes dart away, back to the throng of people whose hopeful stares are on their king.

Despite my best efforts, my gaze meanders back to the stranger.

He no longer looks in my direction, allowing me plenty of time to appreciate the sight of him. He has a haunting beauty that leaves me breathless. He's tall, but a few inches shorter than Shay, and more lithe. His skin has a perfect bronzed glow, a mixture of birth and sunlight. Inky hair is pushed back from his clean shaven, sharp jaw and full lips purse as his cold eyes stare forward. His dark clothing is snug against his body, allowing his lean muscles to make their presence known. A sheathed blade sits on his back.

Who doesn't love a bad boy, am I right? Wait, no. Bad Cara. I'm dating someone. Marcus is a good guy and only yesterday I was contemplating about him being my boyfriend.

I drag my eyes away when the king speaks again.

"All who wish to join the competition, please come forward," he announces with a wave of his hand.

Wait, what competition? There's no other introduction? Aren't those in leadership supposed to give a long winded speech that has everyone zoning out at least three times? The questions burn my throat with the need to ask Shay, but the magic stops me.

The crowd pushes forward like the main band of a concert came on stage, their bodies becoming more sardine-like as they shove themselves closer. Everyone stops when the king raises his hand.

"One at a time," he says with annoyance.

Slower, individuals walk forward to the table one by one to bend over to sign one of the papers on the stack.

Once they are done, the king flicks his hand and the leaf of signed paper floats into another stack, so a new piece reveals underneath.

After someone agrees to whatever contest, they make their way back through the room and leave without a word.

This is completely bizarre. Aside from quick utterances between the king and his subjects, the only sound is the scratch of pen on paper. An eerie feeling seeps into me until I give my body a little shake from the heebie jeebies. One of those intense moments, where you shake all your limbs and shimmy your shoulders to make the feeling go away.

Shay raises an eyebrow at me, the first indication he remembers my existence in an hour, and all I do is shrug at him.

The crowd thins, and soon Shay is dragging me forward by my arm.

Okay, dude, you don't need to manhandle me, thank you very much. It might come as a surprise, but I can walk myself. Sadly, I can't say any of this, so I squint at his meaty hand, hoping the magic will zap him like it's been zapping me.

Nothing. Stupid magic.

Multiple times since arriving, I have still opened my mouth to ask a question, but the magic of our deal forces my windpipe shut each time. Not just blocking my voice, but blocking my air. I have since given up deciding it's not worth it. Also, still ignoring the idea that this is at all possible, but there's no other way to explain what the hell is happening.

We step up to the table ourselves. For the first time, the king looks up from his hands. His piercing green eyes hover on Shay as he raises an eyebrow. "You wish to join the trials?"

"Aye, but via proxy," Shay responds in a way that seems too informal for how one should speak to a king.

The king's eyes rake over me and he grimaces. "With her?" he asks.

"Aye, she owes me a life debt, and this is how I will collect," Shay explains to his king, still too casual.

Awkward, I sing-song in my head.

The king's face pinches as he ponders the idea before he nods. "So be it. Shamus Harbinger of the *Druids*," the king's face sours at the last word, "do you accept all terms with entering the *Naim* Competition?"

"Aye."

"And your proxy?" The king raises his eyebrow at me.

Shay leans into my ear and whispers. "You may speak."

I open my mouth, ready to ask all my probing questions and clarify everything happening, but Shay cuts me off.

"With my next payment, you will tell the king you accept, and after that my payment is for you to sign the document after me. You may do nothing else." His raspy whisper sears through me before he pulls away and straightens.

I open my mouth again, but the static electricity, which I now recognize as magic, zaps me, dislodging a strangled "I accept" from my mouth.

Shay takes the quill and signs his name, and hands it to me. My arm, with a mind of its own, reaches to add my signature under his.

The king flicks his wrist, and the paper soars into the large stack at the other end of the table.

Stupidly and to Shay's horror, I reach out to wave my hand in the air where the paper floated. Everything is solid, real. The table, the pen, the paper, and there is no weird strings making this happen. Holy. Crap. This is real? Like really real? As in, I wasn't secretly drugged, passed out, or something else, but kidnapped to another realm and just forced into a competition?

My chance to ask questions is lost when Shay snags my arm and drags me away from the dais. The king watches our retreat, eyes trained on us, and his attention is broken only when the next fae steps up and blocks his view. Before we can leave the room, a man steps in front of us.

"Are you sure that was wise?" It's the same man from earlier, the pretty one, and it takes everything in me to not drop my jaw. He's even more handsome closer up with the sharp planes of his face, and depthless amber eyes one could get lost in. The smell of sandalwood mixes with Shay's clove scent.

With a full view of him, my eyes snag on the red scars marring his skin. They peek from his shirt and cover the left side of his neck and part way down his left arm.

The man's angry stare pierces me.

I take a step back. It's as though I can see death in his eyes, and right now it feels directed at me.

"Get out of my way, Killian," Shay spits.

"I asked a question," he responds, unfazed by Shay's wrath.

"I am not obligated to answer the questions of a *Púca*." Shay stares down his nose at the man.

Killian's eyes roam over me, paying no mind to the man who still grips my arm, scrutinizing every detail. Every inch of my body he traces sears me and when I can't take it any longer, I look away.

"I simply don't see why you'd risk losing by using someone so… innocent." Killian says the last word like an insult.

"I do not need to explain myself to you," Shay says as his fingers dig deeper into my arm.

I wince from the pain. I bruise easily, so I'm already dreading the dots I'll find on my bicep later.

Killian's relaxed stance goes rigid, his focus lancing to Shay's hand. His eyes move upward until they have me locked in his gaze.

I open my mouth to speak, to say I'm fine, but something to the effect of "A… uh… I… uh…" stumbles from my mouth. Even Shay looks worriedly at me. Thanks for the concern and all, but no, I'm not having an aneurysm, just my brain short circuiting.

"Move before I make you." Shay's hand relaxes, but his attention is back on Killian, and by the set in his jaw, I don't think he is bluffing.

With one last glance my way, Killian moves to the side. Bowing low as he spreads his arm to the door. "After you, my liege." Disdain and mockery drip from his voice.

Shay's step falters, but he composes himself and drags me away.

SIX

"**O**kay!" I pull my arm from Shay's grasp. "I got it. I'm following you. Stop manhandling me like I'm a lost child."

Shay glowers at me, seeming more like a giant shadow with the sconce on the wall backlighting him. "You are a lost child."

I fold my arms. "More like a kidnapped child."

"At least we can both agree that you're a child," Shay utters as he continues down the hall, leaving me to fume at his back.

Once more, I'm left stomping after him through the myriad of halls and staircases. Despite the hundreds of people leaving the throne room after signing up, the halls remain as empty as before. The walls are made of the same cream sandstone, but without windows or natural lighting, the passages feel dark. There's a lack of decor aside from the artistry of the architecture, probably because this giant castle has too many walls to fill them with paintings. Either way, boredom sets in as I follow my captor.

Finally, we stop in front of a broad wooden door.

"This is your room," Shay explains as he grasps the brass handle. The door swings open and my eyes widen at the room in front of me.

It must be, at least, twice the size of the apartment I shared, I mean share, with Shauna. A four-poster, teak-framed bed sits off in the corner to the left. It's covered in ivory sheets. On the opposite side of the room sits a lounge area with a loveseat and armchair in front of a brightly burning fireplace. Pushed against the wall in the far corner is a desk and wooden rolling chair. My eyes trace the rest of the room and find two more doors residing to my left.

I cross the room to the large windows that line the opposite wall. I pull aside large, canary colored curtains to reveal a set of double glass doors. I open them to find a small balcony. I step out onto it, ignoring the pelting rain, and overlook the front courtyard we entered through earlier. Groups of people, who I assume are the other contestants, leave through the front gate. I turn to Shay with a frown.

He leans against the door frame with his arms crossed, watching the people below.

I open my mouth to ask a question, but pause. The sudden lack of breathing has not been a fun experience and one I hope to avoid in the future. I don't feel any magical strain to prevent me from talking, but I'm still cautious.

Shay notices the hesitation on my face and rolls his eyes.

I think that's the most normal thing I've seen him do since I've met him.

He pulls himself upright and takes a step forward. His eyes roam the landscape as rain drizzles on us. "You may talk openly, and I'll answer all your questions on one condition," he says without looking at me.

I raise an eyebrow at him. Yeah, I don't think I'll be falling for any more of his tricks.

He turns to me. "You owe me one more debt, not a life debt, don't worry."

I narrow my eyes.

"One normal debt, but with none of the previous stipulations. A single debt for freedom of questions." He waits as I puzzle over his offer.

This could be another ploy, and from what I understand fae are notorious for that. However, he did technically save my life, no matter how unethical the circumstance of it, and has yet to steer me wrong. Although he also kidnapped me and forced me to enter some kind of competition I still know nothing about. Conversely, it is for the life debt I owe him, so at least that's paid off. But I'm dying to understand what's happening and I can get answers without fear of him continuing to control me. My brain continues to battle itself with what choice I should make, but in the end, my curiosity wins.

I hold out my hand. "Deal."

An electric shock moves up my arm when he shakes it, locking the magic in place.

"Well?" He turns back towards the railing.

"This is all real. Like actually real," I say.

"Is this a question or statement? You're not the most eloquent human, so it's hard to tell."

"Both?" I say with uncertainty. "I'm not on drugs, dead, or in a dream, correct? Like, I'm legitimately in another realm where magic exists?"

"Correct."

For once, I'm a bit lost for words. It's been hours since this all started, if I was on drugs I'm fairly certain it would be out of my system by now. There's no other explanation except… this is real.

I jut my chin at the fae below. "Why is everyone leaving?"

"I assume they are going home."

My brow furrows. Great, I'm so happy he's willing to answer my questions— not. "Can you at least give better answers now?"

He scowls at me. "Maybe you should ask better questions."

I wrap my arms around my midsection and stare across the dreary landscape. Yes, the sky is grey, and it hasn't stopped raining since I've arrived, but I still recognize the beauty in it. The varying greens from the courtyard to the hills and finally the forest. Part of me is sad I don't have a view that overlooks the ocean, but the thought is blown away when a biting wind lashes against me and I'm instantly appreciative to be on this side of the castle.

I take a deep breath through my nose and release it slowly through my mouth. I am so tired. It's probably mid-morning back on Earth, and most of time was spent hiking in heels. Let's not get into how mentally taxing this all is too.

This is real. I shake my head, squeezing my eyes shut, and when I stop I'm still in the same place. Yeah, by this point, I'm 99.99% sure I'm not hallucinating, but it's still weird to admit.

I'm brittle and overwhelmed, and the pull of the comfort of my bed, one I don't know if I'll ever see again, chokes me to where a sob wants to rip out of me. But I don't let it.

"I just..." Tears spring at the back of my eyes. I'm exhausted, I'm confused, and I can't decide whether Shay saved me, kidnapped me, or both. "Please, can you please explain to me what's happening?" My voice shakes as I plead to him. I understand this is real, but I don't understand why it's happening, and to me of all people.

His stern face searches my own. His eyebrows pinch when he notices my light shivering. Although, I'm fairly certain I've been shaking from my soaked clothes for a couple hours, but I wasn't able to say anything before due to the whole magically sealed mouth problem.

"Let's get you warm and then I'll explain." He shuffles me inside and walks to the door in the room's corner.

An extensive bathroom shines with white and grey marble stone. It's larger than my bedroom back home. My eyes dart across the glass shower door, where grey river stones line the floor and walls, before landing on a large tub that could fit four people.

Shay walks over to it, turns three silver knobs, and the tub fills with clear water. He nods at a stack of clothes on the counter. "You'll find clean pajamas there. We'll focus on finding you more suitable clothes later." He glances at my mud coated boots that have seen better days, dirtied pants, and wet shirt. Well, shirt is a strong word to describe this top.

I hide my embarrassment by tilting my head until my hair blocks my face and torso. I forgot I was wearing something closer to lingerie and suddenly feel very exposed.

"Take your time as I have some things I have to take care of. I'll be back in forty minutes." He closes the door behind him, leaving me alone for the first time since I've met him.

I shed my dirty clothes, and the once pristine room is now covered in muddy footprints and flecks of dirt. There isn't a hamper to help contain my messy clothes, so I fold them and put them on top of my boots at the floor beside the door. If I was at home, I would throw them away, but as my last connection to Earth, I can't bear to part with them. I'll clean them in the sink later.

The water laps near the rim of the tub. I twist faucets until it's off, step into the steaming water, and relax into it with a sigh. The tension in my muscles subsides, and the aches in my bones dwindle, but the fatigue of the day grows. Once my chills stop, I lather my hair and body with the soap I find on the side of the tub. Rose floral scent hits my nose and the edges of my lips tip up at the alluring smell. I condition my hair and run a comb I found on the ledge through my tangles before dunking my head under the water.

I stay under, muting myself from the world, with a small hope when I lift myself from the water I'll be back in my tiny apartment. A girl can hope. Again, there's a 0.001% chance this isn't real.

My lungs begin to burn, so with one last prayer, I pull my head up to take a gasping breath, and there's a small drop in my heart at the unchanged room. It was a fool's wish anyways, but that hadn't stopped the hope from creeping in.

Once clean, I exit the water and dry myself with a fluffy white towel hanging on the wall. I grab the lavender colored satin pajamas off the counter and discover it's a camisole with matching bottoms. It seems this top will not be any less revealing than my last, but the excitement of clean clothes overrides my modesty until I don't care.

As I leave the humid bathroom, Shay's head raises from where he lounges on the loveseat. His crossed legs lay across the cushion as though he owns the place.

I waltz across the room and sit in a chair across from him. I don't move, I don't speak. I wait for him to explain everything to me like he said he would.

A few moments pass before he starts, which boils my blood.

Seriously, could this guy be any more arrogant?

With a sigh he explains. "As you know, you are a banshee and we are in the fae realm, *Gon'an'rit*. When I saved your life, you owed me a life debt, which I utilized when I had you sign up for the *Naim* competition. Once it's done, I will take you home." He stares at his nails, bored, as though he has explained everything perfectly and there's no need for further explanation.

Oh, hell no. He's not getting out of this that easily.

"What's the *Naim* competition?" I sit straighter. I demand proper answers this time.

"It's a set of trials, and the winner gets one wish, any wish. It's a combination of the King's powers and the magic within the realm that grants it," he drawls.

"That doesn't sound so bad," I say more to myself, but Shay shrugs at my comment. "How does someone win?" I inquire.

"Well, you must pass each trial, but you are also scored as, oftentimes, more than one fae will pass all the trials."

"So, highest score wins?"

"Essentially."

"And if I don't win?" I chew on my lip.

"Welcome to your new home."

I blanch. "Excuse me?" I leap from my seat and storm over to him.

He watches me with a bland expression, which has my fists clenching at my side. I have no reservations about punching him in his face.

"You said you would take me home!" I scream at him, no longer keeping my composure in place. I am done with this.

"If you won the competition," he adds.

"Screw you! Screw this competition! Screw the life debt!" I holler.

"Ah, ah, ah," Shay wags his finger at me like I'm a child about to steal a cookie. "A life debt is exactly that. A life for a life. I saved yours, so if you do not provide me of something of equal importance or what I deem a fit substitute, your life will be forfeit instead."

"Are you kidding me?" My eyes bulge. "You saved my life, so I can die if I don't repay you? That makes absolutely no sense!"

He shrugs. "I don't make the rules."

"How about, uh, I don't know, you don't kill random people for a stranger and then state you saved my life?" I gape at him.

"Well, where's the fun in that?"

It takes all my willpower not to slap the smirk right off his damn face.

"I should get going," Shay announces as he stands. "I'll have food brought to your room."

"I want to go home. Now." I don't budge, blocking him from the door as I tilt my head back to glare up at his pompous face.

He rakes a hand through his hair with a sigh. "Look, kid," *If I kill him right now, can I owe myself a life debt?* "There's nothing that can be done. I'm sorry. Win the competition, the life debt is paid, and I take you home."

"That's easy for you to say," I seethe, imagining all the ways I would never win against him if I tried to take him. I'm definitely going to start working out as soon as possible.

A hunger pain shoots through my stomach which causes it to rumble through the silence.

He stares at my midriff like it offended him personally before shaking his head. "You're hungry, I'm tired. We can talk more about this later." He grabs my shoulders, and acting like I weigh nothing, lifts me and places me off to his left so he can step past me.

Damnit. He could at least act like he's intimidated. How does my sister do it? It's not like she's a hulking person either, but she still manages to scare the wits out of people.

Shay glances back at me. "Get some rest," and he leaves without another word, shutting the door behind him.

I slump into the chair in stunned silence. Maybe I can follow him, find my own way home. Perhaps there's another fae, a nicer fae willing to help me out. Shay, Killian, and the King flash through my mind, as well as the judgmental stares I got from every fae downstairs. Okay, that might be harder than I thought. Lethargy takes over my body.

I close my eyes and picture home in my mind. I envision snuggling under the duvet from my bed on the stained couch, Shauna's laughter from whatever stupid comedy she chose, and the taste of popcorn as I shove kernels into my mouth. Our usual Sunday night tradition. And I snap my fingers.

There is no whoosh, there's no melting walls, there's no zap of anything, and when I open my eyes, the fire from my prison room waves at me. There's no way I have magic. I would have known before this, right? In the end, I don't even know if I could get home with the magic of the life debt intact. Shay is my sole way home.

My stomach grumbles and I grab it. I wait to hear a knock at the door, for the food Shay promised, but my eyelids droop.

Moving to the bed, I plop on top of the fluffy comforter, and I moan. It's one of the softest things I've felt in my life and I kind of hate how I love it so much. I roll over, kicking my feet until the blanket bunches, so I can slide it up my body. I curl into a ball as the warmth of the heavy blanket seeps into me and place my head on the feathery pillow.

I'll wake when the food arrives. Just a few minutes rest.

SEVEN

My eyes pry open as a stretch works its way through my limbs. Based on the grey clouds peeking through the window, it's morning. I wish I could see what this place looks like with the sun shining. I bet it's beautiful.

My eyes widen when the aroma of coffee hits my nose. I bolt upright, and sitting on the desk in the corner of the room is a tray. I throw the covers off and am across the room in seconds.

A large mug of steaming coffee sits on the platter. I ignore the sugar, but dump half the container of cream into the cup until it's about to spill over. I bend over to slurp at the edge before picking it up to take a fuller gulp. A sigh escapes my lips.

I plop down into the chair, careful of the wheels, and stare at the two eggs, fresh baked roll, and cup of fruit. I lift the steaming roll and press it into the over medium cooked eggs until the center bursts open and douses the bread with the creamy yolk. I take a bite and a moan escapes my lips.

My plate and cup of coffee are empty before I know it. I lean back into the chair with a satisfied sigh, rubbing my taut stomach.

A knock comes from my door and my eyes shoot open.

"Who is it?" I yell, too full to get up.

The door opens, and I spin in my chair, baffled that someone had the audacity to open it before I invited them in.

Shay saunters into the room. "You can't bother to open your own door."

I bristle at his entrance. "You can't bother to say good morning?"

He ignores my comment. Great, the typical treatment from him. Walking towards me, he raises a dark eyebrow.

I shrug him off and relax back into the chair. "I was finishing breakfast."

He glances at my plate, and I shift uncomfortably because it's clear I licked it clean, literally.

"Well, it seems you're done, which is good because you need to get ready for the first trial," he says as he meanders through my room. His hands lock behind his back as he takes everything in.

My eyes widen, "Already?" I only signed up yesterday and Shay and I never even finished our conversation.

He stops and turns to me. "Of course, there's no point in dillydallying. And the sooner this is done, the better."

Isn't that the truth. He wants to be rid of me just as much as I want to be rid of him. I puff out my building tension. It seems there are little options except to finish off this life debt as soon as possible by winning this competition and get back home. Easy peasy.

"I don't have any clean clothes," I say in a dead tone.

He lifts his chin towards the other door beside the bathroom. "Your closet was filled with clothes last night as you slept."

I sit upright in my chair. "You... you were in my room last night while I slept?" I'm horrified a man I barely know was waltzing around my room... as I slept! Completely vulnerable! The nerve of this man.

He scoffs as though I'm the one who said something absurd. "Heavens no, the seamstresses took care of it."

"What?" I screech. "So, strangers were in my room instead?"

"Well, I would have introduced them to you, but you were asleep. So there's no way around them being strangers." He seems unperturbed by the fact he allowed people into my room like it's the most natural thing in the world, which it is certainly not. "By the way, not only do you sleep like the dead, but you snore, not becoming of a young maiden."

I snort at his use of the word maiden, which has him giving me another eyebrow raise.

I'm sure it's due to my other unbecoming sound from a young maiden.

Again, I snicker to myself. Who talks like that?

"Thankfully, Robin Hood, I don't really care what you think," I fume. "But I do care if you're letting strangers into my room."

"Well, nothing we can do about it now. I will introduce you to them later," he states as he walks towards the front door. "I'll be outside while you get dressed. There is something laid out on the chair. Wear that."

He closes the door before I can retort, so instead I resort to flipping off the closed door.

After being so rude and belittling me, he expects me to wear what he's chosen for me? Sorry, bucko, but this isn't the 19th century and you might be surprised to learn women have a mind of their own.

I stomp across the room and fling open the closet door then pause. It's a closet, but an entire room itself. I could throw a dance party with fifteen of my closest friends and still have plenty of room. Well, with the assumption I have friends. Let me rephrase, I could have a dance party with my sister and at least twenty dogs in here!

In the center is a chaise lounge and lining the walls are a myriad of outfits in every color I can imagine. I gingerly run my fingers along the different fabrics of blouses, pants, skirts, and beautiful gowns. Speaking of, I face a slim purple dress laying across the lounge chair. The colors darken on the bodice and become lighter to the bottom; it's like a pansy flower was turned into a dress.

I bite my lip. I have never worn something so beautiful in my life. Of course, Shay had to go and open his mouth, ruining this moment. So with deep regret, I turn my back on the dress.

Shauna always said one of my worst attributes was my stubbornness, but what she never realized is it ran in the family. Who does she think I learned it from?

A pang hits my heart at the reminder of my sister and I press my palm to my chest. I can't imagine what she is going through right now. First our parents, and now me. But what's worse is there isn't even a body to explain what happened to me. She must be worried sick if she hasn't already assumed the worst. Sure she has friends, but I'm her best friend, just like she's mine. I can't imagine her turning to anyone.

I promise I'll make it back to you, Shauna. If it's the last thing I do. You're not alone in this world, or rather all the worlds.

With a deep exhale, I try to push Shauna to the corner of my mind. Compartmentalization at its finest. There is nothing I can do about it now. I need to focus on finishing this competition first.

Perusing the selection, I settle on a green summer dress with a pink flower print. It reminds me of something Georgia O'Keeffe would paint. My sister took a few art history classes and obsessed over her paintings for months before moving onto Frida Kahlo. She probably would've pursued it as a degree if it weren't for me. She had said a couple of classes were enough, how she only wanted to get a taste of college. I can still remember her silence in the final weeks of classes, which is very unlike her.

In a drawer at the back, I find underwear too. As I put everything on, shock stills me at how perfectly everything fits. It's official, fae are completely creepy. I hope they didn't somehow measure me in my sleep.

A shudder of mild panic runs through me.

No, Shay made it seem like they were professionals, I'm sure they found another way.

I run my hand over the smooth material of the dress. This might be the most comfortable article of clothing I've ever worn. I throw on a pair of strappy brown sandals, ignoring the black heels beside the dress. I've had enough time in heels recently to last me a lifetime.

I move to the bathroom where I brush my teeth and hair. My makeup is long gone, but I'm okay with that. My hair is so obnoxiously straight, even with the humidity from the constant mist of rain, I don't have to worry about it getting too frizzy. As I go to leave, I notice my clothes are gone.

Ah, that must be how they know my size.

I open the door of my bedroom, and a triumphant smile crosses my face at Shay's disapproving glare after he scrutinizes my outfit.

"That's not what I laid out for you."

"No, but I have a mind of my own." I try not to grin as his face becomes even darker. "I'm still in a dress. I almost threw on what looked to be riding pants just to spite you." This time I do laugh when he throws his head back with a groan.

"Fine." He pinches the bridge of his nose. "Let's just go. I don't want to be late."

Shay ushers me back to the same throne room from yesterday. The halls all look the same and I have no idea how he remembers where to go. I wonder if there's a map I could ask for, something with big scrawling letters and pictures. There can be a drawing of Shay's annoying face with "Shay's Room" written underneath as though it's an amusement park ride.

I gag at the unintended innuendo. Don't get me wrong, Shay is a beefy, good-looking man, but his personality needs a lot of work. Not my type.

In the throne room, rows of pews fill the once empty center where all the fae stood the previous day. A tingling forms in my chest as we walk down the center aisle. A weird urge pulls my attention right, and leaning against the shadowed walls is Killian. The moment we make eye contact his darkened amber ones snap away.

He crosses his arms across his chest as he ignores me.

Rude.

My gaze lingers for a few more seconds before they drift back to the crowd Shay and I traipse through. All around me people are in gorgeous attire. Maybe I should have worn the dress Shay suggested after all. Don't get me wrong, my dress is beautiful, but others are in frills, silk, rubies, diamonds, and other accoutrements to heighten the opulence of their attire. I'm the only one who downplayed my wardrobe.

Well, me and Killian. Even Shay's not in his leather vest, but has upgraded to a nice white shirt and black trousers with his sword sitting elegantly on his hip instead of his back. How did I not notice this before? I purse my lips. Probably because I was too distracted by his creepiness of letting people into my room last night.

Shay slides into a pew four rows from the front and folds his arms.

I sit next to him and place my hands in my lap. Everyone else sits with their backs straight and hands in their lap. I mimic them instead of Shay, who lounges back with his ankles crossed. I wouldn't be surprised if he flung his arm along the back of the bench to spread his essence as much as possible.

More people file into the room, filling every seat, until people stand off to the sides like packed barn animals.

I peek over my right shoulder, but Killian is blocked from view. I exhale and push away the slight disappointment. It's for the best. I need to know what to expect from the trial and not be distracted by a disarmingly handsome and mysterious man.

The king enters the room, and everyone stands in unison.

"May the blessing of light be on you," his gravelly voice echoes across the hall.

"Light without and light within," everyone choruses back as they lower their heads.

The king sits on his throne, and the crowd follows suit. Well, everyone who has a seat in the pews.

Despite the king's ease as he sits on the dais, his power radiates through the room. He holds everyone's rapt attention.

"Welcome to the start of the *Naim* Competition. It is with tradition we hold this every seven years. As you all know," his voice booms and I listen intently because I, in fact, don't know, "this started thousands of years ago."

I sideways glance at Shay and he picks at his nails. He knows all of this, and since he isn't the one competing, he must not care.

"It started as a way to test the current king and allow for those to oppose his reign a chance to take his place," the king continues. "But as good rulers came to sit upon this throne, the competition evolved, and this long standing tradition allows its winner a single wish. One that will be granted by myself and the magic of the land." He pauses.

I raise my hands above my lap because this seems the time to clap, but drop them with heat tinging my cheeks as I realize everyone else waits attentively.

The king's gaze scours across the crowd, once again pausing on both Shay and me. "Due to our land being at peace, no one has used the wish to battle the king in over 300 years."

At this, the room cheers.

My mouth drops open. Three hundred years? Wait, does that mean he's been king for...

I lean over to Shay. "So, how old can a fae live?" I murmur below the applause.

Shay has no problem hearing my question. "One thousand years is the average lifespan."

I blink at him in shock. "If I'm a banshee, or part fae, will I live longer too?"

I don't know what being a banshee entails yet, and with my human side I don't expect to live for quite so long. I need to learn more about how I'm a banshee, which is hard to fathom because I distinctly remember photos of myself in the hospital with my parents.

"It's not an if, kid. You are a banshee, and yes you will live longer than the humans in your life."

I swallow through a lump forming in my throat. A darkness within me swirls, wanting to pull me under its waves, but I push away the thoughts of how I've already outlived plenty of humans in my life.

"Don't call me kid," I angry-whisper. I cock an eyebrow and lean forward to better see his face so he can't avoid my question. "How old are you?"

"Older than you," he looks pointedly at me, "kid."

"Keep your secrets," I smile at him, "old man."

Shay stretches, putting the back of his head into the palm of interlocked fingers, nearly smacking me in the face with his elbow.

The king snaps his fingers, drawing back my attention, and immediate silence follows as a crystal orb materializes in air to float above him.

"Each trial of this competition holds a value treasured by the fae. Only the strongest of these attributes will make it to the end, and only the best of you will win the final wish. For the first test, Power is tested. Those with the purest and strongest form of magic tied to this realm may continue on. Once your name is called, please step forward and place your hand upon the globe for the true nature of your power to be revealed." Once the king is done speaking, he waves a hand to a man off to the side.

He holds a scroll which he unfolds as he steps onto the dais beside the king. "Clarence O'Malley," his crisp voice announces.

A burly man, who seems to be Shay's height if not taller, steps forward.

I try not to gawk since the name Clarence elicited the image of a grandfatherly man, not a warrior shoved into his finest britches.

He places his meaty hand on the globe without hesitation.

The orb erupts into varying colors until it lands on a crystal blue that brightens the space into the third row.

The king smirks. "Our first contender is very strong and Power is shown both on the outside and within." He looks over to a line of older fae sitting in chairs off to the left I hadn't noticed earlier.

The three of them lean towards one another and whisper amongst themselves.

"Who're they?" I lean to my left and ask Shay. Perhaps the king snapped them into existence like the orb.

A female fae in front of us, whose face is pinched like there's a stick up her butt, turns to hush me.

I stick out my tongue at the back of her head.

"Real mature," Shay grumbles into my ear. "And you wonder why I call you kid."

"Shut it." I glower through my hair hanging between us. I lower my voice when another fae looks our way. "Answer my question."

"The fae council. Since the wish can be used to try to take the throne, an unbiased council is created to score each competitor. It would be unfair for the king to manage this alone and potentially sway who becomes the winner."

"How can a council be unbiased? Everyone brings bias to a situation," I mutter to myself.

Shay harrumphs at my comment, even though I hadn't meant for him to hear.

"How do they choose who's on the council?" I press for more information.

"A fae from each court oversees the competition," Shay grumbles in an attempt to keep his baritone voice as low as possible.

"There's different courts?" I perk up with my inquisitiveness on full display. A dozen questions fly through my mind.

I open my mouth to ask them, but Ms. Stick-Up-Her-Butt turns to angrily shush me once more.

I lean back against the pew, folding my arms. I guess my questions will have to wait *again*.

The first elderly fae, closest to us, is a pale-skinned old man with clear, round glasses over kind eyes and a knowing smirk. He's dressed in purple robes and seems as though he's spent years of his life tucked away in a library. In the middle is an older woman with long silver hair. A dark green dress covers her tanned, slightly leathery skin from years in the sun. At the end, with his back facing the corner, is a man in all black with cropped salt and pepper hair and a goatee to match overlaying his deep brown skin tone. His hard eyes constantly shift through the room, despite making no other movements. But when the female fae asks a question, his lips move minimally to answer, proving he is still fully aware of the conversation. Finally, the fae woman nods to the king and holds up three fingers.

The king nods. "He shall be rewarded 3 points for the first trial and his display of Power."

Name after name is called. The orb projects different lights, which Shay was kind enough to tell me is based around the affinity and pureness of their magic. I didn't even need to probe him for the information.

"This seems rather anticlimactic for a trial," I mumble.

"It's more of a precursor, yes, but since it tests one of the official values of our realm, it still counts as a trial," Shay explains.

I'm in the middle of asking about said values, when the queen of grumpiness turns to hush us. Seriously, what is with this woman? I uncross my legs, and may or may not accidentally-on purpose knock the back of her seat with my foot.

She doesn't react, but Shay frowns at me.

I huff. I'm really not helping my 'I'm not a kid' case.

Despite the overall boredom of the trial, nervousness vibrates through me at the idea of being tested. I might be a banshee, still unconfirmed in my opinion, and not born in this land, with a gift revolving around death. Confidence is not something flowing through me right now.

My hands twist in my lap.

It seems the orb's light differs in radiance between contestants too. Certain colors are favored such as blue, green, and yellow, and the brighter it glows the higher the score the person receives. The light hasn't not shined for anyone, but if it's too dim, the person does not continue in the competition. There have been zero points if it was an unfavored color such as brown, but with a minimal amount of glow they still passed onto the next trial. The majority of fae receive one or two points, and there's only been a handful of threes.

"Killian Mactíre."

Killian stalks down the aisle, watching those seated as though searching for a threat. When he walks past me, his eyes land on me, and half a smirk touches his lips before he continues forward. Stepping up to the orb, he places his hand on it without hesitation and a grey light erupts from it, lighting half the room.

There are whispers through the room and the king stares at him in shock.

Before anyone can react, the old woman raises four fingers.

"He will receive," the king pauses and verifies with the fae counsel as though he may have misunderstood, "four... points for his display of power."

Killian bows to the king before sauntering off stage without a care in the world like he did not just receive the highest points of the day, to everyone's surprise.

Shay shifts, and I look over to see him scowling. "Damn. The *Púca* probably rigged it somehow."

I don't fully understand what he's saying, and based on the steam I can practically see coming from his ears, I don't think it's the time to ask.

More people are called forward with only one more receiving a three.

"Cara Winters."

My muscles freeze. I'm not prepared for this. I can't do this. What if I fail? What if I'm too weak to continue?

I glance at Shay and he raises an eyebrow at me.

"Cara Winters," the man repeats. This is the first time he's had to repeat a name, and as heads turn from side to side in the crowd, my anxiety skyrockets.

I wipe my palms on my dress. It's okay, it's fine. I need to pass. Oh god, I need to pass or I can't go home.

My chest tightens until I'm unsure if I'm breathing. I hope my muddled banshee side helps me not fail the test. Please be enough.

With a deep breath, I stand, and on shaky legs walk to the front of the room.

The king smirks at me, delighted by the terror he sees across my pale face.

Once in front of the orb, my heart rate jackrabbits. I don't know what this will feel like. Will it hurt? Darn, I should've asked Shay more questions.

I gulp as I reach forward. My palm presses against the cool glass and nothing happens. I hold my breath, waiting for something, anything. Another second ticks by.

The smile on the king's face grows before being replaced with gaping eyes.

I squint as a white light emits from beneath my hand, reaching into the second row of the crowd.

"She… receives three points." I can hear the shock in the king's voice as he sees this, as it matches my own.

How could I have any tie to the magic of this realm? Wouldn't I have felt something more if I was one of the few with great power?

I scurry back to Shay, who now sits upright in his seat, smiling widely at the king.

I plop down in my seat and stare at my hands, refusing to make eye contact with anyone. I'm thankful it's done and hopefully no other trials have me going up in front of a crowd by myself.

The last handful of names are called, and the King stands at the end of everyone's test.

He walks forward, his eyes alighting on the globe. He reaches out, palming the floating sphere. A cascade of blinding colors envelops the entire room.

I cover my eyes, and as the light pulses, I look at the king between my fingers. A manic grin covers his face as he stares at the globe with depthless eyes before it disappears.

EIGHT

"Well, that was interesting," I say to Shay as we follow everyone out of the throne room.

"Yes, white isn't a normal color," Shay replies, his brows pinching in thought.

"I was actually talking about the king at the end with all the rainbow colors. It was all whabam and shwoom!" My hands blast apart to emphasize how bright it got. But now that he's pointed it out, mine was the only one that turned white. The king's shock when it was my turn makes sense now.

"Ah, right. He is the most powerful fae in the realm. Thus why he has been the uncontended ruler for hundreds of years." Shay's face puckers like he's tasting something sour as he speaks. Clearly, he is not a huge fan of the king, but everyone else seems to adore him.

"Why... why do you think my color was different?" My fingers toy with the skirt of my dress. I am cursed after all, maybe white is bad. A part of me expected it to be black, but it's presumptuous of me to assume black means bad and white means good. My face pales while I consider that I still have botched magic, and I interpreted it all wrong. What if white actually means I'm evil?

Shay shrugs, "I can't say, but I'm sure we will discover the reason eventually. Perhaps the next trial will be revealing."

I peek over to him. "What's the next trial?"

"Truth." A husky voice says from behind me.

I startle, swinging around to see Killian looming over me. His heady sandalwood scent is so strong I can taste it. My breath quickens and I tear my eyes away from the amber glow of his own. It's like he is staring into my soul every time, as though he sees the darkness that's followed me through life and knows I am not worthy enough to win this competition. Trials for virtues? Unless the virtues are about curses, death, and social awkwardness, I doubt I'll be winning.

Shay scowls. "Don't you have somewhere to be?"

Killian has yet to take his eyes off me. They burn into me even as I stubbornly keep my face downturned. Finally, his overwhelming presence subsides as he directs his focus on Shay.

My shoulders slump from the lifted weight.

"I'm on my way to the *Naim* feast, as all competitors who passed the first trial are," Killian explains.

My eyebrows raise at Shay. I thought we were heading back to our rooms like yesterday. "A dinner?" I squeak as Killian's attention turns back to me, closing up my throat from finishing my thought aloud. I internally groan. What I wouldn't give to have Shauna's charm and confidence right now.

"Aye, it's a celebratory feast for the official contestants. Yesterday was a sign up, but now that the weak have been weeded, the actual competition begins." Shay runs his hands over his red locks.

"Don't be fooled, little rabbit." Killian leans down to me, causing my stomach to somersault. "This may not be an official trial, but the competition is always transpiring."

I nod. *Why can't I talk?* I whine inside. My mouth is dry and my brain feels like mush.

"Stop scaring the poor girl," Shay chides Killian.

Yeah, we'll go with scared. I almost want to laugh, but the swirling emotions constricting my lungs proves I don't know what I feel when Killian is around. My brain fries before I can gather myself.

Killian leans back, his hands stuffed in his pockets. "See you at dinner," he says as he blends into the retreating crowd.

I heave a sigh as my body relaxes.

Shay eyes me suspiciously before shaking his head and moving on. "Let's go."

We follow the crowds to a large dining area. Rows of tables line the center, and along the walls is a buffet for the masses. I curve through the throngs of people, like a child running ahead of their parent, to the mounds of food. My mouth waters as I admire the large bowls of various salads, fresh carved meats, steaming vegetables, and towers of bite sized desserts. Everything is more or less recognizable. Thank goodness there isn't some strange fae diet I'm forced to partake in.

The plate I snagged from the end of the buffet fills within minutes, so I grab a second and load it with desserts. The fruit tarts draw my attention, as well as the miniature crème brûlées.

"Thank goodness you have the best foods from Earth," I muffle to Shay between bites of mini cobbler, too hungry to wait until we find seats to try it.

A rumbling chuckle escapes him, in a condescending way only Shay could manage. "You presume these are Earth delicacies? You should thank us fae for bringing them to Earth for you to partake in."

Yup, definitely condescending, but my ears perk at something he says. "How long have fae been on Earth?"

"Thousands of years. Just because humans do not know of *Gon'an'rit* does not mean we haven't been a part of your society from the beginning. I would say the reason humankind has made the strides it has is because of our influence." His chest puffs up like I should thank him personally.

I roll my eyes as I grab another cobbler, this time I choose berry since I finished the peach.

We head to a table in the corner, and Shay sits in the furthest corner seat, so the least amount of people are at his back. I sit across from him so I can ignore the stares I keep getting from other contestants.

"Why do they keep staring?" I mutter as I poke a piece of red meat covered in gravy. It melts in my mouth, and I moan.

"Probably because of the obscene noises you keep making like your food is your lover," Shay responds.

I glare at him. "They were staring before I started eating. Don't be jealous because food can evoke sounds you can't."

"First, I have no interest in procuring such sounds in another. Second, as I previously stated, white is an uncommon color, and so is having a proxy. The fae that use proxies are the incredibly wealthy, and even then they already have so much that a single wish is of little use to them. Otherwise, most fae are too prideful and enter the contests themselves."

I choke on my food as I try not to laugh. That's rich coming from him, saying 'most fae' like he is not as proud as the rest of them. "Are you incredibly wealthy?"

I'm still conscientious of the fact we sleep in the palace, while everyone else seems to travel from outside the gates.

Shay watches the mingling fae, ignoring my question.

Typical.

"Also, who's stopping me from using the wish for myself if I win?" I swing my fork in his direction.

He presses his lips together. "The contract you sign will not allow the magic of the king and the land to work on you if you try to use the wish. Only the wish I utter will be granted."

"Why?"

"It's written in the contract you signed, and then sealed in magic."

I deflate. There goes that plan. I really need to start reading disclaimers before signing them. I guess trusting him to take me home if I win is the only way back.

I startle when a booming voice echoes through the dining area, and I turn to see the King standing proudly at the head table.

"May the road rise up to meet you, may the wind always be at your back, may the sun shine warm upon your face, and the rain fall soft upon your fields." Once done, the king sits, lifts a turkey leg and takes a bite.

With this, everyone raises their forks and digs in. I turn to Shay to see he's begun eating too, and my face heats at the realization no one else has been eating aside from me.

"Why didn't you tell me not to eat?" I utter with annoyance.

Shay grins before taking another mouthful of mashed potato.

At this rate, I wouldn't use a wish to go home, I'd use it to give Shay a taste of his own medicine.

I glance over my shoulder to the rest of the group, praying no one noticed my lack of manners, and flush when the king is staring at me. I turn back to the table and shrink lower into my seat.

Minutes pass and the awkwardness grows as no one talks to one another, everyone focusing on the feast in front of them. We're competitors, but I'd assume there would be a little more camaraderie.

"You don't wish to eat?" A fae beside me asks. He doesn't turn my way when he speaks, but he fills out his suit. He isn't bulking muscle like Shay, but he has a broad chest and isn't bad on the eyes. Handsome is an ideal word.

Are all fae ridiculously good looking?

He meticulously places the fork he used to eat his chicken down on a napkin before picking up a spoon to take a bit of rice. The food on his plate is sectioned into little piles, all of equal size, ensuring nothing touches.

"Just waiting for others to catch up, I guess," I answer. No need for him to know I lost part of my appetite from the king staring me down. Okay, I get it, white's a weird color for the first trial.

"You'll need your strength," he hums without making eye contact. "If you don't eat, you'll be weak, and if you're weak, you'll fail. You might even die," he states, nodding to himself.

"D-die?" I stutter. Now, I've definitely lost my appetite.

"Oh yes, fae die in this competition all the time. We must weed out the weak." He nods again.

My eyes dart to Shay and he continues to eat as though everything is normal. "I can die in this?" I direct my question at Shay, but the fae besides me answers.

"Oh yes, fae die in this competition all the time," he repeats. "We must weed out the weak." He puts his spoon back in the same place on his napkin when he finishes his rice. Next, he lifts a smaller sized fork to eat the pile of leafy salad on his plate. A brown braided bracelet on his left wrist, weathered from years of wear, contrasts his nice outfit.

Well, this fae is more open than the man I am, apparently, risking my life for. I reach my hand forward. "My name's Cara. Nice to meet you."

He looks at my hand as though it's going to attack him. He relaxes again when I lower my hand.

"I'm Cadan. I'm a *Spriggan* and my orb color was green. I scored a three in the Power contest," he overviews. "How do you spell Cara?"

I smile at him. I have no idea what a *Spriggan* is. Along with a map, I wonder if there's a fae encyclopedia I could borrow. Still, he's definitely the most forthcoming fae I've met so far. "C-A-R-A."

"Our names are similar. Three of our letters match," he dissects the similarities.

"That's very true," I can't help but smile again, "and I think you have a lovely name."

His salad fork pauses midair, and for the first time he turns and meets my eyes. They are all black, which contrasts his pale skin and white-blonde hair sitting messily on his head. Everything else about him seems so put together, as though it all has a very specific place, but his unruly hair has a mind of its own. His unnerving, stark eyes are all seeing, as though depths of knowledge are contained within him, and they warm when he gives a small smile. "Thank you. You have pretty hair," he says. He immediately drops eye contact, shifting uncomfortably in his seat as he turns back to his food.

"Thank you." I smile to myself at his kindness.

"It's often good to respond to an honest compliment with another honest compliment," he recites. "You should do well in the Truth competition."

"Thanks," I respond, not knowing what else to say.

"No reason to thank someone for a statement." He takes his last bite of food and then lines his dirty utensils on the plate in the same order they were on his napkin. Once complete, his dish disappears.

Still without an appetite, I follow suit, even placing my utensils in the same order as the fae beside me, and gasp when my plate disappears as well.

Cadan stares at the spot where my plate was seconds ago. "That's good. Your knife should always be on the left and fork on the right as it matches the hands that hold them." He nods in agreement with himself.

The corners of my mouth tilt up at him. His kindness is like a breath of fresh air. He's the first fae who hasn't made me hate being here.

"I'm done eating, so I must go and rest. I don't want to be weeded out. I'm not weak. It was nice meeting you, Cara." He inclines his head to me before standing.

"It was wonderful meeting you too, Cadan." My cheeks are sore from the huge grin he pulls from me.

With a burst, he disappears in front of me.

My jaw hangs open with my eyes wide. Now, I understand the three score he received in the trial. I open my mouth to ask Shay if he can do that too, but a piercing sound shoots through my head. Doubling in on myself, I grab the sides of my head.

Shay's alarmed face disappears as a concussive blast catapults me towards the stone wall.

NINE

All I hear is ringing. It pings through my brain at an earsplitting rate. Everything is black. There is nothing but death. I can feel it in my body.

"Cara." A rough hand shakes me. "Cara!" My name is muffled.

I open my eyes one by one, and Shay's blurry face hovers over me. My nerve endings electrify across my skin, causing me to close my eyes again to block everything out.

This can't be happening. Not again. Not here.

Shay's hand roughly shakes me again, and I wince in pain. Prying my eyes open, his blurry features come into focus once more. The ringing in my head is so intense I see his lips moving, but can barely comprehend anything.

I focus on his lips.

Cara, get up, I read them as he grabs my hand and pulls me to a sitting position.

The sudden movement increases the ringing in my head. I bite my tongue to keep from crying out. My sharp inhale makes me cough, wheezing out dust from my lungs to float through the air.

I wince when I press my hand to my scalp. Red coats my fingers. I blink at my wet, blood-coated hand in shock. The muffled sounds sharpen, and the first clear thing I hear are the screams.

Shay's lips are moving and I realize he is trying to talk to me.

"What?" I ask, but my own voice sounds disjointed from reality.

Shay hauls me up by the arm, concern etches his face. We use a pillar to hide ourselves and he shoves me behind him as he unsheathes his sword.

I lose my footing and tumble back to the ground.

My palm presses into my forehead. The sound is so painful, nausea twists my stomach. I gulp a couple of steadying breaths before pushing myself onto my knees. Shay is no longer in front of me. My eyes scan the room for him.

Tables are toppled, if not blown to bits. Motionless fae lie on the ground, most likely dead. Some who can stand try to flee, but many are fighting cloaked figures. The King is nowhere in sight.

A shadow crosses over me and I raise my head to see a dark figure. His cloak masks any of his features.

I'm paralyzed as he brings a sword above his head.

I'm going to die. My curse has caught up with me. It's finally come for me.

All I can do is stare as he swings his weapon down.

A body flies through the air, smashing into the man's side. Both of them topple to the floor. The cloaked man grapples for the sword that has fallen from his hand, but the figure on top of him cracks his skull with his elbow. After the fae climbs off of him, he turns to me.

Amber eyes analyze my body, pausing on each bruise and cut. Killian leaps over to me. "Can you fight?"

I blink at him. Fight? With what? I mean, I did take those defense classes, so I guess I kind of can.

I nod, but wince at the movement when a throbbing pain bursts through my skull.

Killian helps me stand, and his gaze sweeps across the pandemonium surrounding us.

My legs buckle, causing me to lean into him, and instinctually his arm wraps around my waist.

"Can you even stand?" His words still sound muffled in my left ear.

I can feel warm blood trickling down the left side of my neck, the opposite side of where I found my head wound earlier. Great.

"Not well, apparently," I rasp. The use of my throat causes another coughing fit into my elbow to cover my mouth. I pull my arm from my face, and blood coats my sleeve. I'm 99% sure coughing up blood is a bad thing.

Killian's face hardens with concern, his teeth grinding until a muscle ticks in his neck. Something shines in his eyes before his gaze sweeps the room. If I didn't know any better, I'd say it was fear.

Let's change that to 100% sure it's a bad thing.

"Follow me," he says, pulling me along with his arm still around my back.

I don't fully register the contact as we walk, avoiding piles of stone and bodies. So many bodies.

A sharp sound echoes in my head, but it cuts off the moment a blade enters a fae's chest. My eyes blur. I can't tell if it's from the emotional or physical pain.

Killian drops his hand, and without his support, I crash to my knees.

He sneaks up behind another cloaked figure and uses the hilt of his sword to knock them unconscious, seeming to be the only fae not aiming for deadly blows. He rushes back to me, and when he helps me stand my legs give out.

He curses before slipping his arms under me to hold me like a baby.

Usually I'd be fumbling with embarrassment, but the pain ricocheting through my limbs has me leaning my head against his shoulder. I close my eyes to help quiet my mind. With a deep breath, I look to Killian. "Leave me," I say with another cough, coating Killian's shirt in blood.

He grimaces at me. "Not gonna happen."

"Where's Shay?" I croak.

"He can take care of himself." Killian glides across the wreckage, only pausing to avoid detection from the cloaked fae.

We are at the main doors when a deep voice calls out. "Let her go, Killian!"

He ignores the voice and doesn't stop, but Shay leaps in front of him.

"Put her down," he demands again.

"She needs medical attention. Move," Killian sneers.

Before Shay can retort, he's swinging around Killian with his sword slashing out.

Killian turns with him, refusing to have his back to Shay, and the movement makes my head pound.

Everything dims, and it becomes harder to breathe.

Killian should have left me. Death has surrounded me my entire life. I am cursed, and it'd be better if I was gone. It'd be easier.

Shay's sword connects with another held by a cloaked figure who had been sneaking up behind us.

Killian hesitates, his eyes sparking with desire to join the fray. He frowns down at me, his hands gripping me harder into me until I'm pressing more firmly against his chest. His torn eyes slipping between me and Shay shows his indecision on what to do.

Shadows press in on my vision.

The worry increases on his face as his fingers dig into my thighs.

"Go!" Shay hollers to us. "Take her, Killian. I've got this!"

Without acknowledgement, Kilian turns from the battle and runs with a scowl etched across his face.

His anger is the last thing I see before darkness takes me.

I awaken to a cream colored ceiling. I hear the soft pattering of rain against a window above me. I brace my elbows, intending to lift myself, but the ache in my body forces me back into the mattress.

A grey haired woman, with pointed ears peeking from underneath her short hair, waltzes over to me. "Oh good, you're up," she says with a warm smile. "The master will be pleased."

Why would the King be thankful that I'm awake? A huge travesty just happened to dozens of fae. I'm pretty sure there are bigger things for him to worry about.

The nurse helps me into a sitting position, but not without plenty of whimpers on my end. My body has seen better days.

"Drink this," the fae woman says as she holds out a cup to me.

I peer inside as I take it from her and see green sludge.

She chuckles at my grimace. "It tastes better than it looks. It'll help repair your body by working with the magic of *Gon'an'rit.*"

Before I can think better of it, I toss the cup back and it oozes into my mouth. It takes everything in me to swallow it. I have no idea what she thinks bad tastes like if this dirt filled concoction tastes good to her.

"Very good." The woman grabs the cup. "I will let the others know you are okay." She whisks away before I can ask questions.

I must have dozed off again because the next thing I know I'm being shaken awake.

"Sir, you really should let her rest," the nurse complains over Shay's shoulder as she looks at me worriedly.

"It's okay," I say with a groan.

She frowns between the two of us. "Let me know if I can get you anything," she tells me.

I nod, but have no plans on taking her up on that. Leftover grit grinds in my mouth from the last time she helped me.

"What happened?" I raise my eyebrow at Shay.

"We were attacked." He leans away from me until he's casually lounging in his seat. He folds his arms across his chest, back in his leather vest with his sword on his back, like he wasn't recently in a battle.

"Wow, your answers are really improving." I roll my eyes. "Clearly we were attacked, but by who? Or why? What happened to me or where am I? And is Killian alright? Answers to any of those would be great."

"Well kid, if you learned to ask better questions, I'd give better answers," he once again chides me.

I stare at him, waiting. I am not in the mood for games.

He releases a deep sigh. "We assume another court attacked. Blew a hole right through the wall on the other side of the dining room. We are investigating who it was as their cloaks were used to mask an affiliation. For you, the nurse said you have a concussion, three cracked ribs, and damage to your lungs, which had them filling with blood." He seems to answer all my questions except the one about Killian.

I prod my chest filled with my wild heartbeat, and pray they aren't filling again. I hadn't made it far in my vet assistant training, but none of that sounds good.

"You've been in a healing sleep for three days. Your lungs are fixed, ribs nearly mended, and concussion should be gone in the next twelve hours. You'll mostly feel bruised now," he amends.

"Why didn't you say that from the start?" I gape at him. Also, wow, can we talk about the healing time? Back on Earth that would've taken months if I hadn't died from it.

He shrugs before looking at me. "Why didn't you use your power?"

I cock my head to the side. I have no idea what he's talking about. Unless he considers my curse a power, but I wouldn't know how to use that. My *power*, I cringe at calling it that, is a signal before someone dies around me. So, yeah, I definitely have no clue what he means.

"Why didn't you scream? Like in the alley," he modifies his question, annoyance tinging his tone.

"If you couldn't tell I was in a lot of pain," I retort. "Plus, when I screamed, I wanted help. I didn't really need help at that moment."

"Considering someone almost killed you, and you had to be carried out or you would've died if not by someone's hands than your injuries, I think that would count as needing help." He props one of his feet onto my bed.

"Wouldn't screaming have alerted the cloaked fae where I was and killed me sooner?" I'm pretty sure prey don't let their predators know where they are by purposefully calling out.

"You truly don't know how to use your *Beansidhe* powers?" He presses his lips into a hard line as though I'm the most idiotic person he's ever met.

My cheeks warm. "No, because until a few days ago I didn't know I was one! For someone who whines about my questions, I'm surprised your listening skills aren't better."

He scratches his chin. "Learning to protect yourself is something we need to rectify as soon as possible." He stands. "You continue to rest. I need to set up some things and then we will start your training."

"That's all? You're just going to leave?" I holler after him. "What training? Where are you going? When can I leave?"

He ignores my questions as he leaves the room.

I seethe as I nestle into my bed, crossing my arms like a child about to throw a tantrum. I glare at the wall across from me until drowsiness presses on my eyes.

First step is getting better. With this goal at the forefront of my mind, I drift back into a healing sleep.

TEN

I stop at an intersection on the path I'm on and re-read the note from Shay. I hunch over to block the rain from smearing the ink.

Left at the fork.

I continue to follow the directions that appeared on my table this morning with breakfast.

After being released two days ago, all I've done is lie in my room. I haven't seen Shay, and food magically appears on my desk three times a day, and disappears once I'm done. It's been boring as there are no books for me to read. Multiple times I considered sneaking around the castle, maybe trying to find a way home, but sleep consumed most of my time to help me heal.

I crest a hilltop and below is the riding ring Shay told me to meet him at after breakfast. The rain is already soaking through my workout clothes, or what I assume is workout gear from its soft spandex-like material. It's black, so neither the rain nor my sweat will show.

My footsteps echo on the path as I reach the arena. I fold my arms over the top of the wooden fence and prop my head on my wrists.

No one is here yet. I didn't oversleep, so I doubt I missed practice.

Off to the right, sitting on top of a small grassy knoll, is a large white barn trimmed in green paint. I perk up at the thought of seeing animals. I wonder if the animals here are different than on Earth. It's close enough that I'm sure I'll hear Shay complaining about something once he arrives.

I bite my lip, but the tug of my heart to meet some furry friends wins out.

I walk along the fence lining the paddock until I have a straight shot to the barn. It takes less than five minutes to reach the stable, and the unique scent of horse washes over me. I smile as I take a deep breath of the earthy aroma mixed with fresh hay.

My comfort zone is dogs and cats, but connecting with any animal fills my soul with a buzz of happiness. In my semester work-study program, there was a month I spent working with a livestock vet. He had no particular office, but would travel to different farms in the area. He drove everywhere, so if the farm was three hours away I didn't need to find my own way which was nice. Chickens, goats, cows, hogs, but I always loved when we worked with horses. They're like extremely large puppies.

One of my most prized experiences, which solidified my desire to be a veterinarian, was when I helped birth a baby horse. My job consisted of keeping the mother horse calm by rubbing her neck, and bringing animals a sense of peace is my specialty. To witness a birth was miraculous.

I really need to win this and get home or I'd lose my spot in the internship. I didn't work this hard for my future, one where I can help my sister in all the ways she's helped me, only to lose it all.

The doors are already open and I get a reprieve from the constant misting outside when I enter. I pass through the center, and each stall holds a horse. Eight are brown with white diamonds on their foreheads and socks on at least two of their feet. Five are all black and three are white with strawberry dapples.

I land in front of a tan horse with a white mane. White speckles that match the mane coat its body. A palomino, my favorite. In my ideal world where I wasn't scraping by to make ends meet for my part of the rent, this is the horse I would want to own. My sister offered to pay for all of it so I could focus on school, but the moment I became a legal adult, I refused. With being a full time student, I became a tutor where it was easy to make money and have a flexible schedule.

"Hey there, beautiful." I lean against the door. I'm unsure if it is a mare or gelding, but it's not a stallion because if it's a male, it's been neutered.

The horse's ears flick back as it listens to me coo. Raising its head, it turns to look at me with one of its brown saucer eyes.

"I won't hurt you," I reassure the beast.

The horse nickers at me before moseying over. Its long neck drapes across the gate and it releases a deep exhale through flared nostrils, blowing my hair behind me.

I lift my hand, fingers flat, and raise my palm to the horse's nose.

It breathes in my scent. Its eye never leaves me, and I can see a dark reflection of myself in the huge pupil.

"There you go." I lean forward and slowly blow into the horse's nose; a trick taught to me by the vet I worked with as a better way for a horse to scent you.

Its nostrils flare as it registers me, and the tail swishes while it stomps its front leg.

I smile as the horse bends its head lower, calming at my presence.

I reach forward and place my hand on its neck, petting in long smooth strokes. I move my hand up until I'm scritching the horse behind the ears then my palm continues down its forehead.

Its eyes droop under my touch as it continues to relax.

I've always had a magic touch with animals, which various veterinarians confirmed after working with them. *A soothing touch*, they called it.

My mind wanders to the dog in the alley as I continue to stroke the palomino. It had lost a lot of blood. My lips pinch when I chew the inside of my cheek. I hope the wound didn't become infected.

The horse blasts more air across my face, and my tight muscles relax with a laugh.

"Ah yes, I have enough to stress about, huh?" I talk to the horse as though it'll respond. "Horses are always so in tune with our feelings. Maybe one day I'll be lucky to ride you, what do you think about that?"

The horse whinnies, which I'm taking as an agreement.

Now all I have to do is learn to ride a horse. I'm sure I can convince Shay to squeeze that into whatever training he has planned for me.

I huff a laugh to myself at the idea of convincing Shay of anything, but my lighter moment quickly ends with a sigh. The wish to ride will stay as nothing but a wish. It wasn't something I had the luxury of doing while bouncing between foster homes in a city, and there's no reason to believe that'll change now.

Low voices murmur at the entrance of the barn.

Shay must've arrived. Took him long enough.

I kiss the nose of the horse, promising to come back again, and meander to the entrance. I'm about to step into the open when I see the backs of two men, neither of which have Shay's crop of auburn hair.

From the golden chest plate, I know one is a guard. His hand rests on the pommel of the sword at his side. Security became tighter across the castle compared to when I first arrived. I passed fifteen guards on the way here. I noticed it when coming to meet Shay, but didn't think much of it. Seems a normal thing to do after an attack.

The other figure is wearing a dark outfit and has two swords across his back. His raven hair glistens from the rain. His deep voice is one I recognize when he speaks— Killian.

I pull back inside the barn door, hiding in the shadows off to the side. I'm not sure if I'm allowed in the barn. Should I thank him for saving me? I don't want to interrupt his conversation. Maybe I'll leave using the back entrance and come through the field. That way they see me coming. I take a step in the direction of the other side of the barn, but pause when I hear a name I recognize.

"I see Shay is using a proxy," the guard gossips.

"Cara," Killian confirms.

"She's quite fetching, wouldn't you agree?"

I hold my breath as I await Killian's answer.

"If you enjoy a curveless, feeble woman."

My heart sinks as I glance down at myself. I mean, he's not wrong, but that's a little harsh.

"Don't act like you don't like it," the guard prods.

Killian grunts. "Needing to save a woman who shouldn't be here in the first place isn't what I would call a good time."

My hands ball at my sides until they turn white. Not wanting to hear anymore, I sneak away. Shauna would tell me it's my fault for listening to a conversation not meant for my ears. But I say, screw that and screw him. Killian Mactíre will not be receiving any gratitude from me any time soon.

I stomp through the fields at the back of the stable until I'm at the bottom of the opposite side of the hill. I unclench my fists with a breath to calm myself before turning to follow the bottom of the knoll back to the arena to meet Shay.

Shay leans against the fence with his hands in his pockets. His head raises as I approach. "It's about time, decide to have a second sleep instead?"

I press my lips in a fine line. I didn't want him to know why I was late or say out loud what I overheard.

He pushes off the fence and with one hand boosts himself over the side to the inside of the ring. "We are still waiting on one other, but we can get started."

I step to the railing and duck between the first and second slats instead of jumping over the top. I am tiny, anything closer to the ground is more my style. Although, I'm guessing what Shay has planned for me today is already not my style.

"Let's start with activating your banshee powers." Shay crosses his arms, waiting for me to do something magical.

I am not in the mood for his games. So, in response, I mimic his pose and cock my hip for good measure.

He sighs. "Well, give a scream, kid."

My eyebrows draw closer to my hairline. "You… just want me to scream? That's all?"

"Well, that's what you've done before." His body is stiff, annoyance radiating from it, as though I'm purposely holding back.

"So you say, I don't know what I did. You are the one who claims I did something. I screamed for help, a guy fell, you killed him, and voila I ended up here. Pretty sure you did most, if not all, of the work." I stare at him blankly.

This is an absolute waste of my time. I shouldn't have even bothered to come. It's not as though Shay has been helpful since he dragged me here. Why should now be any different?

Shay scratches at the scruff on his chin. "Have you experienced anything odd in your life? Anything that is your normal, but weird to others? Maybe something developed in later childhood?"

My face pales. A ringing that isn't there echoes through my mind along with flashes of people falling to the ground from heart attacks, car crashes, faces turning blue from choking on food. Endless images of death from my life makes my head spin. My curse, it's the only thing I can think of, but there's no way I'm comfortable telling Shay. It took years for my own sister to believe me.

Instead, I fill my lungs through my nose, open my mouth, and scream at the top of my lungs.

Shay's eyes narrow as he watches me.

My chest compress as I scream until I gasp back a lungful of air.

"That's not it." Shay shakes his head.

I throw my hands into the air. "Well, I screamed. I don't know what I've done, or how I did it, or what I'm aiming for!"

"*Beansidhes* are not only known as predictors of death, but can bring unconsciousness to their victims." Shay circles me as he looks me up and down. "Your scream didn't incapacitate me. You should have knocked me out. Have you ever known a death to happen before it occurs?" He stops in front of me.

"No!" I rush out. Crap, I didn't mean to shout at him, but it's a touchy subject. My instinct to hide away takes over and the internal walls build in my mind, putting barriers up against myself and the world.

Shay scrutinizes me.

My hands twist in front of me, and I stretch my fingers to make myself stop. Could I look anymore guilty? Maybe I should tell him? He said this is normal for banshees, right?

I shake my head to myself. There's no way that much death is normal. There's no way losing a childhood friend because you mentioned someone would die, for her dad to then have an untimely stroke downstairs, is normal. The two years after the incident is a bit of a blur, filled with a darkness I still try to fight off today. The fear she had in her eyes, a fear directed at me, still haunts me. That was the last time I tried being close to anyone outside of Shauna.

"Hmm," Shay muses. But before he says anything more, his gaze looks over my shoulder. "Ah, there you are. Her powers are a bust," his eyes lock on mine, "for now."

"I guess it's a good thing I'm here then."

I cringe at the husky voice behind me, and it takes everything in me not to storm away when I turn to see Killian leaning on the fence.

ELEVEN

Killian gracefully swings over the fence. He stalks toward me, and I take a step back. His predatory eyes roam over me as he stops in front of me. "Let's see what you're capable of, little rabbit."

His eyes gleam as he unsheathes his swords.

I glance at Shay, who frowns at Killian.

Killian clucks his tongue, bringing my attention back. A sword tip points inches from my chest. "Never take your eyes off the enemy." With a knowing smirk, he flips the sword and catches the tip without cutting himself, holding the hilt towards me.

My fingers wrap around the grip and when Killian lets go, my arm drops from the unexpected weight. My other hand reaches out to double grasp the sword, but the top still drags through the dirt.

Killian holds up his other sword in his left hand, pointed slightly upward. He lunges forward and I skitter back.

Using every feeble muscle in my body, I lug the sword in front of me. The clang of his sword against mine shifts the heavy burden to the right and my body follows. I stumble forward until I catch my footing and swing back around. My arms already burn from propping the sword.

Killian prowls in a circle around me, and I shuffle with him, never taking my eyes off my opponent.

I run at him, hoping to catch him off guard, but he sidesteps and I tumble past him. I turn back around in time to see his sword barreling down at me, but I barely meet it with my own.

The force of this hit knocks my sword from my hands and it clatters to the compact ground. My chest tightens with failure, and tears of frustration threaten me. My teeth grind together for a distraction against my building emotions.

Killian faces Shay. "I don't know how you expect us to teach her before the next trial."

My nails dig into my palms as I scowl at them. Who do these men think they are? I'm a foster kid from a city on Earth, when the hell was I supposed to learn how to sword fight? I taste blood from where I've bitten through part of my cheek.

The pain is sobering.

I bend down and pick up my sword, and before I think better of it I'm moving forward and swing my sword like it's a baseball bat.

Shay's eyes widen as Killian leaps out of the way at the last second, but not before the sword tip slices through the billowing sleeve of his shirt.

"Fighting dirty, I see." Killian's finger prods at the new addition to his clothes.

There's no blood. A part of me kind of wishes I had drawn the tiniest bit to put him in his place.

"Never take your eyes off the enemy," I throw his words back at him.

His golden eyes darken, and in a flash he disappears from in front of me.

I open my mouth to speak, but cool steel presses against my neck, silencing me.

"Don't tempt me, little rabbit," he breathes across my ear as he leans over me from behind, causing a shiver to run down my spine. "You know nothing."

His open ended statement hits home in a way he may not realize. Actually, knowing him, he knows exactly what he's saying and how much it would hurt. He sees me as this meek, pathetic, human girl who doesn't belong here and has nothing going for her. The worst part was, he isn't wrong.

I squeeze my eyes tight.

Screw that. Screw him. Screw Shay, this place, my curse, and everything that has brought me to where I am. I'm about to lose everything I've worked for because of them.

I slam my elbow backwards into his ribs.

Killian hisses as the momentum pushes him away from me. The blade moves with him, nicking my neck, but I use the moment to duck under and away from him.

"My regrets to you thinking you need to teach some feeble, curveless woman," I spit in his direction.

The slight tensing of his body is the only indication he realizes I'm using the same words he spoke to the guard. His eyes harden while he massages where I hit him.

"I do not wish for your help and you're relieved of the misplaced duty to save me." I square my shoulders and walk away from them both, squeezing back between the wooden rungs and traipsing back to the safety of my room.

Shay calls after me, but I ignore him. His attention diverts to Killian with a load of cursing.

I don't dare look over my shoulder, but the hairs stand at the nape of my neck with the feel of Killian's burning gaze as he follows my retreat.

I'm halfway back to the castle when I notice a small grouping of fae gathered near a wall. They form a semi-circle, but I can't discern what they surround.

"Did you cheat?" One of them shouts.

"Nah, he didn't cheat. He's too stupid to do something like that," another adds.

"He can't even look at us," another chimes in. "How does he expect to win?"

Another bursts out laughing. "Look at this idiot fae."

Everyone joins in the heckling and laughter, but it teeters off after a few beats.

"Why is he laughing with us?"

"Because he's crazy," another answers.

"I don't wish to be called crazy," a voice pipes up from inside the half circle. "I have a different wish."

My body stiffens at the sound of Cadan's voice. I trudge forward until I can see his tousled blonde hair and depthless eyes as he scans everyone's shoes.

"Oh yeah? What's your wish, dumbass? To be normal?"

"You wear two different shoes." Cadan points towards one of the fae's feet. "Do you not have money to buy matching shoes? Were they given to you?"

"Shut it! Who the hell do you think you are judging me?" He retaliates before stepping forward to raise his foot, shoving it into Cadan's chest.

Cadan's back hits the wall, and he curls in on himself.

My own chest tightens at the impact.

"He's so weak he can't even stand up for himself. He's going to die in the competition," another laughs.

"Maybe we should convince him a little harder to drop out early."

Others murmur their agreement.

I run at them, my slight frame easily slipping between two of them. Spinning around, I hold my arms out to the side to block them from Cadan.

Two of the five men seem like brothers, both bulky with shaved heads and blue eyes that match. The other three are just as large. One has a serpent tattoo running up his arm to his neck, the next has a scar across his cheek, and the final fae, who seems to be the least feral of them all, stands with his fists clenched at his sides.

"Planning on punching me and my friend?" I goad the last man. I must have a death wish. There's no way I can take on these five massive fae. But there's no way I'm leaving Cadan defenseless.

One brother laughs. "Who would be friends with that idiot?"

I glare at him, widening my stance to further cover the fae at my back.

"Screw you," I seethe through clenched teeth.

Scarface smirks with too much delight in his eyes. "Well, if you're offering." He takes a step forward, and the others follow.

Cadan grasps my hand, but I never take my eyes off the enemy.

"It's okay, Cara," he claims from behind me. "It's okay. I'm okay. I'm not weak."

My grip tightens around his fingers. "This is not okay," I announce to the others just as much to him.

"If you give us a reason, we can forget all about that weak fae behind you," Serpent licks his lips. "I'm sure you can think of a few ways to distract us." He gives a wink, and the burn of bile climbs up my throat.

My sister is right, it seems there are disgusting people no matter where you go. But Cadan's presence reminds me there are good people too.

Scarface takes another step, one step too close.

I am not feeble.

I drop Cadan's hand, ball my fist, and with a running jump, slam it into his face. A curse slips from my lips from the impact of my bone hitting his radiating up my arm.

"You bitch." Scarface grabs a handful of my hair, pulling upwards until I'm on my tiptoes.

I attempt to ball my fist, but moving my fingers sends a sharp pain through my hand.

He gives another yank, and my hands reach up to pry open his chubby fingers. I push the pain of my hand to the back of my mind, but his fingers don't loosen. A cry rips from my mouth when he tightens his hold further.

There's an echo of a snap of fingers, and I fall to the ground.

Scarface is grabbing his hand as welts form on his fingers. "Damn bastard!"

Cadan crawls over beside me. His depthless eyes are wide in bewilderment. His right hand rubs at his brown leather bracelet, twirling it around his wrist.

"Seems we have two idiots on our hands," one of them taunts.

I'm pretty sure they're the idiots since it seems they can't be more creative with their insulting names.

They've now circled us, creating a pentagon. There's a chance I could evade them and slip away, but Cadan's too big for that.

"We don't need them smart for a good time." A brother's beady eyes trace over my body.

"That bitch is mine," Scarface fumes.

"Let's teach the idiot asshole who's in charge."

A sharp inhale fills my lungs. "Cadan, go," I whisper. I know he can disappear; he did it at dinner. "Go and I'll follow." I push conviction into my tone, hoping he will hear the confidence I don't fully have in myself.

Cadan shakes his head.

Suddenly, a blur of motion couples with grunts from the men. They crumple to the ground and the whirling brown mass moves swiftly between them.

I gape at the unconscious men now littering the ground.

Killian stops in front of me, eyes jumping between me and Cadan.

All I can do is stare in shock at how fast he took down those five fae. "Isn't it a low blow when the enemy doesn't know you're coming?" I ask in annoyance.

"Would you have rather I left you to their wiles?" He retorts, but when he says it malice shines in his eyes.

When I don't answer, he extends his hand to me, but I swat it away. "I told you I didn't want your help."

Cadan and I climb to our feet.

I shoot Killian a loathing look before turning to my friend. "Are you okay?" I ask him.

"You're kind, much nicer than I expected someone from Earth to be," he replies.

I give a small smile. That was more of a backhanded compliment, but I'll take it as long as it means he's fine.

"All the fae I have met so far have been douches," I respond. That includes the bullies on the ground, Killian who stands there watching us, and Shay who leans against the wall like this is the last place he wants to be. But then there's Cadan. "Except you. You are the only kind fae I have met." A wide grin crosses my face.

"All fae are different," Cadan adds.

"Just like humans," I agree.

"I need to go." Cadan runs a hand through his unkempt hair. "Thank you, Cara."

"No problem! You're my only friend here. You can always ask for my help." I give a thumbs up like I'm part of a political campaign.

Honestly, could I be anymore awkward? This is why I'd prefer the company of animals, so I can avoid these moments.

Cadan stutters, and again I am consumed by his depthless black eyes when he looks at me. "I'm your friend?"

My heart squeezes in my chest at his hopeful expression. "Of course."

He gives a small smile to himself and then disappears.

I blink at the empty spot. I guess I'm not the only one who lacks friendship in their life. I simply hope I can be worthy of Cadan's friendship.

I move past Killian, pretending he doesn't exist. I can't believe I found him alluring.

I stomp over to Shay who still relaxes against the palace wall. "Can we go—"

"Let me see your hand," Shay interrupts.

With an eye roll, I raise my left hand and flex my fingers. "All good. Now can we go?"

He reaches down and grabs my right, causing me to flinch.

The skin of one of my knuckles burst open earlier and now a patch of dried blood coats the back of my hand. Three of my fingers are swelling, to where they are starting to look purple and even though Shay touches me gently, it still sends pain through my hand.

"You need to ice this," he states.

"Is it broken?"

My lips press in a line at Killian's voice behind me. Why is he still here? No, why is he here at all? I told him I didn't want his help. Scurry on home, fae boy.

Shay prods my hand, ignoring my pinched face of pain and anger.

"Sprains and bruising, but no broken bones," he decides, dropping my hand. "Come, let's go ice it."

"He's not coming, right?" I tilt my head in Killian's direction.

Shay's jaw ticks, but amusement lights his eyes. "It would be better if he takes you to the kitchen to find you ice."

"What? Why can't you just do the finger snappy thing and have it appear?"

Shay's face darkens at my question. "Killian, accompany her to get ice."

"No!" I cry at Shay's back as his brooding self walks away. "I don't want his help! I don't need his help."

Shay doesn't reply, doesn't turn back, and now I'm left with the last person I want to be near.

I face Killian, and his eyes twinkle with mirth, which only makes me want to scream at the top of my lungs.

"Follow me," he says.

And, begrudgingly, I do.

TWELVE

The scuffing of our shoes against the stone path interrupts the silence. Rain droplets drip from my hairline down the planes of my face.

I narrow my eyes at Killian's back.

His wet shirt clings to the muscles of his back, flexing with the swing of his arms.

I tear my eyes away. Why do the pretty ones have to be jerks? At least my new found annoyance helps make me less brainless around him.

For a brief moment when cresting a hilltop, I see past the wall where waves of rolling green land are interrupted by the tree line of the forest Shay and I had walked through when we first arrived. Above us, four seabirds hover on the ocean breeze, allowing it to carry them effortlessly. I wrap my arms around my waist, shivering as the wind tears through my soaked clothes. A hiss escapes my lips when I rub my bruised hand over the goosebumps on my arm.

Killian's head turns minutely, a reaction so small I would've assumed he had spotted something to his left, but there is only the stony wall of the palace we walk beside. He says nothing and trudges on.

"I miss the sun," I whine to myself. The enamor of the greenery is wearing off. I'm done with this dreary weather. What I wouldn't give to feel the warmth of the sun on my face. I tilt my head upwards, envisioning the basking light, but instead am met with a cold plop on my cheek.

"It wasn't always this way." Killian speaks so quietly I'm unsure if I imagined the response in my head.

We reach a weathered wooden door, and it groans as Killian pulls it open. He steps aside, waving his hand for me to enter first.

How unexpectedly chivalrous of him. However, I'm determined for him not to see me as some damsel in distress. So he can take his 'Ladies first' and shove it where the sun doesn't shine.

I fold my arms, lifting my chin in defiance, until he gives a shrug and steps inside first.

Ha ha! I win!

I smirk when I head into a small entryway filled with hanging coats. I don't care how petty I'm being.

The warm air smells of freshly baked bread, causing a sigh to leave me after I breathe it in. The warmth permeates my cold clothes and settles into my bones, causing a quick shiver through my body. I turn, in hopes Killian didn't see, but of course he's looking straight at me with an unreadable expression.

He snaps his fingers and a warm tingle covers my body.

I want to hate the feeling and bite back the soft moan on my lips. Unease from his magic coursing over me follows the sensation; I enjoyed the feeling a little too much. I glance down to find my clothes are dry and my silky hair draping over my shoulder is too.

The fae can dry themselves with magic, but Shay left me soaked to the bone for hours when we first got here? What an a-hole.

Killian pushes past me and opens another swinging door.

The kitchen is bustling with people, flitting between each other with trays, dishes, and ingredients. They move like a choreographed dance with a random "behind you" called out here and there.

Killian joins the fray, putting his hand lightly on the shoulders of the workers to signal his presence, and moves swiftly into a walk-in freezer.

I squeeze into the corner, pressing my back against a wall, and hold my injured hand to my chest.

A female fae with blonde hair in a braided crown swirling into a tight bun, and the world's most perfect curves, pulls freshly baked rolls from the oven.

I don't swing that way, but if I had my sister's taste… just saying. I'll settle on a girl crush. I may not wish to do her, but I can sure wish to be her. She has my ideal body; what I wouldn't give to look like her.

I blink away my thoughts as the aroma of coffee wafts across the room. My eyes scan the area and snag on a brewing pot. The trickling rich brown liquid has my mouth watering.

"Would you like a cup?" A plump woman with rosy cheeks and a kind face stops in front of me. She wipes her hands on her apron as she waits for a reply.

"That'd be wonderful." I brighten with a smile, although I could hug this sweet woman for offering me coffee.

She nods before heading off. "Any sugar or cream?" She hollers above the menagerie.

"Extra, extra cream," I call back.

She passes off the mug to the gorgeous blonde who pours a dash of milk into the cup.

"A little more, if you don't mind," I plead.

She smirks to herself before adding three more tablespoons.

Perfect.

She glides over to me with the mug and a kind smile touching her lips.

I reach with my injured hand, but the flexing of my fingers reminds me why we're here in the first place. With my left hand, I grab the cup. "You are a lifesaver."

My heart pangs when the words slip out of me. The last person I said that to was my sister the day I got abducted.

"Of course. You new here?" The blonde asks as she moves to the counter to place rolls into a basket. "I haven't seen you before."

"Yeah, you could say that." I take a sip of the steaming coffee and almost tear up at its mouthwatering earthy flavor.

"My name's Marley." She flashes me a smile.

"Cara." I take another sip. This girl is beautiful and kind? Don't get me wrong, I'm all for female empowerment, but if she's ridiculously smart or bad ass then I'm giving up.

Before the silence can get too awkward, Killian appears at my side, ice pack in hand. He grabs my hand without a sound and places the pack on my knuckles.

I take another gulp of my drink to hide the blush creeping on my cheeks as he continues to hold my hand in his.

Damn, and here I thought I was becoming less of a bumbling fool around him. It's not as though he's choosing to hold my hand. I trace over his features through my eyelashes. I mean, he's not *that* good looking. There's a crook in his nose, as though it was once broken and hadn't healed properly, and the scowl he seems to have is creating lines between his brows. My eyes trace over the red marks on his neck; it's like his skin is unblemished. But then I see his strong jaw, his full lips, and hair I want to run my fingers through. There's a harshness to him, but he's gorgeous.

Ugh. I shake my head in hopes the thoughts fling from my brain.

"I can hold it myself," I manage to mutter and reluctantly lean to put my coffee cup on a table beside me.

He opens his mouth to respond, but then he's being hauled away from me.

I catch the ice pack as it slips off.

"Killian, my dear boy!" The motherly woman who offered me coffee pats his cheek. "Come now. Why're you so stern this morning? Here, have a muffin." She snags a blueberry muffin off the counter and shoves it into his hands.

"Thanks, Mrs. Hennessee." He gives a hint of a smile.

"And one for your friend," and she hands one to me too. I balance it between two fingers while I continue to hold the ice.

"We aren't friends," I grumble to myself. She doesn't hear me, but I see the flick of Killian's eyes in my direction.

"Tell me, how is the contest going? I'm sure you're in the top," Mrs. Hennessee continues as she tidies the counter by putting away pans and assisting Marley with assembling baskets of baked goods.

"It's going fine." His deep voice is soft when he speaks to her. Without hesitation, Killian steps forward, grabs a basket and starts arranging different scones with containers of butter and jam.

Mrs. Hennessee smiles at him approvingly. "Well, I'm sure you will beat all of those weaklings in no time."

Killian's hand pauses over a muffin.

"Mom!" Marley looks over, mortified. She leans closer to her mom to throatily whisper, "Cara is a contestant too."

Mrs. Hennessee turns to me. "Oh, I'm sorry, dear. It's nothing against you, of course. It's just our sweet Killian deserves this."

"Stop it," Marley pleads to her mother as she shoves another roll in a basket. "It's not our place."

I shift on my feet, putting the muffin beside my coffee to flip the ice pack to the other side. A tingle in my chest has me raising my gaze.

Killian creates baskets of food, arranging them in a delicate formation. Despite the tenseness between the bickering mother and daughter, he continues to focus on the task at hand. His shoulders relax the longer he works. He's done with his fourth basket when he finally looks up, his golden eyes brushing against mine. His hands continue to work beneath him, having memorized the pattern, as he studies me.

My lungs tighten with a breath I don't release. When I do exhale, his amber eyes drift to my lips, causing them to stop working once again.

"Your mother is doing well." Mrs. Hennessee places a hand on top of his, making him pause.

His face shutters at the mention of his mom, but the emotions swirling there are whisked away as his face hardens once more. "Can you be sure to take her an extra scone?"

Mrs. Hennessee nods, her eyes shining with sorrow.

"I'll be sure to make it cranberry. Her favorite, right?" Marley asks with an apologetic smile.

"Yes, I'm surprised you remember." He stares intently at her.

Marley lips upturn in a soft smile. "Of course I remember."

"Thank you." Despite his frown, Marley nods, understanding the sincerity in his voice.

Mrs. Hennessee sighs as she looks back and forth between the two of them. "It's a shame you two didn't work out."

"Mom!" Marley's mouth is hanging open, matching my own.

My eyes bounce between the three of them.

Killian is back to arranging the food, avoiding eye contact with anyone. Marley and her mother are having a staring contest, communicating without words in a way only family can.

I'm certain Marley could get any man she wanted, so why in the world would she pick Killian? Maybe that's what has his panties in a bunch. She probably realized she was too good for his morose self and dumped his butt.

"What, honey? Can't a mother want her daughter to end up with someone as strapping as Killian?" She shakes her head. "And you two were such a beautiful couple."

"Killian and I are better as friends." Marley purses her lips. "We always have been."

"I really thought that after Roisin—"

"We should get going," Killian cuts in. He closes in on me, causing his sandalwood scent to wash over me.

Marley glares at her mother before turning to Killian. "I'm so sorry, Killian." She reaches forward but before she can touch his arm, he steps back.

"It's nothing." His harsh tone rebuilds the walls that weren't there moments ago.

"Oh, Killian." Mrs. Hennessee steps towards him with tears in her eyes. "I'm so sorry. I spoke out of turn."

"It's fine," he replies, his tone softening.

"It's not," Marley butts in, stepping towards Killian. Her eyes search his face, as though she's looking for a man she knows is there but can't find.

"Take a muffin for the road?" Mrs. Hennessee offers the one she handed him earlier.

"Of course, thank you." He leans down and gives her a kiss on the cheek. "Don't worry. I'm fine."

She smiles but wipes a stray tear from her cheek. "I have no doubt about that, my boy. But I want the same happiness for you I would want for my own child."

He shifts from one foot to the other, shoving a hand in his pocket. "If either of you need anything, please let me know."

The two women nod, their mannerisms mimicking each other, and showing the family resemblance.

"Thanks for the ice," I pipe in, unsure if I should break whatever situation is occurring in front of me.

"Of course," Marley replies with a smile back on her face. "It was lovely to meet you."

"You are welcome anytime," her mother adds.

Killian places the hand on my lower back and ushers me back the way we came.

"Do you know how to get back to your room?" He asks once we are back outside in the rain.

"I think I'll manage."

He frowns at the melted bag of ice in my hand before peeling it back to inspect my fingers. "The swelling has gone down."

Unsure what to say, I settle on a shrug. Internally, I groan. It wasn't a question. What kind of response is a shrug? I'm an embarrassment to heterosexual women everywhere.

His lips flatten as he stares at my hand before he scopes our surroundings. "Are you sure you'll be okay?"

I roll my eyes. "I know you see me as some weak girl that can't take care of herself, but I've done pretty well so far in my life."

He steps closer, making me tilt my head back to look up into the sharp lines of his face. "Do you consider getting caught and brought to the fae realm against your will doing pretty good?"

I open and close my mouth a few times before I release a huff.

His amber eyes glisten while he lifts his hand to take a bite of his muffin. His Adam's apple bobs when he swallows. "Not feeling so confident now, are you, little rabbit?"

I fold my arms. "Stop calling me that. I'm not some helpless animal."

He leans closer to me, bringing his heady scent with him and whispers against my ear. "Make me."

If I could melt into a puddle, it would happen in this moment. I bite my lip as I work through the fuzz of my brain.

He straightens, bringing the muffin back to his mouth, the corners of it tilting up.

My teeth clench at the sharp reminder of his horrible personality.

"Even if I needed help, you are the last person I would ask it from," I quip. Throwing my hair over my shoulder, I march away from him to the safety of my room.

THIRTEEN

A yawn drags from my lips, the onslaught of bare, stony walls hypnotizing my mind back to the lull of sleep.

"At least cover your mouth," Shay comments from beside me.

"If I was able to drink my coffee before you dragged me away, maybe I wouldn't be so tired," I grumble as another yawn makes itself known.

"It's not my fault it took you so long to get ready."

Earlier this morning, to my surprise, he had swung by to fetch me for the next trial. "It is your fault that I didn't know there was another trial today. Isn't there a pamphlet or something I can have? It's not as though you've been very helpful. A palace map and a fae directory would be useful too if either of those are lying around."

Shay side eyes me. Scratching his head he lets out a puff of air. "Today's trial is truth."

"Okay, and?" I push him for more.

"I don't know," he grinds between clenched teeth. "I'm not used to playing host. I don't know what to tell you."

"First, it's your fault you're playing host because you're the one who dragged me here. So, don't take it out on me," I quip as I pull at the itchy sleeve of my dress. "Secondly, assume you need to tell me everything."

"Real helpful, kid."

"About as helpful as you've been, old man."

A smile almost seems to tip the corner of his mouth, but he quickly smothers any ounce of humor he may possess.

"The virtues tested every seven years always remain the same, as does the first trial. The first trial is the initial weeding out the weak. After that the trials represented by the different courts happen; this next one being truth. There is no exact time table, as the trials are decided along the way and different trials need different levels of preparation. Typically fae are told the day before, but sometimes the morning of, for when a trial will be. So, more or less, anyone competing has to be ready at any given moment."

"That doesn't seem fair."

Shay studies me from the corner of his eye. "It's a power play."

I look at him with wide eyes. "From the King?"

He nods. "Having his subjects be able to do his bidding, even last minute, in a situation like this helps set the precedent of who is in charge."

I contemplate this for a few moments. This fits with the leader I have been momentarily around, but the deferential treatment the fae people give makes him seem more of a savior than how Shay describes him. At times, it's as though Shay has a deeper understanding of the King than anyone else.

"So, what exactly is today's trial?"

"Another power play by the King. We were only told this morning no less, and I know what virtue, but we will not know the exact test until he wishes to divulge the information upon arrival."

Great, more secrets. At least this time it's not from Shay's doing, but it still irks me to no end going into these situations with little to no information.

He must see the annoyance on my face because he adds onto his explanation. "Truth, today's trial, is meant to reveal a fae's true self. Previous tests have been drinking truth serums, revealing your darkest secret with the use of torture. Or something as easy as expressing your feelings to loved ones."

I blink at him. "You're telling me this could range from telling you 'Hey, I don't appreciate you taking me to the fae realm' to being tortured until I unveil sides of myself I don't want any living person to know?"

"Pretty much," he shrugs.

I smack his shoulder, which causes a wry smile to escape his lips. "Don't act like this isn't a big deal!"

He stops in the middle of the empty hall and turns to face me. "You're right. This is a big deal. No one knows your true self but you. This trial is about revealing that to others. It's uncomfortable and difficult, but to understand someone's true essence is of great importance to the fae, especially if a fae is to win something as important as the *Naim* Competition." His face darkens with the next statement. "But never let your guard down, Cara. Allow your true self to be seen, so we can move onto the next trial, but be wary of those who learn it. For it can always be used against you."

All I can do is reply with a nod because in this moment, Shay's showing a piece of his true self. One that worries, one that cares, and it juxtaposes the pompous fae I have known up until now.

We continue walking until we enter a courtyard residing on the opposite side of the palace from my room. Due to the throne room still in shambles from the attack, the procession is taking place in a different area.

Archways give accessibility to the open walkways that provide cover from the drizzle falling from the sky. Dotted throughout the open square are empty stone benches with small puddles on top. In the center of the courtyard sits a marble fountain. Lily pads speckle the water's surface, which shimmers with every drop of rain.

Above the water sits a statue, with weathered grey spots dripping down its exterior, of a man on a large horse. One foot is in a stirrup and his other leg swings over the back of the horse. It's unclear if he is mounting or dismounting. A woman stands to the side, partially covering her face with splayed fingers as she looks to the man.

Shay's rumbling voice snaps my trance. "It's one of our land's greatest tales of both love and tragedy. Oisín," he nods at the man, "was a human who saved Niamh, the woman, from her father. Despite her being cursed with the head of a boar, he married her, breaking the spell her father had bestowed upon her. They lived together in *Gon'an'rit* for three hundred years, but Oisín wanted to return home. Niamh's love for her husband outweighed her fears, and she granted him leave to take her white steed. But she warned that if he stepped foot on the land of Earth, time would catch up with him and bring about his demise."

The rain drips down Niamh's face, depicting an image of her crying for the man she loves.

"Is he leaving or coming home here?" I ask, never taking my eyes from the statue. My heart yearns for this to be the moment before their happily ever after, but Shay's somber voice has it beating in worry of the opposite.

"In the story, he came across someone in need of help. While assisting with the removal of a large stone, he fell to ground, withering away within seconds."

"And what happened to Niamh?"

Shay shrugs. "It's only ever been told through Oisín's perspective. Only Niamh herself knows."

Niamh is small in comparison to Oisín and her horse. Through the veil half covering her face, it's still obvious she has long flowing hair. Her thin frame bends in on itself, which I can only assume is from grief. Oisín's broad shoulders and tall frame rule over her small demeanor. Even the statue's focal point is the male perspective, leaving Niamh as an afterthought.

"Do you think she still lives?"

Shay emits a chuckle. "This story has been passed down for thousands of years. Unless she can live two to three times longer than any known fae, I highly doubt it. And if so, she'd be nothing but a frail old woman now."

My arms encircle my midsection. Warming myself against the onslaught of wind through the small area, and from the heartbreaking story carved before me.

"How is your hand?" Shay breaks through my thoughts.

I flex it between us, showing the normal sized fingers with cuts now scabbed over. "Better."

"You won't need it for today's trials, but that's good. We need to start up your training again soon."

I groan while throwing my head back. "Didn't we realize training was useless already? Why even worry about it?"

"Well, I'd prefer to give you a fighting chance." Shay leans his shoulder against a pillar at the edge of the open courtyard with his arms folded and crossing one foot over the other.

"Are there trials dedicated to sword work and screaming?" I chuckle, envisioning a scream battle. Killian would look ridiculous.

"No, but there is a trial based around the virtue of strength, which usually is some kind of physical battle."

My eyes widen at Shay's stoic face. "I have to battle someone? Oh, hell no."

Shay eyes me derisively. "All you have to do is live, kid. We will condition you to that point."

"All I have to do is live," I parrot. Easy for him to say like it's no big deal when he's not the one risking his life. "We?" I place my hand on my hip and cock my head. "Neither of these things are instilling confidence in me." Perhaps Shay was too self-indulged to hear when I told Killian I didn't want his help anymore.

Speaking of, I haven't seen him once while we've been waiting, and usually I see him creeping at one point or another. I scan the area, but I recognize no one, not even the crop of messy blonde hair. Sadly, Cadan is, also, nowhere in sight.

"Stop fidgeting." Shay frowns as I scratch the sleeve of my navy blue dress.

"Well, the lace isn't the most comfortable thing in the world," I grumble. "Why did I have to wear this again?"

Shay convinced me to wear this when he arrived unannounced this morning. To my displeasure, I learned too late this is the most uncomfortable garment in the closet. Knowing him, he's retaliating from the last time I didn't wear what he'd chosen for me. Jokes on him because after this fail of an outfit, I won't be making this mistake again.

"Modesty and elegance are a good first impression," I deepen my voice to say in unison with him.

He frowns at my mockery of him. I meant it as a rhetorical question considering he's said that about ten times since this morning.

An annoyed chuff has his nostrils flaring and, like the child he continuously reminds me I am, I stick my tongue out at him.

Take that for modesty and elegance.

"May the blessing of light be on you," the King says as he steps onto a balcony overlooking the area where we all stand.

"Light without and light within," I murmur with the crowd.

Shay arches an eyebrow at me.

"What? Don't you want me to fit in?" I tease with an innocent bat of my eyelashes.

He shakes his head before returning his attention to the king.

"Today's trial is about truth," he echoes through the open space.

My stomach tightens at the thought of the trial. To show my true self. Not ominous at all. Opening up to complete strangers, or anyone for that matter, is definitely outside of my comfort zone. Plus, how am I supposed to show my true self to others when I'm still figuring that out myself? Isn't that what your twenties are all about?

"When your name is called, you will be escorted into another room where your test will take place," the king announces.

My eyebrows pinch at Shay. I wonder if we can bring a friend. Well, maybe 'friend' is a bit of a stretch. Once more I search the area for Cadan. The crowd is too thick, and with everyone standing plus my short height, I can barely see anything. I already have to stand on my tiptoes to get glances of the king on the balcony above us.

"Lie and you forfeit your place, but those truest to themselves will receive the most points. Let us begin." He waves forward the same fae with the scroll from the last trial.

The fae announcer starts calling out names, but instead of calling us one at a time, he calls groups of five.

Hopefully this goes a little quicker and we can get to lunch where hopefully there'll be some coffee.

A smile toys my lips when my name is called after Cadan's.

Shay gives my shoulder a quick squeeze before directing me towards a doorway at the end of the courtyard.

I bite the inside of my cheek as my stomach squirms and don't realize Killian's name's been called too until I almost run into him at the door. My face flushes as I step in line beside him.

"Hello, Cara," Cadan's sweet voice comes from my other side. His dark eyes make momentary eye contact then drops down to my knees. His right hand toys with his bracelet.

"Cadan!" I beam, "I'm so happy you are in my group."

"We should be tested separately," Killian's stern voice says from the other side.

"No one is talking to you." I raise my nose while I refuse to look at him.

"Has Killian upset you?" Cadan asks. "Were you not thankful when he helped us?"

"Well, I… yes, but you see, he…" I fluster. Cadan doesn't beat around the bush, something I appreciate about him, but less so at this moment.

Killian chortles beside me, which earns him an extra squinty glare from me.

"Follow me," a female fae with her brown hair curled into a bun and clipboard in hand announces to the five of us.

In a line, we all follow. The first is a small fae girl with light freckled skin, who seems to be no older than sixteen, but I know fae age differently than humans. In contrast, she's followed by an elderly fae with dark skin and white hair and a cane in hand to help him hobble along. After him, Killian walks through the doors, followed by me and then Cadan.

As we walk, I admire the burgundy suit of the woman who leads us. I would kill for a pair of pants right now.

I pull at the itchy lace again. I hope I'm not having an allergic reaction to whatever tormenting material this dress is made from.

"Enter through here and take a seat," the female fae commands as she opens a door.

"We're not being tested alone?" Cadan questions as we step through, and his fingers find their way back to spin the bracelet around his arm.

"That is correct." The woman closes the door behind us.

Killian's face sours, going so pale he could match my own skin tone.

I would normally take pleasure at his discomfort, serves him right, but nausea roils through my stomach too. I don't want him knowing my secrets any more than he seems to want me knowing his.

We all file into our seats in the order we walk in, Killian sits to my right and Cadan to my left. The chair creaks beneath me as I cross and uncross my legs.

"We will bring in a *Korrigan*," the woman looks at my raised eyebrows and answers my unspoken question. "A water sprite that can see the truth within the past, present, and future." With a nod to someone in the shadows off to the side, a crystal tank rolls out.

The blue water glows, casting a light across the room.

Five fae guards line each side of us, no longer hidden by the darkness, holding spears in their hands and swords on their hips.

Cadan taps his finger in a pattern on his knee and whispers to himself.

I can't hear what he says, but I watch his lips move in unison with his hand.

Conversely, Killian sits silently beside me, his own hand tense on the hilt of his sword as he scans the room.

I twirl my black hair around my finger and squint through the bright light of the water.

Inside is a small, but beautiful woman. She's no more than twelve inches tall and she pulls herself up the side of the tank, so she can rest the side of her head in the crook of her arm. Long pointed ears stick out of her golden hair that floats in the water around her, shimmering with the same radiance as the water she bathes in. As her hair swifts to the side, my eyes bulge when I realize she is naked.

My lap suddenly becomes very interesting, and I pay strict attention to the eight loops of hair I wrap around my pointer finger.

"The female body makes you uncomfortable?" A bell-like voice chimes through the air.

Lifting my eyes from my tenth loop of hair, I'm struck by the *Korrigan's* red eyes. I gasp as they pierce through me.

Her tinkling laugh rings through the air at my reaction, showing her razor-sharp teeth. Once her chuckling dies down, her piercing eyes home back in on me to wait for an answer.

"N-no," I mutter.

"Hmmm," she tilts her head. "Not quite a lie, but not quite the truth. So, is it just me?"

"No," I say with more conviction in hopes she won't see through my lie. I don't want to offend the fae before me.

"That is a lie," she sneers. "Do it again and I may request that delicious finger you have wrapped in your long hair like a present for my afternoon snack." She twirls her own finger through her golden hair floating at the surface of the water.

I shudder as I quickly unwind my finger. My hands fist into the folds of my dress to hide my fingers.

"What I mean to say," I start but hesitate when her beady red eyes make contact. "I-I have no problem with the female body, but I was merely surprised by your nakedness."

"Truth," she sighs. "I guess I will have to wait on a banshee delicacy."

A shuddering breath leaves my lips.

The *Korrigan's* attention draws to a fae at the end. The mousy girl is in a simple green dress and her innocent eyes widen under the scrutiny of the water sprite.

"Let's start with you," she chirps. "What are you?"

"I'm… I'm a *Brownie*," the girl squeaks.

"And why would a fairy maid join this competition?"

"For a house of my own," her soft voice carries through the dead quiet room.

"Lie!" The *Korrigan* shrieks. "Chop off her hair. It'll be a perfect thread." Her maniacal laughter fills the room at the girl's shocked face.

A guard steps forward and unsheathes his sword.

"No! Please!" The *Brownie* cries, but the guard wrenches her head back and with a swipe of his sword her long curly brown locks turn into an uneven bob.

The *Korrigan* cackles as tears well in the girl's eyes.

"You are ashamed of what you are," she says as her red eyes penetrate the girl who now huddles in on herself.

"Yes," she sniffles.

"Truth. I'll ask again, why're you in this competition?" The *Korrigan's* arm sways back and forth over the side of the tank, boredom written across her face.

"I…I…"

"If you cannot speak truth, even when caught in a lie, you do not deserve to be in this competition."

"No, please! Ask me anything else," the *Brownie* pleads as she claps her hands together at her chest.

The *Korrigan* shakes her head, her long locks swishing from side to side, displaying small moments of nudity. "You!" She points her finger directly at the young girl. "You are ashamed of what you are. You wish you weren't a *Brownie* and want to be something else. You fear being a housewife or maid throughout your life. You would try to change innately who you are well before asking for the independence of your own home!"

She breaks down into tears, covering her face with her hands.

"The truth of yourself is the only way to find true power." The water sprite clucks her tongue. "Take her away. Maybe next time you join these trials, you will do so for something of more value."

My stomach drops as they whisk the girl out of the room. I have spent my entire life hating the curse I seem to carry, and now it could be my undoing. And if I fail, I will never go home.

The *Korrigan's* attention turns to Cadan, and I suck in a breath. What will the wretched creature do to him?

"You are different," she states, but poses it more like a question.

"Everyone's different," Cadan answers without hesitation. "I believe differences should be celebrated and valued rather than ostracized and demeaned."

The *Korrigan* narrows her eyes until they are nothing but red slits. "Truth."

My fists ball so tightly, my nails dig into my palm.

"If it were possible within the wish's power, would you change yourself?"

"No." Cadan doesn't miss a beat. "I would wish for others to see me as I truly am rather than through an altered lens of what they think."

"Truth," she sighs. "And finally, what is your biggest regret?"

Cadan's face pinches as he thinks. "I regret cheating on my final exam in my fae diplomacy class."

My jaw drops. Cadan's biggest regret is cheating on an exam? As in biggest regret in life? There is no way that would be anyone's main regret, not with some crazed truth telling fae there to uncover the lie. My heart stings at the thought of losing Cadan in the competition, and a pit forms when I remember what the *Korrigan* did to the *Brownie* when she lied. I rack my brain of ways to help him, but I can't think of anything. This isn't the same situation as the bullies outside the castle. There's a good chance she will exert her wishes on me if I try to intervene. I don't want to lose my hair, my finger, or whatever she comes up with. I gulp. I don't know if I'm a good enough person to—

"Truth. You shall move on," the tiny fae says, but her eyes flick to me.

"If he had been lying, would you have taken his punishment for him?" The sprite directs her questions to me now.

I still. I can't believe that's the first question. She must've seen the turmoil on my face or maybe it's part of her power. Either way, I know the truth.

I hang my head and whisper, "No."

I don't dare look at Cadan or Killian, knowing the cowardice they must see in me.

"But you didn't even know what it was," she haughtily laughs. "So quick to make presumptions about yourself and others."

I fold my arms over my chest, not that they'll protect me, and wait for her next question. I don't want to communicate with this creature more than I must.

She closes her eyes and takes a deep breath, leaning towards me as though to scent me. "What are you?" Her singsong voice breaks the silence.

I roll my eyes at this question. Talk about an anticlimactic follow up. "I thought I was human, but I'm actually a banshee, or *Beansidhe*."

I want to make sure I'm thorough to not give her any reason to say I'm lying.

"That is not completely true," she immediately responds as though she knew what I'd say.

My eyebrows raise, "I'm not lying." If I'm not fully human, but not fully banshee, then what am I?

"I never said you were," she continues. "What you said you believe, therefore it is a partial truth. But there is so much more to you. You are correct you are not human, but you are not fully *Beansidhe* either." Her tiny finger taps her lips in thought with her eyes unfocused. "You'll soon discover the truth, no need to spoil the fun." She laughs to herself as though she watched the funniest thing happen before her.

I open my mouth to demand her to explain, but she is onto her final question before I can utter a word.

"If you could make a wish for yourself instead of another, what would you wish for?"

My mind immediately travels to being at home with Shauna—eating pizza, having a glass of wine from Shauna's persistence, and watching trashy TV shows. But I know that's a lie, and the *Korrigan* will too. It may be what I want most right now, but it's not the wish I have held onto for over a decade.

"That I wasn't cursed," I mutter.

The *Korrigan* smiles, her sharp teeth gleaming from the light of the water. "Truth, but a partial lie again."

I gape. What the hell? How could that be a lie?

"Since you gave two half-truths, which means there is one full lie." Her eyes dip to my fingers twisting in my lap. Her tongue licks her lips, and I freeze when I realize her intent.

"A truth is truth," Killian speaks up.

The water sprite hisses at his interruption, but he ignores her.

"It's still truth if the person knows no different. You cannot use your sight into our past, present, and future to create a lie one doesn't know exists. At no point has she knowingly lied, thus why you have not been able to condemn her." His voice is powerful as he makes his claim.

The *Korrigan* gives my fingers one last mournful gaze before the red beads snap to Killian, filled with vengeance. "Very well. What do you desire most?"

He swallows. "For my mother to be free."

"Truth."

I suck in small breaths of air as I listen to their exchange.

Where is his mother? Earlier he asked the cooking staff to take her an extra roll. Does that mean she's locked up somewhere in the castle? Is that why he joined the competition? I secretly hope the fae will ask any of these questions for my own curiosity.

"What is holding you back in your life?" The *Korrigan* smirks.

Killian goes rigid. "My... mother," he seethes with his admission.

"Truth." Her eyes twinkle with mischief. "What is your biggest nightmare?"

"Myself."

The *Korrigan's* sharp-toothed smile spreads wide. "Truth."

FOURTEEN

"What're you still doing in bed?" Shay pulls open the drapes uncovering the dreary day.

Grabbing the comforter, I tug it further over my head, burying myself from the world. There is no reason Shay should be bothering me this morning. He said he'd give my hand one more day to heal before training, otherwise we only had some fancy dance tonight. Apparently, it's a tradition after the second trial.

Ugh, the last thing I want to do right now is go out in public and deal with the world. A shiver runs through me remembering the evil little face of the *Korrigan*. After the fifth competitor made it through the *Korrigan's* questioning, we were marched from the room. Killian disappeared immediately, and Shay whisked me away before I could speak with Cadan. I'm 75% sure after my first confession in the trial, my friend count of one in this realm is now at zero. I wouldn't blame him either; nobody wants a disloyal friend.

I bite my cheek to force the tears from falling. I feel so stuck. I don't understand how I'm going to make it through this entire competition. Even if I manage to make it through without losing a finger or my life, I won't be able to go home unless I win. My hope of returning dwindles with each passing day, and I want nothing more than to stay curled in bed all day and ignore my present life.

"Get up," Shay demands as he snags my covers off me. "It's almost lunch. Did you acquire your laziness from the humans?"

"Why're you being such a prick?" I cry as I reach for the blanket, but he pulls it further from my reach. "Oh wait, I forgot who I was talking to."

"Is that any way to speak to the person who will take you home if you win?"

"The key word there is 'if'." I lie back onto my pillow and wrap my arms around my bare legs in a fetal position. "What're you even doing here anyway? I thought my next requirement wasn't until tonight."

"You need to get ready for tonight." Shay saunters through the room, running a finger along the mantle of the fireplace. He inspects his digit, and frowns at whatever is on it. Wiping his finger on his trousers, he moves back across the space to me. "You need to be fitted for your gown. It is one of the most prestigious galas this court has."

I bolt upright. "You made it sound like some boring dance! Also, '*this court*?'" I mock his deep voice, "Are you ever going to expand on that? Do these other courts have royalty too or is this kingdom the main one? Will they be there? Oh! And are there fancy fae dances I need to know?" I spew everything in a single breath, but my brain is already gearing up with other inquiries.

His bland stare combs over me, and my satin nightgown suddenly feels too small. "I thought we were done with all your questions."

The minutes tick by as I wait for an answer, any answer to any question.

"If I answer, will you oblige me by getting ready properly for tonight?" Shay sighs while pinching the bridge of his nose.

"Deal." I slap my hand over my mouth, but it's too late, the magic zips through my bones. Damn, I need to be more careful, especially with Shay.

"There are four courts that have developed over time and where we get our virtues from. *Ulster*, a court known for its truth and wit. The older gentleman on the fae counsel for the competition is their representative. *Tuatha*, which is a court of courage and strength."

"Let me guess, the scary warrior guy on the counsel is the representative?"

"Do you want me to answer your questions or are you going to keep interrupting me?"

"Go on," I grumble.

"The warrior is in fact from *Tuatha*. The next court is *Fenian*, known for their wisdom, and represented by the female fae. Finally, we have where we currently reside, *Rímor*, the strongest court. We are known for our power. *Rímor* is also known as the court of the kings, so we are the ruling court, although there is lesser royalty at the others."

"And the ball tonight?"

"The royalty is invited, but they rarely show unless they are competing themselves. But none are this year. And, yes, there are fae dances, but I do not expect you to participate." The final sentence he scrunches his face like a terrible smell accosted him.

I'm a bit offended how the idea of me participating in fae dances is so terrible to him. Based on that reaction alone, maybe I'll try to learn one of the dances and join the fray. Although, his reaction *is* warranted. I have no doubt I'll be terrible, and yet a small smile toys at my lips. Me botching a dance and pissing off Shay would be worth the mild humiliation.

There's a knock at the door and Shay, with his entitlement on full display, answers my bedroom door.

Three fae filter in.

"Ah, the seamstresses are here." Shay moves aside for them to enter. "I told you I would introduce you to them so they weren't strangers." He gives a roguish smile at me.

Self-conscious about my state of dress, I pull up the sheet to cover my body.

"I'm Aoife, a flower fae." A petite, curly haired redhead in a tulle blush-colored dress bows her head. "This is my sister, Aisling," she points to a fae with matching hair, but her face is covered in freckles. Her dress is similar, but with a higher neckline and turquoise. "And my brother, Aydan." The final fae's red locks are cut short. He is thin and wispy like his sister's and wearing an emerald suit.

"I believe these belong to you," Aisling says as she steps forward offering a bundle of clothes. Her voice is light, reminding me of the wind on a spring day.

I choke up as I grasp what she hands me. My clothes! But instead of being covered in mud, they are clean and smell of lavender. I hug them to my chest and take in a deep breath. "Thank you."

The three of them nod in unison.

"I'll let you get to it." Shay heads to the door.

"Wait, you're leaving?" I holler at him.

"I feel no need to see you in your underwear," he comments as he waltzes out of the room and shuts the door as he leaves.

My face heats, more from annoyance than embarrassment.

Aydan gives an apologetic smile. "We were told you knew we were coming. We are nothing but professional."

"And I have the most ravishing idea of a dress for you," Aoife beams.

"Especially now that we've seen your eyes," Aisling chimes in.

"If you could please stand on the stool." Aydan dips down to place a wooden frame on the ground.

"O-okay." I swing my legs over the mattress and pad across the cool floor.

"And don't worry, you can stay in your camisole." Aoife adds.

I wasn't planning on getting out of it, but whatever. I follow their directions, and once I'm on the step stool, they flitter around me—taking measurements, holding fabrics next to my face, and pinning swaths of material atop my clothes. Within a half an hour, weaving through their craft at a speed that is beyond anything I had seen on Earth, they slow. I have to remind myself, of course this isn't humanly possible—they're fae!

"The two of us will finish the dress in the corner, if you will please bathe and then Aisling will do your hair and makeup," Aydan interjects their process. Within a minute, I'm left in only my nightgown as the fabric they pinned to me seems to melt away into his hands.

I'm ushered into the bathroom, where they allow me privacy for a quick bath. Slipping back into the bedroom, Aisling greets me with a bright smile.

"If you'll sit in this, please." Aisling's chipper-self bounces over to my desk chair, which has been moved closer to my bed. While I plop down into it, she withdraws a small suitcase and opens it on my bed before ruffling through it.

I spend the next five hours being poked and prodded. Food gets delivered and I'm allowed a semi-break, although my arms, waist, and bust are continually reassessed as I shove food into my mouth. Considering they've measured my stomach four times, I'm reconsidering the second slice of cheesecake. It was accompanied with coffee and a note that said, "Consider me a life saver" in swift cursive writing. I assumed it was a special treat from Mrs. Hennessee.

Once I am done eating, Aisling does the finishing touches on my makeup, including lipstick, and last minute additions to my hair. By this point, I am zoned out.

I daydream what Shauna is up to and how behind I am in my university classes until I'm fighting tears that'll ruin my makeup. So, I refocus on the other virtues Shay revealed to me earlier— wisdom, wit, courage, and strength. I have already done the trials for power and truth. I wonder what the others will entail. Goosebumps cover my arms as I pray they aren't anything like the last. The sinking in my gut has me believing I won't be so lucky. Cursed is how I've always been, and I'm sure this will be no different.

"All done!" Aoife claps as her face beams with pride.

"You look dazzling." Aisling's eyes are wide as she takes me in.

"Our best work yet," Aydan agrees.

I step in front of the mirror to find a stranger staring back at me. My hair is a myriad of braids with baby's breath flowers placed throughout it. The smoky eyes and bright red lipstick is dramatic, and my eyes pop in a way I wished for when I was younger. My floor length aubergine gown tightly fits my waist, but has added layers of tulle to the skirt and a slit up my right leg. The sweetheart neckline bodice has black beads sewn into swirling flowers tapering off at my hips. The moment I blink, so does the figure before me. When my hand smooths down my hip, so does hers. That's the only proof that it's me. I'm like a panther, sleek with a dark beauty. There's no rabbit present here tonight.

"Wow," I breathe.

"I agree." Shay's deep voice reverberates behind me.

I turn to see him smiling at me, a genuine smile. He wears a dark suit, his curls well hydrated with no noticeable frizz, and his tie is a deep plum.

I narrow my eyes at his attempt to match me. This isn't prom. I never went and I never felt the need to go. If he pulls out a corsage right now, I will refuse to accompany him.

"I'm not your date." I lift my chin to signal his matching ensemble. If anything, our relationship is more equivalent to colleagues.

"No," he agrees, "but I want them to know you are my proxy."

Wow, I wonder if he gets all the ladies with such romantic sentiments like that. I smirk to myself. My plot to annoy Shay with my horrendous dancing is not out the window yet, and with these comments I'm even more determined to put him in his place.

"Shall we?" He holds out the crook of his elbow.

I step forward gracefully, or what I hope appears to be, and place my hand on his arm with the largest fake smile I can muster. My cheeks ache within moments, but his unnerved glance only makes me grin harder.

142

The siblings were kind enough to find me decadent wedged heels when they saw my disdain for the strappy death traps they originally handed me. Granted, it only gives me four extra inches, but at least now I'm only a foot shorter than him.

With one last farewell to the three fae, Shay whisks me off to not only my first dance, but my first fae ball.

FIFTEEN

String instruments serenade the fae as we walk down the hall to a set of open double doors. The melody floats through the air, beckoning everyone closer. A group of girls behind us giggle from the anticipation, but my stomach sours as nerves twist through me.

Stepping into the ballroom has me tripping over my feet. Silks hang from beams on the ceiling and wrap around pillars, twisting with floral arrangements. Floating through the air are what I thought were fairy lights, but to my disbelief are real fairies. They are tiny and emit a bright light.

One zips in front of my face to join others dancing high above us. They have wings and everything! Classic, stereotypical, Tinker Bell worthy fairies! Across the chatting crowd, where fae pick at finger foods and waltz in the center, is a raised dais where a quartet plays an enchanting song. The throne beside them is empty.

Everyone is breathtaking, dressed in their best, and their fae elegance makes them ethereal.

Shay's unimpressed grimace is the mirror opposite of my wide-eyed wonder as we move through the throngs of attendees. The buzz of excited energy has me bouncing on my feet, to Shay's dismay, which makes it all the sweeter.

Okay, I may hold small grudges causing slight vindictiveness. But who wouldn't with a man who struck a deal, which caused them to leave everything they knew behind without their knowledge? Granted, he wasn't the worst company, but I wouldn't call him the best either.

"I feel like I'm in a different century being here," I comment. "I guess there's no reason to advance at the same rate as Earth when there's magic."

Shay haughtily laughs. "Earth has its own magic."

I cock my head. Is it because they visit so often or am I missing something here?

He leans against a decorated pillar to finish his thought. "Technology is its own form of magic. Invisible currents in the air so people can talk across the world. Having a single database able to hold the entirety of the human knowledge for anyone to access and learn. To have multiple tons of weight hurtling at hundreds of miles per hour, thousands of feet above the air for faster transportation. We may not have the same technology you do, but that is because it's Earth's own form of magic. Trust me, I've tried bringing items back to this world and they never work."

"I never thought of it that way."

"Most take for granted what they've been raised with," he adds.

I smile to myself as I envision Earth from his point of view. I never thought Earth could be viewed as someone else's mythical other realm.

He stiffens beside me, causing my forehead to wrinkle in concern.

"May I have this dance?" A stentorian voice asks to my side.

I jolt, to his pleasure based on the predatory smile on the King's face while extending his hand to me. His hair is in its usual ponytail, but a more intricate crown with red gems sits on top of his head. The regal outfit he dons shimmers with gold against green.

Shay steps in front, blocking me with his right shoulder. "We have only just arrived. Perhaps allow her a moment to enjoy the festivities."

The King gives him a slithering stare. "Are you saying dancing with your king is not the best way to enjoy this extravaganza?"

"You're not my king," I murmur under my breath.

Shay steps sideways, knocking me slightly to quiet me.

I press my lips together. They're always getting ahead of themselves.

The King leers at me, not having missed my comment.

My hands twist behind my back.

"Shall we?" The King offers his hand again. This time when the King gives Shay a sharp look, he steps aside.

I place my shaking hand in his cool one. The crowds party as we cross to the center of the room. My stomach hollows from all the attention. My plan was to slightly embarrass myself to annoy Shay, not to make an utter fool of myself in front of every fae present.

The King swings me in a circle, twirling my skirt and allowing my beaded bodice to glisten in the light, before placing his hand on my lower back. Delight flashes across his face when he sees my pale-faced terror.

"We all must keep up appearances, dear. Try smiling," he croons in my ear.

"I... I don't know how to do these dances," I admit as my face heats. I hate admitting weaknesses, and this seems like the last man that should know mine.

"Don't worry, my skill will mask any of your ineptitudes." His hands tighten on me as we spin across the dance floor.

Butterflies erupt in my belly from the euphoric floating sensation. My feet trace the ground as the King directs us. Laughter bubbles up my throat when I realize I am not tripping, but soaring.

The King's strong demeanor initially scared the other dancers away, but after a minute, others join without missing a beat.

"How has your time in my kingdom been, Ms. Winters?" The King peers at me while keeping his head held high.

"It's been fine... sir." I press my lips in a tight lipped smile when I realize I don't know how I'm supposed to refer to him.

The King chuckles, "King Harbinger will suffice."

My ears perk at the familiarity of his last name, but I can't seem to place it. Shay must have called him that at some point and I didn't pick up on it.

"It's uncommon to have a proxy for these competitions, especially someone of your... background." His eyes sweep over my body. His hold stiffens, pinning me in place when I squirm under his gaze.

I gracelessly shrug, unsure how he expects me to respond.

"How did you meet my son?"

"Son?" I raise an eyebrow. "I don't think I've met your son."

He scans the crowd until they land on Shay. "Hmm... interesting, he didn't tell you of our relationship. Usually I'm the hesitant one."

I blanch. "Shay's your son?" My voice is high pitched and I inwardly cringe with how I just spoke to King Harbinger.

Oh my gosh, Harbinger, I knew that name from signing the contract. I mentally face palm myself. It's Shay's last name.

The King studies me as the pieces fall into place in my head. "He should be so lucky to have my name." His voice is harsh as his eyes narrow at the crowd.

I shift under his grip, uncomfortable at our closeness. I feel like a gazelle in a lion's den. A very ungraceful, awkward gazelle. Definitely the one at the back of the herd that gets eaten.

He refocuses on me. "Answer me. How did you meet?" His slight kind demeanor from before has evaporated.

"He... he saved my life. On Earth," I add.

He raises a thick eyebrow. "Curious. Why did he do that?"

"He says my magic called to him. I screamed when I was being attacked," I utter.

"Ah, your magic does have a distinct smell," he notes as his nostrils flare with a deep inhale.

"Yes, of rain. Your...son," I choke on the word at Shay's further betrayal, "told me."

"Rain is the overpowering scent, but there is more." His face hardens. "The fact he can only detect the scent of rain truly shows how weak he is."

"Is that why he didn't join the competition himself?" I blurt out. It's something that has nagged me for a while. He has the infallible confidence, it never made sense that he would put the fate of winning in my hands. Now, to know he is the son of the strongest fae in the realm, it makes even less sense to me.

The King gives a deep chuckle, one that more closely resembles a growl than a laugh. "I believe the reason he joined at all is the better question."

Unease coils around my lungs like a boa constrictor, making it difficult to breathe. I should be avoiding the attention of the King, the most powerful ruler for hundreds of years. His keen interest is already much more than what I am comfortable with.

The melody comes to a crescendo ending, and King Harbinger drops his hands with a curt nod. "I'm sure we will be seeing more of each other soon."

My mouth opens and closes as I search for what to say. Should I smooth things over? Tell him there's nothing to worry about because, let's be honest, there's not. I have no chance at winning.

This realization is like a sucker punch in the gut, interrupting my breath with its truth.

The King smirks when he notices the change in my demeanor, once again taking pleasure at my discomfort.

"Have a good night, King Harbinger," I mutter with a small bow before hurrying away.

Once off the dance floor, I head straight to a waiter walking with a tray of drinks. I pluck off a golden goblet. Inside it sloshes an iridescent red liquid. I bring it to my lips and sip. It tastes of the sweetest strawberries, but the smooth burning sensation of alcohol warms my throat down to my belly. The giant gulps I take help ease the tension in my body. I place the empty glass on the tray and grab another. The server's eyes widen in alarm, but he presses forward through the crowd without a word.

"You shouldn't drink fae wine so fast," Shay's deep voice chastises from behind me.

I swing to him with a glare. "Now you are willing to open up and offer advice? Anything else you care to share while you're at it?" I spit at him.

He glowers at me. "He told you."

"He told me," I confirm. "But why didn't you?"

"It's not of importance." He shrugs nonchalantly.

"You are the king's son," I simmer, "the most powerful fae in the realm, and you chose a person who has spent their entire life thinking they were human to be your proxy in a magical competition? Seems pretty damn important to me," I whisper-shout.

Fae around us aren't outwardly watching us, but they tilt their heads in our direction to listen better.

Shay grabs me from under my arm and totes me off to the side, away from prying ears. Once in the shadows, he drops my arm. "Listen, my father," he says the word like it's acid on his tongue, "is taking an unexpected interest. But it will pass, his attention never strays on me for very long."

My heart clenches at the hurt I hear in his voice, but I don't pry. I am familiar with the walls I see shuttering around him as he speaks, with the awkward shifting as he admits this much.

"All I want is honesty," I say.

"Thankfully, that's not a fae virtue," he remarks.

I roll my eyes. "But truth is." I take another swallow of the delicious wine. "Weren't you the one who said how important showing someone your true self is?"

"I, also, said that those who know your true self can use it against you." His lips flatten when I take another sip.

Warmth spreads through my body as the first glass of fae wine gains traction. Soon I am fanning my face from the unbearable heat. "I think I need some air."

"I think that's a wise idea. I'll accompany you."

"No, no," I swat his arm. "I can handle myself, Prince Shay." The overemphasis of his new name prompts a horrified face from him, which has me bursting into giggles.

"Go get some air," he grates. "I have some things I need to take care of."

"Yeah, yeah. I'm sure there're lots of princely duties at these events." I wave my hand at him.

He grunts before stalking off.

As I walk the outskirts of the room, I use the wall three times to steady myself before I find the open doors leading to a balcony. I grin at the tingling sensation electrifying my body.

Fae wine is amazing; Shauna would love this.

I traipse onto the balcony, slipping on the slick ground from the constant precipitation. I stabilize myself by grabbing onto a vine wrapping around the balcony's awning.

Wine sloshes onto my hand.

Giggling, I tip the cup back and finish my beverage. I turn in a circle, using the vine once more to stop myself from falling as my feet tangle around themselves.

Everyone is inside, including the servers with the trays. I frown. I don't want to be holding an empty cup all night, and I don't want to go back into the sauna of a ballroom.

I weave over to a dark corner and place the cup down, nudging it so it's against the wall, then scurry away so no one knows it was me who put it there.

The cool drizzle feels blissful against my heated skin. Wisteria blooms around me, filling the air with its rich scent. I close my eyes and listen to the swaying music.

Nothing beats home, but right now, this is a close second.

I lean on the balustrade, looking over the side at a beautiful garden expanding before me. Roses, manicured bushes, dirt and stone pathways twisting together like a maze, and willow trees with swaying boughs dancing in the breeze. On the far side of the garden, a fountain sits in the center of wildflowers. The serene scenery calls to me.

To my right is a marble staircase. I glide over to it, we'll ignore the one stumble, and enter the estate below.

My fingers brush along the dewy leaves as gravel crunches beneath my heels. I grab the skirt of my dress and swish it from side to side as I meander through the gardens. I hum to myself as the strings of the dance become more distant, beginning where the tune left off and making it my own. The night has become foggy as the clouds settle closer to land, keeping the air moist, but thankfully no droplets of water to soak through my dress. The palace creates shafts of light that filter through the cloudy veil encompassing me.

I listen for the trickling water at the end of my path to help guide me.

With all the fae partying inside, there is a calm stillness out here. The bushes become wildflowers of purples, blues, and yellows speckling the green grass. The trail curves into a circle and at its center sits the fountain.

I wander to the fountain's edge and sit on the cool marble. My dress is dark enough that the water dampening my bottom shouldn't show. I dip my finger into the clear water and am surprised by how warm it is. Koi fish leisurely swim closer, curious as to if I have food to offer them. I twirl my finger through the water, hoping it enamors them enough to swim closer. But, alas, they do not. Skittish little creatures.

The statue is weathered like the one from the courtyard, but mossy along the bottom where it meets the water. I can tell it's Niamh on the platform. The same long hair cascades down her backside and her mournful, empty eyes stare off into the distance. The pain in her face matches the other too. This time, her hands clasp over her heart instead of hiding her face, as though she still holds out hope.

"You shouldn't be here."

I jump at Killian's gravelly voice as he steps out from the shadows. He's dressed in an all-black tux, including the shirt and tie. His eyes are the brightest part about him.

I grab my stomach as I giggle to myself. Seems the fae wine is still coursing through me.

Killian raises his dark eyebrow at my reaction, which makes me laugh harder.

"May I?" He points to the seat beside me.

I scrunch my nose at the wet spot beside me. "I guess."

He lowers himself so he sits foot away, but his back is straight as a plank of wood.

Liquid courage gets the better of me, and I lean forward and squint into his face. "How do you know Shay?"

"He's the prince." Killian pulls at the black jacket. His fingers dip into his unbuttoned collar to pull the tight fabric further away from his skin. My eyes trace his movement, glimpsing the crimson scars on his upper chest. Noticing my gaze, he drops his hands.

"You'd think with how Shay acts, he'd be a little more… involved," I attempt to put delicately.

"He's a bastard prince," he admits.

"Are you allowed to say that about royalty?" I snicker to myself. "Isn't that treasonous or something?"

He flinches at the word treason, and my eyebrows scrunch together.

"What I meant was that his mother was not queen," he amends his statement, continuing to watch the darkness of the gardens.

My jaw hangs open in shock. "But… but…" Spit flies as I hunch over in laughter.

Oh dear, this wasn't funny, like at all. Why am I laughing? But learning more about Shay from the King, and now Killian. To have truth be a virtue, and revealing one's true self, but be surrounded by secrecy. It was too much, and all I could think to do was laugh. Not an appropriate reaction, but I couldn't stop it.

I sober, pressing my fingers to my mouth. My cheeks redden from my inappropriate response. "Anything else?"

"His history isn't my place to divulge. If you didn't know he was a prince until now, he did that for a reason."

"What about his history with you? You seem to know him more than only him being the prince," I observe, the giddiness leaving my body as the mood becomes more serious with my question.

Killian's jaw clenches and eyes dart sideways at me. "It's…. complicated."

I fold my arms and stare pointedly at him. He is not getting out of this that easy.

"Let's play a game, little rabbit," he offers with a smirk. "An answer for an answer."

I shake my head in exasperation. Not this again. "You're no better than Shay," I say.

"I take offense to that." Killian narrows his eyes at me. "Well? Do you want to play?"

"Fine," I huff. "You first." I gesture in his direction.

"What do you miss about Earth?"

I don't even need to think twice. "My sister." My hands fall to my lap as I bite my trembling lip. "How do you really know Shay?"

Killian ponders for a moment, finding the right words. "We... knew each other as kids."

My head tilts as I try to read his stoic expression, but he gives away nothing.

His amber eyes consume me as he asks his next question. "What would you do if you won the competition?"

I shrug. "It doesn't matter because the wish is for Shay."

"If it wasn't." His heated gaze sears into me and I feel hot once more. This time, there's no outdoors to escape to.

"All I want is to go home," I sigh.

"Won't you be taken home in the end?" Killian searches my face, and I merely blink at him. His lethal beauty numbs my brain. I jerk when he clears his throat, prompting me to answer.

"Umm... uhh... sorry, what?" My hands squeeze together at my humiliation.

"Isn't Shay going to take you home once it's done?" He repeats, mirth sparking in his eyes.

"Oh, yeah. Well, only if I win."

Killian's amusement sours. "Damnit," he hisses under his breath. His concern over this has me shifting in my seat. He probably has drawn the same conclusion as me, the chances of me winning are slim.

"You can't trust him," he adds. His eyes bore into me, imploring me to trust his word.

I numbly nod. I don't understand their history, and I don't know if I can trust anyone, but Killian's sincerity and concern throws me into blind acceptance. "Why did you stand up for me at the trials? I didn't need your help."

"Seemed you did. You didn't get kicked out of the competition," he glances at my hand, "or lose any fingers."

"Yeah, but I got zero points from the judges. I could've handled it myself." I lean away and trace patterns in the water again.

"Still better than the alternative," he retorts.

I don't respond. He's not wrong, and despite my pride, I don't know what would've happened if he hadn't intervened.

We sit in silence, not even the wind moves.

"It is quite beautiful, even if the constant rain gets annoying," I say as I appreciate the blooming flowers.

"It used to be a lot more beautiful." His eyes trace the same path mine do, but a frown mars his striking features.

"You've said something like that before," I recall. "What do you mean by it?"

"*Gon'an'rit* used to be magical the moment you stepped foot in this realm. We'd have impeccable seasons, the sun casting such a light upon the land all the creatures would come out to bask in it. The nights were perfect, showing millions of stars until the velvet sky seemed to be coated in glitter. The colors… they were vibrant, almost like they had a life of their own. I could wander the meadows and forests for hours looking upon this realm." His eyes are distant as he speaks, seeing memories that I can only use my imagination for.

"What happened?" I whisper, afraid to break his reverie. This is the most he's ever spoken. At least not without somehow insulting me.

My breath catches when his dark eyes, no longer the usual golden color, snap back to me, pulling me into their depths. "Something is wrong with the magic of the land."

I shake my head at his words. "The magic seems fine to me."

He sighs and leans back, using his flat palms against the stone to support him. "You simply have nothing to compare it to, but I can feel it, and most can see it even if they choose not to."

"It sounds like it was lovely."

His burning gaze studies me, as though he is stripping away my layers. He's a predator, watching each breath I take, lingering to search for my weakness.

I shudder under his penetrating stare, and my chest tingles as he leans towards me.

I grasp the skirt of my dress as his intoxicating sandalwood scent wafts over me.

"You shouldn't be here, little rabbit," he purrs.

His obnoxious nickname for me breaks my trance. "I am. Not. A rabbit." With murder in my eyes, I poke him in his hard chest with each word.

His hand envelops mine, stopping my physical assault, but not my verbal one.

"I'm not some defenseless animal that needs taking care of! Stop acting like you need to save me. I never asked for your help. In fact, I explicitly told you not to help me. So, stop it, and stop treating me like I'm some distressed, helpless pet!"

"You do not know the nightmarish creatures that live in this land."

"Oh, yeah? Like you?" I throw the truth he admitted in the second trial in his face. I expect him to flinch, but instead he yanks my hand.

I tumble forward, using my other hand to brace myself against his muscular chest. My shocked expression meets his stern one.

"Yes, exactly like me," he sneers. He leans forward to whisper in my ear. "I am a *Púca*, a fae made of your worst fears." As he speaks, he transforms. His burnt caramel eyes turn bright green, his broad shoulder thin, and thick black hair turns into a brown pixie cut.

I gasp as Shauna sits before me, but when she speaks it's not with her chipper confidence, but with warning malice. "I am darkness. I am death."

Her eyes sink into her face and flesh begins to rot. She emits a shuddering, a painful sound. Under my hand, blood pools on her chest.

I scream, peeling my hand back. I look at it, but my hand is clean of her blood. Shaking, I glance up, and Killian's firm form is back to normal.

"What the hell." I brush a tear from my eye. "What is your problem?" My voice is weak, exactly the way Killian sees me.

"You do not understand this world, Cara," he explains. "It's dangerous and I'm not even the worst creature out there. Sometimes those you least expect are the ones who will hurt you the most."

As I stand in a huff, so does Killian. I cross my arms, pushing down the sob that wants to tear from my chest. He has officially ruined the one good evening I've had since arriving. "Leave."

There's a flash in his eyes. Regret? Sorrow? I don't have time to figure it out because it's soon masked by a predatory smile.

"I said leave!" I scream, a stray tear springing free. I brush it away just as quickly, angered by my obvious weakness.

He hesitates, but he shuts down any potential emotions until his impassive face stares down at me. "Did you know when a rabbit gets caught, they scream?" He doesn't wait for me to respond as walks away and melts into the darkness.

I watch the shadows for any movement, but after a few minutes of nothing, I collapse in on myself with a gasp.

I will leave this wretched place if it's the last thing I do.

SIXTEEN

The briny air slashes across my face the moment I step outside the palace. I brace myself against the wind as I turn to head to the training ring.

My arms are still sore from training with Shay yesterday, but I guess there's no rest for the wicked. At least Shay was kind enough to drop off a soothing balm for my muscles last night.

"Cara!" A male voice hollers across the breeze.

I push my hair out of my face, using the back of my hand to block the rain from hitting my eyes as I look off to the right.

Cadan jogs over to me, waving his hand.

My heart pounds from my anxiety escalating through my body. I haven't seen Cadan since the second trial, not even at the fae ball. I was worried he was avoiding me, not that I'd blame him.

His pace slows until he stands before me. His focus is on my chin, the closest he's come to direct eye contact outside of the momentary spurts.

"Hey Cadan," I say in a shy voice.

His eyebrows knit together as he scowls at me.

My stomach drops. I knew I messed up at the trial. I would take whatever verbal lashing he wanted to give me.

"Are you mad at me?" he asks.

"W-what?" I utter in complete shock. "Why would you think that?"

His depthless eyes move between my two shoulders as he formulates his thoughts. "Your greeting was unnatural for you."

"Huh?" Still confused, my head cocks to the side.

His lips pinch together. I can see the turmoil on his face while he figures out what he wants to say to me. He presses his left wrist into his side, twisting it side to side to use his thigh to wind his bracelet.

"I'm not good at social cues, so maybe I'm wrong. But when you spoke it was different. Usually you smile 'til your eyes crinkle on the side. I understood those as signs of happiness to talk to me. But just now, your eyes went wide and you took a step away from me. Those are movements associated with fear and anxiety." His finger taps the side of his leg. "Although, I guess that would not make you mad." His eyes flit to mine for half a second. "Are you frightened of me?"

A few seconds of silence pass between us. I close my mouth as I emerge from my stupor, realizing he's waiting for my answer.

"No, Cadan, not at all." I take a step closer. I hadn't even realized I had stepped back from him earlier.

"Then why'd you greet me differently?"

"I... I thought you were mad at me," I admit.

Now it's his turn to tilt his head to the side. "What'd I do to make you think this? I called for your attention and came over to you. These aren't actions associated with someone who's mad."

A low chuckle escapes me. "Yeah, I guess you're right. It wasn't your actions. I thought it was my actions."

"I don't understand."

I sigh, "I thought you were mad at me from the second trial. When I," I hesitate. I didn't want to remind him of a reason he should be mad at me, but Cadan is a candid person and he deserves for me to be forthcoming. "I said I wouldn't stick up for you at the trial."

He blinks before explaining his own thoughts on the matter. "But the trial was not about standing up for someone else. The trial was about telling the truth. Why would I be mad at you for telling the truth?"

"Because a friend is supposed to help their friends, no matter the circumstance." I scuff my shoe at the ground, kicking nothing in particular.

"Friendship shouldn't only be about help, but about accepting someone for who they truly are. I accept you, Cara. I accept and understand your fear of the *Korrigan* and how that would make you not help me. I don't blame you." He nods along with his statement.

"I accept you too, Cadan," I whisper, peering through the tendrils of my hair that blow across my face.

A small smile toys at his lips and the pressure that was building inside of me releases a little. I should have spoken with him sooner. His honesty and lack of playing games, unlike other fae, should have given me confidence to seek him out.

"Where're you going?" He changes the subject, eyes skimming my black workout clothes.

"Training with Shay," I mutter with distaste.

"Won't your hair get in the way?" He watches me fight with my hair when another shift of wind has it scattering around me.

"Yeah, I'll put it in a ponytail."

"What kind of training will you be doing?"

"I don't know. Probably combat or sword work, maybe try to get my powers to manifest." All of those sound like a terrible way to spend my day. I can think of a dozen other things I would rather be doing.

"If you don't know how to use your powers, why'd you join the competition?"

"Life debt," I say.

He nods like I've given him all the answers.

"Speaking of my powers," I shift on my feet, "the *Korrigan* said my claim of being a banshee was a half-truth. What do you think that meant?" Cadan is one of the most knowledgeable and forthcoming fae here, maybe he can help me understand myself better.

"You smell of *Beansidhe*, but something more. The scent is reminiscent of nutmeg, but a little mustier. It's muted, so I'm not completely sure."

"Join the line," I sigh. "One more mystery for me to solve. Anyways, I should get going to practice."

Cadan shakes his head. "Your hair will get in the way."

I give a shrug. "It's fine. If it gets too windy I'll put it into a bun."

"Neither of those will work. An assailant can use your long hair against you, especially hair as long as yours. It'll be easier to grab if you try to move away or they can use it in a painful way to bend you to their will."

My eyes widen at his deduction. It's something I should've realized before with some of my recent encounters of the male variety. Thankfully, Shay hasn't done that yet, but that doesn't mean he won't and it doesn't mean another opponent won't in the competition. If Cadan can think this way, I'm sure some of the more brutish competitors will too.

"A crown braid weaving close to your scalp would be best," he adds with a nod of his head.

I chuckle to myself. "Sadly, that is not in my skill set. I can do a normal braid down my back, but I have a feeling that isn't any better."

He shakes his head. "It's not. But I can do it."

I raise an eyebrow at him.

"Come." He walks towards the step of the door I exited through, sitting inside the archway to block the wind.

I follow him, and he points at the floor in front of him. I oblige by sitting with my back to him. I feel his fingers pause above my hair, questioning the physical contact, but with a deep breath, he plunges his fingers into my hair, separating and molding pieces together with finesse.

"How did you learn to do this?" I ask, my curiosity rearing its head, especially with the messy hair Cadan always sports.

"I have four older sisters."

"Four?" I can't hide the shock from my voice. That means there's at least five of them. Five kids. I can't imagine. I'll have one, maybe two, max three, but only if I find the right person. Bless the women of the world who have more than that. They are super powered warriors in my eyes. I hurry to conceal my judgement. "Any brothers?"

"No, just myself and my four older sisters." His fingers weave through the strands of my hair. He's so delicate it feels like a scalp massage, causing me to close my eyes with a smile.

"I have an older sister," I murmur.

Cadan doesn't say anything, but it's the first time thinking about my sister doesn't hurt, so I press on.

"She practically raised me. She's my best friend and I miss her dearly."

"Where's she now?"

"Back on Earth," I sigh. "What are your sisters like?"

"The oldest is a mother, she's pregnant with her third child. My two middle sisters are twins and are the reason I know how to braid hair. I spent my childhood with them dressing me like I was a doll. I never thought anything about it until I went into public one day with makeup and braided hair. A group of kids from school saw me and started bullying me, taunting at me, laughing," he pauses. "The youngest of my older sisters was walking by and ran over. She stood up for me, just like you did. When we got home, she washed my face of the makeup and blood. I told her I didn't want my longer hair anymore, and without hesitation she got a kitchen knife and chopped it off. She's the strongest person I know. Although, it was the first time I ever worked up the courage to have my hair cut. It wasn't the best experience, a complete overload for me, so to this day it's difficult for me to manage my hair."

Tears press against the corners of my eyes. "My sister is the strongest person I know too." I fumble for the right words to say. "I'm sorry you went through that."

"You didn't do it," he shrugs, "there's no reason for you to be sorry."

"I'm still sorry it is a pain you went through." I wish I had the power to take away pain, to take away painful memories.

"I'm not sorry." Cadan's fingers toy with the ends of my hair, seeming to weave them through braids he's already created. "It made me stronger. It made me appreciate my family, their openness and acceptance. The world can be cruel and if I continued to be protected from that then I wouldn't know how to appreciate the good."

I remember the reason he joined the *Naim* competition, which was revealed during the second trial, how he wanted the world to accept him for who he is. "Have you had a lot of, uh, difficult moments?"

"Of course," Cadan says as though it's a given. "Don't most people? Just because my moments aren't the same as yours, doesn't mean we both haven't gone through our own versions of difficulty."

"I hope you have had more good in your life, to help balance it out." Because I sure haven't and I hate imagining Cadan's life filled with pain.

"Plenty." I can hear the smile in his voice. "Recently, I met you. You remind me of my sister and have brought good into my life."

He gives me too much credit, but I can't help the warmth blooming in my chest from his words. "I'm glad I met you, Cadan. You're my one good thing in this realm."

"All done," he says. His hands drop away, so I reach up to feel the work.

Braids of various sizes weave over my scalp, with a pile of intertwining tendrils toppled near the crown of my head. It's intricate but sturdy. The wind has nothing on this.

"Thanks," I whisper.

"You're welcome."

I turn to Cadan, his darting eyes meeting mine before staring at his hands. "I should get going. Thank you again, my friend." I grasp Cadan's hand.

He stills at the contact, clearly uncomfortable. I drop his hand, but before I do he squeezes my hand as he nods his head.

The moment I pull away, he snaps his fingers, disappearing.

My voice is hoarse by the time I'm done screaming.

"Again," Shay demands.

"I've been screaming for the past hour," I huff as I lean against the wooden fence of our training ring, sweat sliding down the nape of my neck. I'm fairly certain Shay is punishing me for being late to practice. I raise my head and let the pattering rain cool my face, opening my mouth for the moisture to soak into my dry mouth.

"And you still haven't used your power, kid." Shay folds his meaty arms over his broad chest. "Again."

"Holy hell, Shay," I fume. "How many times do I have to tell you I don't know how to use my powers? Are you secretly deaf or something and have only been reading my lips this whole time? Or are you just dense and don't understand when a woman is talking to you?"

He opens his mouth, but I cut him off. I'm so ramped up that I step forward until I mirror his pose, face red as my voice raises.

"Or is it that I'm a human? Oh wait, I know," I smirk. "The wondrous prince of this land views everyone else as nothing but a servant to his needs. That's all I've ever been to you, so how could I possibly have my own opinions or know what the hell I'm talking about when it comes to my own body or abilities? Heaven forbid you actually try to listen to anyone but yourself. Although, it doesn't even seem your father seems to care what you think, so maybe it's just your way of taking your daddy issues out on everyone else."

I can tell by the tick in his jaw and the way his hand squeezes his bicep that the last part of my rant gets to him.

"Maybe you are nothing but a fae as weak as a human who is destined to be no one, and taking you on was an utter mistake. Maybe I shouldn't help you and let you perish in this competition so I can be rid of your petulant self." Shay's face stays solemn as he says this, giving nothing away of his genuine feelings.

"Seriously, what is your problem?" I scream. "You literally stole me from my home!" My voice continues to raise. "Not only have I asked for none of this, but you tricked me into it! You are nothing but a selfish prick!" By the end, my voice is a shrieking mess, which causes Shay to double over with his hands covering his ears.

I gasp, moving a step forward.

"Well, it's about time," he says as he stands upright. "It took you long enough."

"I... I don't even know what I did." I gape at him while he moves his jaw from side to side as though he's popping his ears in an airplane.

"Often powers are tied to our emotions." He rubs his chin. "It's something we learn at such a young age, when we have yet to school our feelings. By the time a fae is an adult, separating magic and emotions is second nature and not something we need to mentally do anymore. But since you've never had this training, even though you're an adult, we have to treat your training like you're a child. I did not consider this before." His eyes brighten at his realization.

"Great," I roll my eyes. Just what I needed, to be treated like a child on top of everything else. His nickname for me will take on a whole new meaning, exactly what I wanted.

"Again," Shay demands.

I spend another fifteen minutes trying to use my powers, often with Shay saying things to rile me, but I fail to replicate my power.

"Okay, that's enough for today," Shay claims as he tosses me a bottle of water.

"Oh, thank goodness." I collapse onto the ground as I chug the crisp water.

"My turn?"

I turn to see a devilish grin bloom across Killian's face as he leans on the fence, and I promptly groan aloud as my head lolls back. You've got to be kidding me.

"I thought you said I was done for the day," I give Shay my best attempt at puppy dog eyes.

"With working on your banshee powers, yes," he nods. "But we still have to make sure you can defend yourself in combat."

"Or at least not get yourself killed," Killian chimes in.

I flip him the bird as I finish the last of my water.

His eyes harden and Shay stares at me with delight dancing in his eyes.

"Good. Use that feistiness to beat him." Shay extends his hand and helps haul me up. "He could use it. He's a little too cocky for my taste."

"That's rich coming from you." A wry smile tugs at my lips at his disgruntled look.

"Either way, you need the practice," Shay responds.

"If it's so important, why don't you show me how it's done?" I goad. "Big strong prince like you should easily take him down." If I'm being honest, I could use a longer break too.

Killian chuckles off to the side as he brandishes his sword. "I'd like to see him try."

Without a word and murder in his eyes, Shay pulls his sword from his back and swings it side to side as though testing the weight. Satisfied, he takes a leap towards Killian, crossing a fifteen foot gap without even a running start.

My mouth drops open, a slice of fear for Killian pierces my chest momentarily, but it evaporates when metal on metal rings through the air.

Killian spins away, moving so swiftly the dirt under his feet is barely disturbed.

Shay lunges again, but Killian sidesteps him and swings the sword at his back.

The sword whizzes over Shay's head as he ducks and rolls, coming up quickly to face Killian. Their steps mirror one another as they circle each other in unison. Their moves are so stealthy, I can't even hear the crunch of gravel.

Killian swings his sword at Shay's side, but he parries so quickly it's like he knew the move was coming.

Immediately, Shay counters with a twirl, the tip of his blade aiming to cross Killian's chest. This time Killian avoids the attack like they are in a synchronized dance.

Again and again, they strike and counter, the only sound is when their swords clash. After twenty minutes, I finally see beads of sweat forming on their foreheads. With one last leap from Shay, he comes crashing down on Killian, who easily crosses his sword to block. They stand face to face, their breathing unaffected despite the immense physical labor they've endured.

"Draw," Killian mutters.

Shay's eyes narrow. "Draw," he agrees before stepping back.

In unison, they bow to one another.

They turn to me, scowls in place, when I start clapping. "Bravo! Bravo! Encore! Encore!"

Shay stalks over and throws his sword beside where I sit. "You're welcome to try."

I grasp the hilt, but grunt when I'm unable to lift it with a single hand.

Killian steps up beside him, "I have a better idea."

He pulls a second sword from his back, one that resembles his own but is much smaller. He twirls it in the air before giving it a light toss. It flips in the air, and he expertly catches the blade without cutting himself in order to pass it to me with the handle in my direction.

I brace my arm, preparing for the heavy steel's weight, but when Killian let's go, my arm barely budges in the air. The sword is light— swift— something that my weak muscles can acclimate to.

"It's called a short sword," Killian explains. "After our last session, it was clear a regular sword was too heavy for you."

"Smart," Shay nods.

Killian gives him a menacing look. "I know."

I pop onto my feet and swing the sword from side to side.

Shay moves off to the side as Killian shuffles me to the center.

He takes me through some basic drills, allowing me to adjust to the feel of the sword and practicing basic maneuvers. After ten minutes, a dull ache seeps into my arm, but it's not enough to where I need to use the support of my other hand.

"It fits you well," Shay announces from the fence. "Try to attack him."

"With pleasure." A predatory grin spreads across my face.

Killian's eyes narrow at me, but the corners of his mouth tip up.

I swing my blade at Killian, which he easily avoids, but I turn with him, no longer dragged around by the weight of my weapon.

He brings his sword down on me, at a quarter of speed he used on Shay, and I parry him. His eyes darken as we continue to roll through different motions. He starts to quicken his speed. I proudly block most, but he begins to land some blows as he lets loose his expertise. He never cuts me, but uses the flat edge to whack my shoulder, side, and, at one point, my bum. With my tendency to bruise, I have no doubt I'll have pretty purple marks by the end of the day.

With a screech, which to my satisfaction gets a flinch from him, I run at him. I swing my sword, slicing at his head. He quickly ducks and swipes his leg.

Before I realize it, I'm dropping my sword as I fall backwards. The air slams out of my lungs when I hit the ground.

Killian pounces on top of me, bringing the tip of his sword to my chest. He looms over me, nothing but a dark figure.

You do not know the nightmarish creatures that live in this land; his voice echoes in my head.

My lungs burn as I attempt to suck in breaths of air while the image of his face morphing into my sister's and her moans of death invade my mind. The rot. The Blood. A whimper escapes my throat as tears blur my vision.

Killian's body goes rigid as he takes in my face. He bounds off of me, putting distance between us. He sheathes his sword as I sit up. His eyebrows pinch in worry while watching my unsteady movements.

I wait for him to ask if I'm okay, but when I look at him, he avoids eye contact as he runs his hand through his raven hair.

The gravel grates underneath Shay's shoe when he walks over to me. He regards me with a frown.

It's then that I realize I'm trembling. I wrap my arms around my body, hugging myself to hold still.

"What did you do to her?" Shay accuses as he careens towards Killian.

"I didn't do anything," he mumbles, avoiding eye contact by inspecting the barn in the distance.

"The hell you did!" Shay steps closer, causing Killian to stand taller so they are face to face.

"Back. Off." Killian seethes through his gritted teeth.

"What did your *Púca* do to her?" Shay hollers. He speaks to Killian as though his fae species has a mind of its own.

"I didn't do anything!"

Shay points in my direction. "Look at her! Clearly you did something!"

I shrink under their scrutiny.

"Have you ever thought uprooting her to do your bidding is the real problem?" Killian counters as his hand covers the hilt of his sword.

"I'm not the one she needs to be careful of," he says in a deep rumble with his fists clenching at his sides.

Killian's jaw ticks. "I think you're exactly the one she needs to be careful of."

"I think I can take care of myself," my shaking voice has them turning in my direction. When I stand, my wobbly legs almost give out.

Killian takes a step forward, but Shay's withering glare stops him.

"I think we've had enough practice for today," Shay says as he steps in front of Killian, but still watching me, daring either of us to object.

"Fine with me," Killian's tenor voice drips. He turns towards the fence, effortlessly leaps over it with his hand barely touching the top plank of wood, and stalks towards the forest in the distance.

Shay now moves towards me, but I hold up my hand.

"I'm fine."

"Let me escort you—"

I shake my head and turn my back. "I'm fine," I grit through clenched teeth.

I head back to the palace. The rain falls harder as I move across the grounds, soaking through my sweaty outfit. A few guards nod at me as I pass, but I ignore them. I focus on putting one foot in front of the other. Once I'm back to my room, I shut the heavy door behind me.

Leaning against the cool wood, I slither down it until I place my forehead on my knees. A shiver wracks through my body as I cry.

SEVENTEEN

I shuffle forward with the rest of the crowd, although the contestants have thinned greatly after the second trial. Less than half the amount of contestants remain.

The patch work in the throne room is now complete, but the material is lighter compared to the original stone. The blast that had crumpled the wall and part of pillars is still apparent.

Everyone shifts nervously with the reminder of what occurred the last time we were in this room. Well, that and the fact we're all here for the next trial. Or, maybe, that's just me.

Shay passes me a flute of champagne, and I shake my head.

He leans down to whisper into my ear. "It's customary, and an affront to the king if you do not drink."

I gingerly take the glass. I don't want any alcohol in my system with the next challenge about to begin. However, I don't need any more animosity or unwanted attention from King Harbinger either.

Thankfully, for this upcoming trial I could wear a pair of jeans, laced boots, and a green blouse. This outfit most resembles what I would've worn on Earth, and I feel more like myself than I have in weeks. I have no idea when jeans showed up in my closet, but they were a welcome sight this morning when I went to get ready.

More or less, I've lived in my workout clothes over the past week with Shay taking me through an intense training regiment, focusing on working with the short sword since my banshee abilities are still acting shy. Killian, luckily, stayed away during this time after the incident in the ring. Sometimes during training I would get tingles in my chest, which would distract me, and quickly result in Shay besting me, but when I'd search the area I never saw anyone.

The King steps forward on his dais and raises his glass.

I raise my own, and my arm aches from all my recent sword work. I will need another ice bath at the end of today. I've never worked out so much in my life.

"A toast to our contestants who have made it this far. Continue to prove yourselves, continue to prosper, continue to represent the best quality of the fae!" King Harbinger brings his champagne glass to his lips and takes a sip.

Everyone follows suit, mimicking the action of their king.

The champagne bubbles against my tongue, but it tastes like I took a bite of a crisp autumn apple. I take another sip, along with the other fae.

"This is delicious," I whisper to Shay.

He gives a tight-lipped smile, his eyes strained with a secret.

"What is…?" I sway a little and grab onto his arm. "Woah, I think this is stronger than the fae wine."

Shay says nothing, but braces me by putting his hand on my back.

"Whatsh happnin," I slur as I peer at a blurry Shay.

Again, he doesn't speak, instead using both hands to steady me.

"I…" But before I can finish, Shay's arms tighten around me as everything goes black.

❧

My eyes blink as the room comes into focus. I push my dark hair from my face and sit up from where I'm sprawled across a stone floor. I stretch a kink in my neck by rolling it side to side.

"Hello?" I say to the empty room. "Is anyone there?"

No answer.

What the hell happened? Was it the same men as the last time? Is Shay okay? I'm beginning to think that room is as cursed as I am.

This room is smaller, more the size of the living room in the apartment I shared with Shauna. Random pictures hang on the wall. There's a bookcase, a desk covered in papers with a wooden chair, and a velvet armchair in the center with a coffee table beside it. Across the space are an assortment of tchotchkes— an owl statue in the corner, a sundial despite being in a room without windows, a globe, and a typewriter— to name a few of the random items. A light switch is positioned next to the single door.

I startle when King Harbinger's voice echoes through the room, despite not seeing a speaker. Ah, right. Magic.

"Hello contestants," he says. "Welcome to your third trial, the test of wit. You must escape your area. The first forty contestants to do so will move on. Good luck."

Forty? That's a third of the current contestants! Weren't these trials supposed to slowly whittle us down? I guess eventually it'll get down to a single person, so major cuts would have to happen at some point.

I pick myself up.

Okay, I need to be within the first forty people out of this room. I snicker to myself when I realize I'm essentially in an escape room. To think Shauna and I once paid two hundred dollars to do one of these for her birthday. Why spend that kind of money when all I needed to do was get kidnapped, taken to another realm, and coerced into a potentially life threatening competition?

I laugh inwardly and shake my head. The fact I'm starting to find my predicament amusing is something I should find more worrisome. My therapy bills are going to be insane when I get back to Earth.

Shauna and I surprisingly did pretty well at the escape room, having solved it with twenty minutes to spare. I could do this.

I walk over to the only door. It's worth a shot.

I twist the handle, but it doesn't budge— locked. There is a place for a key, and I'm positive I need to find a key somewhere in this room.

I crack my knuckles as I scan the room. A four combination lock fastens a desk drawer.

Bingo. Why do these things always start with some kind of lock? I wonder if the fae stole this concept from humans or if they taught it to us? My hope is for the former as that'll give me an advantage having grown up on Earth.

I realize the wall decor is almost all acrylic paintings. There's a ballerina, a cityscape, and, funnily enough, a fairy sitting on a log, but there's a single poster of varying flowers. I step closer to the poster to inspect it.

It's scientific, each flower drawn in immense detail in rows and columns, with scientific names scrawled underneath. I review each word, looking for a pattern in their names, repeating words, but there's nothing. I study the flowers next, seeing if the number of petals or leaves match, but again there is no pattern. Finally, I realize they are in different colors. However, the colors repeat and despite there being various colors with the greens of their stems, the colors of the petals themselves perfectly match in shade even if it's a completely different flower. The red hue of a carnation doesn't flawlessly resemble that of a rose in real life, but on this poster it does.

Red, yellow, purple, and blue is the order of the colors in the top row. There are four colors, the exact amount of numbers I am looking for.

I rush over to the lock and enter 3-6-6-4, the number of letters for each color.

Nothing.

Next option. I count the number of red flowers, seven. I enter that. Five yellow, two purple, and six blue. The lock clicks open.

"Yes!" I cheer to myself.

I pull it off and open the drawer. Inside is a plain white piece of paper, with varying lengths of rectangles cut out of it.

Well, this is wildly unhelpful. I place it on the desk and turn to continue searching for more clues. My eyes snag on a familiar item. Against a wall in the corner, metal gleams from my leaning short sword. My scabbard lies on the floor beside it.

Odd.

With a shrug, I intuitively tie my scabbard around my waist and put my sword where it belongs on my hips. A welcome weight.

I scour the room. Approaching the bookshelf, I pull off books. Perhaps there is a hidden second room and pulling a book will unlock it.

Cliché? Yes, but sometimes that's what you can expect from an escape room.

One after another I pull them and they land on their spine or fall to the floor, never triggering a hatch. On the second shelf from the bottom, I pull a book. Still nothing, but a dog-eared page catches my eye. I yank the book from the shelf and open it.

A picture of Niamh and Oisín is on the marked page, their arms wrapping around each other in a lover's embrace. The colored drawing shows detail the statues have yet to express, such as Niamh's golden hair. They are vibrant and alive, and it's the first time I've seen love in Niamh's eyes and devotion in Oisín's instead of heartache and longing. Beneath it is a printed script. It's a variation of their story that I already know, but the size of the words seem perfect for…

I dash to the desk with the book in hand. I slam it onto the table, papers fluttering to the ground. I retrieve the random piece of paper from earlier and place it over the passage. The empty boxes snugly fit to a subset of words.

The more there is, the less you see.

Crap. Shauna was always better at riddles than I was. The more there is, the less I see. Water? Well, there was no water in this room, not even a faucet, so that didn't make sense. I rack my brain, twisting my hair around my finger. I turn in a circle in hopes of finding inspiration.

Our first Halloween in our own apartment, Shauna and I built a fort in our living room. It was something we had done as kids when our parents were alive, but our foster families were often too strict to allow us childish fun. So the moment we had our own place, it was a way to commemorate everything we had been through. We had ordered delivery pizza and binged on candy. Late into the night, Shauna thought it would be fun to tell ghost stories. She turned on the flashlight while it was pointed at me, blinding me with the light. It took me a few seconds of blinking to get rid of all the spots. So, maybe the answer is light?

I study the room and study the light switch, but there's no way to make it brighter. I search shelves and drawers, but there seems to be no other light source except the one overhead. My attention diverts back to the light switch. If not light… darkness?

I walk over and flip the switch. The room goes pitch black, almost. Glowing arrows run along the ground leading away from me from where I stand.

"Check mate," I whisper.

I follow the glowing green arrows, the same look as glow-in-the-dark stars, but painted by hand instead. They move up the wall and point under the globe. I lift it off the table, and underneath is a big glow-in-the-dark circle. Shadowed in the center of the light is a key. My fingers grasp the cool metal, and I follow the arrows back to the switch.

After flicking the lights back on, I push the key into the lock of the door. Relief washes through me as I hear the bolt slide open.

Honestly, this wasn't that hard of an escape room, or maybe I have an advantage the others don't.

I twist the handle, and this time the door swings open without hesitation. Stepping into a hallway, and I look from my left to right. This was unexpected. What do I do now? Shouldn't Shay be waiting for me or the King? I needed to have some firm words with Shay too. He gave me a drugged beverage and didn't warn me.

Jerk. Although, when it comes to Shay and the fae, I don't know why I'd expect any different by this point.

Across from me, the snick of a lock sounds and the door swings open. Another contestant with green hair and pointed ears steps out. He looks at me for a split second, but I don't have a chance to ask anything because he turns and sprints down the hall.

The trial isn't over yet.

Grey stone surrounds me, which leads me to believe I'm no longer in the cream colored castle. Lanterns light the otherwise dark hallways, an eeriness creeps in since there are still no windows, but instead rows of doors.

As I walk the hall, I try the handles. Many are locked, and the ones that aren't hang open, revealing rooms matching my own. I test to see how similar they truly are by turning off the light in a few rooms, and it reveals the same glowing arrows.

After wandering by myself for a half an hour, I hear voices. The hall of rooms stopped a while back. It seems they set this building up like a maze since I have come across multiple dead ends, needing to turn back to follow a different path a few times.

I creep forward, unsure who lay ahead. A door to another room appears. It's cracked open. I peer into the slat to find two figures hunching over a giant puzzle on the ground.

I breathe a sigh of relief.

Killian's and Cadan's heads pop up at the sound.

I smile, more for Cadan than Killian, as I walk inside, and push the door behind me.

"Wait!" Killian launches up, hand outstretched.

The door clicks shut, and the sliding sound of a bolt moving into place follows.

"I told you the mechanism would lock us inside," Cadan says as his eyes move back to the puzzle in front of him. He's crouched with his arms hanging over his knees as he studies the ground.

Killian rakes his hand through his hair. "Yes, Cadan, you were right, but Cara didn't know that."

"It's pretty obvious by looking at the mechanism," Cadan explains.

"Perhaps for you, but not for everyone," Killian huffs as he sits back down on the opposite side of the puzzle.

Cadan reaches forward and moves a piece to the left. The puzzle is an assortment of squares the size of a hand, with two missing slots.

"They can move into different spots, but they can't be pried up." Killian explains to me as I cross over to them. "We believe it makes some kind of pattern or picture, but we don't know what."

"Why'd we get locked in?" I ask.

Cadan points to another door across the room. "The contestants can't move on until the puzzle is solved. I waited five minutes at the locked door, trying to figure out how to get in before Killian showed up. Together we spent another ten minutes searching before the door opened itself. We saw retreating figures on the other side of that door, but it shut itself before we could follow." He trails off as he reaches forward again to move a yellowed square one spot closer to Killian. Nothing happens, so he keeps studying it with a blank expression. Absentmindedly, he fidgets with his bracelet.

Killian picks up where Cadan left off. "He assumed the door would lock us in as well. So, we didn't shut the door to be safe."

"Assumptions are something accepted as true without proof," Cadan states. "I made an educated hypothesis as I had proof with what I witnessed and the style of the lock on the door."

Killian holds up his hands. "My apologies," his attention moves to me, "he made an educated guess and was correct."

"Hypothesis," Cadan and I both correct at the same time.

Cadan's dark eyes meet mine for a split second before he gives a small smile and refocuses back on the puzzle.

"Either way, you locked us in," Killian says.

"Whoopsies," I add, unsure what else he wants from me. I point to a wooden pole in the corner. It's the only other item in the stark room aside from us and the puzzle. "So, what's the stick for?"

They both shrug.

"So far it's served no purpose," Killian responds.

I sit on a third side of the square, steeple my hands with my elbows on my knees, and press my fingers to my mouth as I study the puzzle too.

We are silent as we all think through possibilities. Every once in a while one of the men reaches forward and moves a square, but there's no signifier the action is correct.

"How did you both get out of your rooms so quickly?" I'm surprised they had made it out before me considering I thought I had been pretty quick. Plus, it's insane there were already fae ahead of them too. I mean, made some mistakes, but not fifteen or more minutes worth. People can only move so fast.

"I zapped out," Cadan states.

My mouth pops open. "You used your magic to get out of the room?"

His dark eyes glance at me. "They said to get out. I did. Although, my magic only worked for the room, not the entire building. I tried." He restudies the obstacle in front of him, his mouth moving with his thoughts.

"I started moving things. After five minutes, I found the key under the globe." Killian raises a knee and rests his arm on it.

Seriously? He merely moved things around? Any idiot could have done that. It completely defeats the purpose of this trial. Someone isn't getting full points this round. Can someone be docked points?

"I don't think that counts as wit," I mention, not bothering to hide the annoyance in my tone.

"What's more witty, little rabbit, solving some puzzles or finding a faster way to get out?" Killian smirks at me.

I purse my lips, choosing to ignore his presence again, so I can study the colored squares. Something tickles the back of my mind. Something about this puzzle is familiar.

I move to my knees, retracing the colored squares, counting how many there are in total.

"We're missing a red piece," I mumble.

"What?" Killian says, raising his head.

I scoot forward and start rearranging the pattern. I smile to myself as it matches what I remember in my head.

"What do you see?" Cadan asks in an awed tone, but there's a bite to it.

Someone's a little jealous I figured out something before him.

"It's the poster," I explain.

"What poster?" Cadan wonders.

Killian's eyes widen as he realizes the same conclusion. "The flower poster in the room."

Seems he wasn't completely obtuse during his five minutes of knocking things over in the room like a caveman.

"Yes, it's the same hue of colors, and the same number of each color," I explain. "You two would have noticed it sooner had you taken the time to solve the puzzles."

I pause as my hand scrapes an empty spot at the end of the fourth row. "We're missing one. There's only six red, but there should be seven."

"There." Killian points to the ceiling corner, but I don't see anything but more grey stone.

Poor Killian is losing his touch. The enclosed space must be getting to Mr. Cranky Pants.

I cover my mouth as I try not to laugh to myself.

Cadan's lips twitch as he tries not to smile like he's in on the same joke.

Killian notices and glares at us. "Look *on* the stone."

Cadan nods. "It's the same size."

"I still don't see it." I squint at the ceiling.

Killian sidles up next to me. He leans in close, and my nerves flare at his proximity, making my chest tingle. His sandalwood scent fills my senses, and I shake my head to clear it when he points his hand out in front of my face.

I follow the rippling muscles of his arms, ignoring the swoop of my belly, to the tip of his finger. Following the pathway he points, there's a square stone attached to the ceiling. It's the same grey color, but also the same sized square as the puzzle. It seems to be glued or locked in place.

"How much do you want to bet it's red on the other side," he breathes in my ear, causing a shiver to ripple down my spine.

He's a jerk. He's a jerk. A pretty jerk, but still a jerk. There's no attraction. Nada. Zip. Zero.

I jump up and move to the stick. "How much do you want to bet we need to use this?"

"There." Cadan points to a small hole next to the square. A perfect match to the diameter of the stick.

"But how are we going to get up there? It's probably twenty feet above us," I observe.

"If Cadan's goes on my shoulder and…"

Cadan cuts off Killian. "That won't work." His eyes shift from side to side as he calculates a plan in his head.

Silence descends upon us as we all try to determine our next steps.

"I have an idea," Killian says, running his hands through his hair. He eyes me and Cadan warily. "Try not to freak out."

I take a step back, remembering the last time he did something unexpected. If he has to warn me this time… unease flashes through my body and seizes my muscles.

They evaporate the moment Killian reaches over his shoulder, grabs his shirt, and hauls it over his head. Hard muscles line his torso, strong shoulders leading to a dense chest and taper into a six pack which drifts into a v lining his hips. Red scars mar his left side. The ones noticeable on his neck and shoulder cover the entire left side of his chest and run halfway down his side and stomach. The shiny skin is made more apparent against the brown, smooth skin on his right side.

His fingers undo the button of his pants and move to the lining of his underwear. I sharply inhale as he tugs, spinning around to face the wall.

A blush consumes my face, and I cover it with my palms. Not that I saw anything, but I'm sure he noticed me ogling him.

Magical electricity ignites through the room, raising the hair on my arms. The air becomes chilly and the light flickers as his dark powers seep outwards. There's a whoosh.

Out of the corner of my left eye, Cadan scrambles backwards until his back hits the wall. He drops into a ball, closing his eyes, and starts muttering. "The bird of darkness is not real, the bird of darkness is not real, the bird of darkness is not real." He white knuckles his leather circlet like it's a lifeline.

Curiosity getting the best of me, and I peer over my shoulder. My breath holds as I brace myself for the same fear I felt the night of the fae ball.

On the ground stands the largest raven I've ever seen. Its ebony black feathers shine in the light. But instead of beady black eyes, they have an amber tint.

"Killian?" I ask.

The black bird squawks back as it flares its wings. It's easily a five foot wingspan, one that is way too big for a normal raven.

I peek over to Cadan who still whispers to himself, eyes closed, as though trying to fend off the darkness he speaks of.

But I'm entranced. Killian's darkness speaks to my own. I step closer, extending my hand as I bend down. "Killian?" I breathe.

He flaps his wings, launching himself into the air, and he careens towards me. I don't flinch when he comes closer, my second nature near animals taking over, even if this isn't a real raven. Killian swoops, his talons snatching the stick, and he pulls it from my hand and flies to the corner of the ceiling.

With measured beats of his wings he hovers below the hole, and with the help of his beak and claws, he manages to fit the wood inside. There's a groan of stone on stone, and the puzzle piece falls from the ceiling.

Killian drops the stick to catch the square with his talons, but misses.

My feet are moving before I realize I'm running, pushing me to get the stone before it smashes against the floor.

I'm going to miss it!

Panic sends adrenaline skyrocketing through me and the balls of my feet press harder against the floor and I propel into a jump. I soar through the air. My fingers snake around the sharp edge of the square.

It cuts my palm.

I ignore the pain, pulling it into my chest to protect it. I curl in on myself just as my shoulder slams into the wall. I fall into a heap on the ground.

EIGHTEEN

"Cara!" Killian's husky voice reverberates through me. I wince as I sit up, a radiating pain moving from my shoulder down my back. I pull the object clutched to my chest away to see the missing puzzle piece still intact. A relieved sigh leaves my lips.

"Are you okay?" Killian asks as he gently touches my shoulder, eliciting a painful yelp from me.

I tilt my head up to him with a mixture of disappointment and relief his clothes are back on. His sharp features darken with concern as his eyes scan my body, logging where I'm hurt.

"I'm fine," I say.

"You don't look okay," Cadan adds over Killian's shoulder.

I search for his dark eyes, but he doesn't maintain eye contact for long. "I could've said the same thing about you a few minutes ago."

He hangs his head. "I knew it wasn't real, but I couldn't control myself."

Killian gives him a remorseful look. "Sorry, that form is particularly difficult for fae to be around."

"What does that mean?"

"Ravens are representatives of darkness and death, often accompanying those who have passed," Cadan explains. "They're a bad omen and often nothing good follows after their appearance"

"Mixed with my powers as a *Púca*, the fear of death can become particularly strong for fae." He frowns at me. "Although, I'm unsure why it didn't affect you."

"You already used my biggest fear against me," I accuse. "I guess after that an oversized bird isn't all that scary."

His eyes harden. I swear a glimpse of remorse flashes across his face, but he says nothing. He hasn't apologized once for what happened, and that speaks for itself.

"Let's finish this," I say as I stand. Piercing pain radiates down my back, causing me to gasp as I brace against the wall.

Killian reaches for me, his hands pausing inches from my skin.

I hold the stone square out to Cadan. "Put this in the missing spot in the fourth row."

Cadan takes the piece and walks over to the puzzle, bends down, and places it inside. There's a fizzle of magic, and the piece disappears along with the stick on the ground. They reappear in their original spots in the corner and on the ceiling, and as the colors on the floor rearrange themselves back into a mixed order, the far door opens.

Cadan smiles at me in triumph, but Killian's eyes are dark with worry.

"Let's go." I push myself off the wall, biting the inside of my cheek to mask the pain on my face from my injury.

Killian follows a step behind me. The hair on the back of my neck stands on end as I feel his eyes bore into me.

The three of us walk into another hallway and the moment we do, the door begins to shut as the original one opens.

"Finally!" Someone shouts on the other end.

Over my shoulder, a bustle of fae cross into the room, their sharp eyes noticing us before the door clicks shut and locks in place.

As we walk, we come across multiple forked pathways, sometimes with two paths to choose from, but other times there are as many as four hallways. Each time Cadan confidently strides forward like he's following a known route.

Killian and I don't question it as we follow him, but after a half hour of walking and not understanding if we are getting more lost or not, I speak up.

"How do you know where you're going?"

Cadan stops, turns to me, and cocks his head. "You don't see them?"

"Uh," I side eye Killian, who shakes his head. "No?"

Cadan turns and keeps walking, which again we follow without question. At the next area that splits into three passages, he points at a small etched crown on the ground, no more the size of a quarter, where it meets the right-hand wall of the left passage.

I inspect the same spot of the other areas, but there's no marking. How Cadan had noticed such a tiny detail, I have no idea.

"They were present starting at the doors of our individual rooms," he says.

"Oh, cool." I purse my lips. That would've been nice to know when I was taking all those wrong turns earlier.

As we continue on, my legs ache and my shoulder throbs, but I push forward without a word. Sweat beads on my forehead, and I focus on breathing slow and deep through my nose in an attempt to cover my sharp inhales of pain.

A dead end greets us after our next turn.

"This doesn't make sense," Cadan furrows his brows as he searches the area. He walks to the crown insignia on the ground, which is in the middle of the wall at the dead end. "It should've led us to the exit."

Killian has yet to take a step away from me. "Let's take a break and then we'll figure it out." His body shifts onto his right foot, the one closest to me.

"I'm fine. I don't need your help," I grumble as I step away from him. I don't care whether he realizes he's still trying to take care of me or not because I'm noticing and it's annoying me.

"I don't think you are, little rabbit," he says as he looks at the area of my body that hit the wall.

A buzzing sound echoes through the room.

We all freeze, waiting for something to happen, searching around us, but when nothing happens we relax.

"Well, that's annoying," Killian mentions.

"Aw, so sweet you can recognize your own kind." I flash a smile at him as though it was a genuine compliment.

In all honesty, it is an obnoxious sound. It reminds me of the horrible rattle sound the ice maker of my fridge would make in my apartment after the ice machine broke.

The noise grows. There doesn't seem to be a pattern, sometimes it's a short blip and other times it elongates. Random pauses occur, but then it makes a bunch of clipped sounds in a row.

"It's Morse code," Cadan realizes with a nod.

"What?" I scoff. "Well, since I wasn't born in the late 1800s, I'm of no use."

"I don't know Morse code either," Killian adds.

"Unsurprising since Morse code doesn't revolve around scaring the crap out of someone." The moment I say it, a bit of guilt runs through me. He's never seemed proud of his abilities, and he admitted as much at the truth trial.

I stare at my toes. My pain is making me irritable. Plus, I'm still mad at Killian for what he did to me. With those two things combined, Killian may want to back away before I bite his head off.

Killian ignores my comment and leans on the wall across the hall from me.

"I knew it. Definitely Morse code," Cadan murmurs with the nod of his head. "It's been a while, so it may take me a moment, and I don't have a piece of paper to help me."

I smile at Cadan, forever impressed by his abilities. "Let me know what I can do to help. I can try to remember the letters or something."

"Thanks," Cadan replies as he sits with crossed legs and closes his eyes. His eyebrows pinch as he concentrates on the sound.

After ten minutes of the horrendous sound, Cadan speaks. "Okay, got it!"

I stand upright with anticipation, trying to cover my wince of pain. Killian straightens too, but frowns at me having not missed my reaction.

"I remember the sequence for the letters. So I can start decoding now."

I deflate, slumping back against the wall. I'm going to rip my ears off if I have to listen to this buzz much longer.

"Okay, I found the start of the message," Cadan announces. "The first letter is… O."

"Got it," I say as I tap my foot. Please be a short message. I don't know how many letters I can memorize.

Cadan opens one eye and stares at my shoe.

"Oh," I whisper. "Sorry." I stop my nervous tapping and slide down the wall, finally deciding to sit and rest, and grunt from the pain.

Killian's body stiffens as his head twists to scan the hall.

I follow his stare, but see nothing.

After a few heartbeats, voices echo towards us. Killian and I look at one another before bounding up.

We turn to face the hall as six burly fae round the corner. They stop in their tracks and smile. I recognize three of them— Scarface and the twins who attacked Cadan. The others include a woman whose fingers have claws at the end, and a seven foot tall man with all white irises. Although, he appears not to be blind by the way he homes in on me. The last is a bald man who looks like an ex-MMA fighter.

I shift, moving in front of Cadan as he babbles out the letter 'i'. I'm unsure if I missed a letter earlier, but I store it in my memory.

"What do we got here?" Scarface leers as his eyes devour my body.

Killian growls beside me.

"Careful, wolf boy," the woman licks her lips. "Or I'll have to teach you some manners."

"Back off," I say. "Let us finish decoding the message and we can all move on together." I hold my hands up in a placating gesture. Hopefully, a compromise will help dilute the building tension.

They laugh, the twins going as far to throw their heads back.

"Only forty move on," Scarface explains. "We aren't going to be risking our chance when we don't know how many have already made it through."

"A coded message," the white eyed man says with a smirk. "Thanks for the help."

Scarface doesn't take his eyes off me, but speaks to his friend. "You got this?"

White eyes nods his head, and closes his eyes like Cadan to concentrate on the sounds.

Cadan still continues to announce letters behind us, and I pray he is keeping track because I'm definitely not anymore.

Without warning, the other five launch themselves at us, pulling out blades and weapons hidden on their bodies.

Ringing erupts in my head. A gasp forms on my lips with the distraction pulling my attention away from the threat coming at me.

Killian shoves me behind him, the movement sending scorching pain through my shoulder. He parries one of the twins and sinks his blade into the one who looks like he fought MMA.

Blood gurgles at his lips.

Killian jumps out of the way as Scarface brings down a mace, pulling his sword out of the fighter who falls to the ground dead.

He doesn't get away unscathed though, as the second twin swipes a blade down his back. Killian hollers in pain, but returns the blow with one of his own, moving across the twin's sword arm, which causes the twin to drop his blade.

The clawed woman scurries past the scuffle, her sights set on Cadan.

I step in between them, widening my stance to block her view. I may not be there for my sister, Marcus may have moved on, and missing so much school may have hurt my chances for my future, but I'll be damned if I'm idle during a trial again. I can no longer sit on the sidelines of my own life, or I'll continue to get dragged through it, losing myself along the way. There's no time like the present to become the person I want to be.

I withdraw my sword, but my shoulder does not cooperate with the added weight, and I choke as the pain forces me to drop my arm.

She roundhouse kicks at my hand, knocking the blade across the floor.

The clattering sound draws Killian's wide eyes to me. "Cara!"

I have no time to respond as I duck from the woman's claws as she swipes at my face. I hit the ground and roll, but not without the pain knocking the wind out of me.

Killian grunts from behind me.

The girl's claws seem to grow longer and she flashes me a predatory smile.

They outmatch us. I'm in too much pain to do anything and Cadan is too busy decoding the message to help. His face scrunches, worried about the situation as much as I am.

The ringing heightens in my mind.

Oh no. I pale while a pressure builds in my chest, lifting my hand to my head as the girl prowls closer to me. More people are going to die, and based on our odds, it's going to be us. I have to do something.

I fill my lungs through my nose, open my mouth, and scream the loudest I have in my life.

Everyone bends over, covering their ears, but I don't stop. My piercing sound renders the white eyed man unconscious first, then the woman in front of me.

Killian fights the sound, trying to step closer to me. I see his lips moving, but I can't tell what he's saying. The next to fall is Cadan, which gives me pause, but the others aren't unconscious yet, so I push my scream further.

Next to go down is the twins. I continue until I'm red in the face. Blood pools from under Scarface's fingers. He looks at me, eyes wide with horror before blood drips from their corners like tears. His eyes roll in his head as he collapses.

I finally stop, heaving in breaths like I've run a marathon.

Breathing just as heavily, Killian falls to his knees.

As I glance at everyone, and terror fills my body, I begin to shake. A step closer to the woman reveals her eyes are open and unblinking. Her chest doesn't rise.

"They're...they're..." I stammer.

Killian rises and moves closer to me, wrapping his arms around me as my legs give out.

I grasp his shirt, taking in his stricken face as tears well in my eyes. "They're... dead. Are... is this part of my powers?" I choke out.

"It shouldn't be." He grimaces. "Predictor of death and causing unconsciousness, but nothing more." Blood trickles from his right ear down the side of his face.

My hand raises. My fingers swipe at the injury I caused, smearing the blood. I press my face against his chest as my tears fall. I really am cursed. He tightens his hold on me, but then I gasp and push him away.

"Cadan!" I run over to my friend, who lies motionless on the ground. Oh god, Cadan. A sob wracks through my chest as I fall beside him.

Killian kneels on the other side.

"Is he..." My throat closes before I can finish my thought.

Killian presses two fingers where Cadan's jaw and neck meet. "There's a pulse."

A relieved sigh escapes me, but tears continue leaving tracks down my cheeks. "How will we get out... without... him?" I blink through my blurry vision at my incapacitated friend. To know I did this to him is too much to bear. All I want to do is curl up in a ball and fall asleep, to escape this nightmare, but I can't. At least not yet.

"He finished decoding the message before he passed out," Killian says.

"But I didn't hear the letters. I didn't memorize them like I told him I would. We're back to where we started."

Killian shakes his head. "I listened."

I rub my sniffling nose on my sleeve as surprise fills me. I have no idea how he was able to pay attention while fighting everyone.

"I just don't know what to do with it," Killian admits.

"What was the code?" I hiccup as I try to calm myself. The best way I can help Cadan is to get him out of here.

"*Oscailte* says me."

The moment Killian finishes the phrase, the stone wall with the crown shudders, and the scraping of stone sounds as it slides open, revealing a ramp.

"Can you walk?" Killian's worried eyes bounce between me and Cadan.

"Y-yes. Take him." I gesture to Cadan and another sob escapes my throat. "What about the others?"

Killian shakes his head. He won't say it to me, but that's all I need to know the truth. They're gone, and it's my fault.

I've never killed anyone before. Even though we were being attacked, it doesn't feel right. This is the first time in my life my curse caused death by my own hands.

Killian hauls Cadan over his shoulder, and I stand to follow.

"W-why didn't you..." I trail off, unable to utter 'die' out loud.

He pauses before advancing up the ramp. "We're similar, fae of death and darkness, whether we want it or not. It must've given me an advantage to your power."

We walk in silence. Every once in a while, I reach out to Cadan's lolling head and feel for a pulse. It's weak, but there each time. I haven't stopped crying, even if it's silent now.

I cover my eyes as we step outside. The natural light, even with the clouds, is almost too much to handle.

Cheers and applause radiate from around us. I turn in a circle and realize we exited from underground into an arena filled with a fae audience. Off to the side, twenty other fae competitors wait, drinking water and talking amongst themselves. A few look immaculate, but many of them have ripped clothes and blood across them. I'm unsure if it's theirs or their foes, but either way, my stomach churns. They pause when they notice us and give a nod.

A team of fae wearing white hastens to us, including the nurse who took care of me after the attack.

Killian explains what happened to them, which causes them to shoot worried glances in my direction. I shrink away from their stares.

"You did it!" Shay's booming voice comes from above. I search the stands above me and find him leaning over a railing with his arms crossed over a puffed up chest of pride. "Good job."

I nod before mindlessly walking away. I barely register Shay telling me to wait because the King has to announce the winners.

I don't care anymore. All I want is my bed.

I cross the arena towards the exit, focused on the palace in the distance, as tears continue to cascade down until they drip off my chin.

NINETEEN

A knock sounds on my door.

I roll over, ignoring it. Squeezing my eyes shut I try to fight the images bombarding me. Scarface's eyes bleeding before they roll in the back of his head, him collapsing seconds later… dead. It's all my fault. Banshees are meant to forewarn death, but I bring it. I shouldn't exist. My powers shouldn't exist. It's because of me that Cadan almost died. It's because of me people *did* die. I'm a murderer.

The word murderer echoes over and over across my brain. I need sleep. I want to sleep. It's the only reprieve I get from this nightmare.

Another knock sounds. This time louder and more persistent.

It takes my entire willpower to drag myself out of bed. I don't even manage to turn on a light.

Shay stands on the outside of my door and frowns. "What're you wearing?"

I glance down at a white shirt and pink shorts. Stains cover the shirt. I can't remember the last time I changed my clothes.

Shay steps around me into my chambers. "And what's that smell?" He flicks on a light. He says nothing at the dirty dishes, still filled with food, lining my desk. Instead he turns, as though it's normal to have dishes piled high in your bedroom. Normally, they'd disappear once all the food is minimal, but they all hold portions close to the original amount, so they've rotted in the corner.

I pull at the hem of my shirt, mildly embarrassed.

Shay's brows crease, and he opens his mouth, but snaps it shut when he thinks better of it. He rubs his chin as inspects me. "You haven't been showing up to training."

"No," I mumble.

"I've knocked on the door." His gaze snags on my hair. "What happened to your hair?"

I reach up and feel the rat's nest I once called hair. I don't think I've brushed it at all recently. When did he knock on my door? Everything feels like a blur after the last trial.

"And the door was locked," he says with irritation grating his voice.

"Don't you have a key?" He is the prince after all. I don't see why a locked door would stop him from barging in like all the other times.

"Magic solidifies the lock when someone doesn't want to be disturbed. I don't have the power or key to override it," he explains.

"Oh."

"It's time for the next trial." His eyes are hard, filled with a judgement I can't place. Probably concerned I won't pass and he'll lose his wish.

"What?" My head feels foggy when I try to think back. I didn't realize that much time had passed. "But the other trial just happened."

"The third trial was over a week ago."

I fail at holding back my surprise. Another week gone, another week I'm behind in school.

Bile burns my throat with the flash of a memory of bodies lying at my feet. The last thing I want to do is go to the next trial, but I don't have the willpower to fight with him about it. I need nothing short of a miracle to get me through this competition. So, who cares anyways?

"I'll go get dressed," I murmur.

In my bathroom, I find some training clothes on the ground. I sniff them and they smell alright, so I throw them on and sweep my hair into a ponytail. Without bothering to check myself in the mirror, I return to join Shay.

He gives me a once over and frowns. He does that a lot. Clearly disappointed by me. It's understandable, but I never asked for this, so that's his problem if he regrets choosing me as his proxy.

He unveils my sword and scabbard from behind his back.

My shoulder has healed, but a dull throb radiates when I see the metal in his hand. I swallow my imaginary pain, but the clenching in my heart doesn't cease.

He steps forward, and my stomach rises into my throat when the weight of my weapon rests on my hips where he attaches the scabbard. "You'll need this."

I can't respond. All I want to do is rip it off and throw myself back into my bed, but I don't, which Shay interprets as acceptance.

Without speaking, we leave my bedroom. Guards ignore our presence when we walk by them. Outside the palace, Shay moves along a path that takes us to the arena from the previous trial.

My steps falter.

Shay looks over at me. "Everything okay?"

I nod my head as I try to push away the image of Cadan's lifeless body. Not only am I a murderer, but I nearly killed my friend. The one I meant to protect.

He places a hand on my shoulder, halting me. He turns me to him, and reluctantly, I peer into his stricken face. "What's going on?"

"Nothing." And it's true. That's exactly how I feel. Death's filled my life for so long I don't understand what I'm living for anymore. I am alive to be some player in a game I never wanted to be a part of in the first place. I am alive as a place setting, where my life could be taken at any moment, and for what? Someone else's glory? It doesn't matter anymore; my life never did. None of it matters. I don't know why I'm still trying to win this stupid competition. The chances of that happening are so slim, I can kiss going home goodbye.

I realize Shay is speaking to me, but I missed everything he'd said. Tuning back in, I hear him ask, "Cara, are you even listening?"

I nod. "Sorry, I didn't sleep well." Which is a total lie. All I've done is sleep since I made it back to my room.

Again, he frowns at me, his permanent look for me.

I press my lips together in what, I hope, appears to be a smile. Based on his response, I failed, so I throw in some teeth for good measure.

"Are you good to do this?" He folds his arms across his broad chest as he studies me.

"It's not like I have a choice," I say under my breath, but follow it with a confident "Of course."

He eyes me suspiciously before inclining his head once and continuing forward.

At the arena, the remaining contestants line up at one end of the oval area. Nausea threatens to empty my already vacant stomach as my eyes move down the row. I don't see Cadan anywhere.

The cheers from the stands join the buzz in the back of my head. I ball my fists, already knowing the deaths which will follow the sound. I bite the inside of my cheek to hold back my tears.

I can't do this. I don't know my powers well enough to know who it'll be, but with the sound starting so early can only mean there will be multiple fatalities.

My brain fuzzes over, shielding me from my dread. Everything becomes muted like I dunked my head underwater.

Everyone around me hollers, "Light without and light within," which pulls me back to the present.

I squint into the stands and see the King talking, and all the fae watch him with rapt attention.

"It's with my regret our 40 contestants is officially down to 39. One is still in a coma and has yet to awaken despite our best efforts." King Harbinger's gaze moves along the line of contestants until they land on me.

He's talking about Cadan. He's out of the competition. He lost his chance for a wish, and it's all my fault. My heart pounds in my chest and I squeeze my fists until my nails dig into my palm. The pain helps distract my thoughts.

The King sweeps his hand over all of us as he returns his attention to his people. "This is the trial of strength. Our arena has been turned into that of a battleground. There are fields, outposts, a small forest, a creek leading to the pond, and an assortment of other features for our warriors to utilize for their advantage."

Currently, we stand in a grassy field underneath where the King speaks, but over my shoulder, not far away, are all the things King Harbinger mentioned. I don't see the pond, but I assume it's in the wooded area which begins a hundred feet behind me.

The King continues, "This trial will last until we have ten contestants left. After, only two trials remain— Courage and Wisdom. Today, there are no rules, anything goes. Death is not necessary for victory, being incapacitated is enough to remove someone from the competition."

The contestants shift and many of them grab for the weapons on their bodies. One contestant holds a spiked mace.

My stomach churns and I fight the urge to throw up when the memory of blood oozing from orifices it shouldn't assaults me.

I follow suit and unsheathe my short sword, holding it at my side. At least I understand why Shay was such a stickler with training. Too bad I haven't attended any recent sessions. Maybe it's for the best. Whatever happens, happens.

"May good luck be with you wherever you go, and your blessings outnumber the shamrocks that grow. May your days be many and your troubles be few, May all God's blessings descend upon you, May peace be within you, May your heart be strong, May you find what you're seeking wherever you roam," King Harbinger announces.

The moment he's done, everyone erupts into motion, becoming blurs of bodies. Some clash together in immediate combat while others run to fortify their safety.

Instinctively, I bring my sword up and fall into a defensive stance.

The buzzing intensifies in my head, and I press my palm against my temple. To my left, I watch in horror as an axe lodges into someone's back.

The fae falls onto their face, dead.

My face pales, terror lancing my spine.

Another fae cries out as a blade swipes across their midsection, spurting blood all over the green grass.

My muscles react without thought and I run. Away from the battle. Away from my past. Away from everything. As I near the trees, the piercing sound intensifies in my skull.

I stutter to a stop when the pounding in my head is so great I want to unleash a scream of pain. I clamp my mouth shut, horrified at what will happen if I do. It increases to an unbearable pitch, and I fall to my knees with a cry. The wet grass soaks through my pants.

This isn't worth it. This is meaningless. I'm meaningless. Nothing but a pawn.

I watch as a red haired fae runs at me, raising his axe above his head.

This is it. Screw Shay's wish, and screw this life. All I want is for my pain to stop. All I want is to be at peace.

I don't flinch as he brings his axe down on me. I close my eyes, yearning to be released from this hell.

But nothing happens.

There's a brief grunt followed by a large thump.

I peek through my eyes to see Killian straddling the fae on the ground to my right.

The fae reaches for the axe lying beside him, and as his fingers grace the hilt, Killian brings his elbow down and cracks him in the temple.

With his opponent unconscious but not dead, Killian peels himself off him. He turns to me, and I gasp at the anger I see in his eyes.

"What're you doing?" He accuses as he retrieves his sword off the ground. He glances at my hair before his dark gaze settles on my face.

I shake my head. How do I put into words what I'm feeling? How do I make someone else understand? My throat constricts so even if I found the words I wouldn't be able to speak them. I cover my face in shame. For what I did, and for the dark thoughts flitting through my mind I can't admit aloud.

Killian takes three long strides and drops to one knee in front of me.

In the distance, the battle still rages, but the sounds barely reach me.

He grips my face in his hands and pulls it up until I look at him. His amber eyes search mine. His features are hard and the scowl doesn't leave when he speaks. "Why aren't you fighting?"

My tongue is as useful as a lead weight in my mouth. Why was he asking me this? Why did he care? The only person in any world that cares about me is back on Earth and probably thinks I'm dead. It would be so much easier if it were true.

His eyes bore into mine, looking into my soul. It's like he can see every thought and feeling while words fail me.

There's a ripple in my chest, but it dissipates when Killian jumps up and leaps over my head. Metal clings together at my back, but I simply sit there while the world unfocuses around me.

Another opponent runs at me, using Killian's distraction to take their opportunity to end me.

I imagine Shay screaming at me from the stands. I'm sure if I listen closely enough I would hear his curses for me to fight, to win. My small sword sits beside me. I don't remember when I dropped it. All I need to do is pick it up and block. A technique he ingrained into me, something we practiced hundreds of times. I stare at it, willing my hands to move and grab it, but the need evaporates.

It's better this way. If Cadan can't get his wish, I don't deserve to win either. In the end, my curse will always be what wins, and it's about time it takes me.

A thud sounds from behind me, and within seconds Killian is upon the fae in front. In his act of desperation, he isn't as careful this time. When he runs across their front, he slices their neck so fast the person doesn't have time to respond. Blood gurgles from the wound as the body crumples to the ground.

Another death, but the ringing in my head hasn't stopped.

At least it was a quick death.

"Get up," Killian demands from above me.

My blank stare grazes his silhouette.

"Get. Up." He grabs me from under my arm and hauls me to my feet.

I trip into him.

He catches me around the waist.

A male fae with pointed ears, battle leathers, and a long sword heads straight for us, but with Killian's back turned he doesn't see him.

No. I can't lose anyone else. I may not care what happens to me, but I can't stomach anything happening to Killian. I shove him to the side, sticking my foot behind his ankle so he falls to the ground so he can't intervene.

The fae has nearly reached me, his sword a barrier between us and ready to pierce my gut.

I ball my fists, bottling my fear for Killian and anger at myself until I unleash it with a scream.

Now ten feet away, something easily crossed with a large jump, the man drops his sword, followed by a crash to his knees. He covers his ears, but I don't stop. I don't stop until he slumps face first on the ground.

I stare blankly at his unmoving back, not a single breath taken. I'm a monster. What's worse is I don't even feel bad for this death. I feel empty. At most, I'm thankful I protected Killian for once.

"Walk," Killian says, glancing only briefly at the dead fae.

I can't will my legs to move. He wraps an arm around my waist, and I don't stop him while I continue to stare at my victim. Partially coherent, I allow Killian to half carry me into the small wooded area.

My shoes soak up the water as we slosh through the creek. The water never goes above our knees while we trek upstream.

"It'll help cover our scent," he explains as he continues to drag me.

I stumble along, my mind blank aside from the pinging of death. My feet catch on a rock and I fall onto my hands and knees, soaking most of my clothes. I sit back and stare at my blood-ridden palms, cut from the rough rocks.

The water tinges pink from the scrapes on my knees. Their burning sensation is dull through the fog of my mind.

Killian scoops me into his arms. The faint memory of him carrying me like this in the throne room surfaces, and like last time, I rest my head against his hard chest.

His head pivots when shouts erupt from behind us. His hands grip me harder as he runs along the stream.

I close my eyes, focusing on his breathing, on his heart beat, to muffle the wretched sound in my head. After five minutes, I shiver from my wet clothes.

Rushing water roars ahead, and I peer through my lashes at a waterfall. Unexpectedly large, and the creek has turned into a small river without my knowledge.

Killian trudges on, hopping through a boulder field lining the bank of the waterfall. He tilts his head into the air and sniffs. Satisfied, he continues forward.

The rushing water grows more intense and relief washes through me, relaxing my muscles, as it helps mask the ringing.

Pressed against the slick rocks, Killian moves closer to the waterfall. The parts of my clothes that were dry before are now completely soaked.

I worry about the algae-covered rocks, wondering if I should ask Killian to put me down so he doesn't slip, but I trust his balance here a lot more than my own. It'd probably make it worse for both of us.

He manages to slip behind the cascading water without any problems.

"Can you grab the lip there?" He acknowledges a flat stone area six feet above us.

"I think so," I mutter.

He shifts my weight, so my feet plant in his palms.

I reach upwards while he lifts me. My fingers clutch the rough edge and my arms strain to pull me up.

Killian shoves my feet so his arms stretch out above his shoulders, but with his strength, he's a solid base so I never waiver.

Using my elbows, I'm able to pry myself further until I hook a leg over the side. I roll onto my back, away from the ledge, and pant as the sting of my palms pierce through me.

Killian hauls himself over the edge, landing gracefully onto his feet, before prowling deeper into the small cave he's found for us.

I'm unsure how long I've been lying in the same spot, zoning out on the rocky ceiling. It could've been minutes or hours.

A small drip falls and lands on the ground beside my face. The continuous pattern distracting me until the curse has become nothing but a light throb in the back of my mind.

"You need to get warm." Killian's face comes into view as he stands over me. His hair falls on either side of his face, hiding it in shadows.

I blink and watch as another droplet of water falls into the puddle beside me.

"Come on, little rabbit." Killian squats beside me.

I turn my head to him, his blurry form coming into focus. He's wearing battle leathers, his sword on his back, and mouth is set in a grim line.

"Why?" I ask.

He angles his head to the side.

"Why do you keep helping me?" I rasp. I don't understand. I've asked him time and time again to stop. But he doesn't, even at the risk of his own life.

His eyes harden and his scarred skin pulls taught when he runs his hands through his hair.

My bottom lip trembles and I turn my head in the opposite direction before he sees the tear slip out. I really am nothing but the weakling he said I was, and I keep proving him right.

He reaches out, cupping my cheek to turn my face back to him. His thumb wipes the tear off my cheek. "Why didn't you fight?"

He knows I'm capable of more. He helped teach me. He's the one who gave me my sword.

A frown crosses his face at the shivers wracking my body. "Seriously, get up. You need to get warm."

I use my elbows to push myself off the ground since my hands still sting from the cuts on my palms.

Deeper in the cave, Killian has started a fire. Considering there's stone and water everywhere, and no wood for ignition, I have no idea how. It floats a few inches off the ground, burning bright and warm. The beauty of magic lightens the dark cave.

On trembling legs, I draw myself closer to the warmth, but Killian stops me from collapsing next to it.

"Strip."

I spin, gaping at him. "Excuse you?"

"You need to get out of the wet clothes or you'll never get warm."

"Can't you simply dry me like last time?" I wrap my arms around my middle as quivers wrack through my body.

"My magic is acting finicky," he grumbles. "I need to figure out what's going on," he whispers to himself. While he says this, he takes his sword off, lying it against the wall. Next, he peels out of his leather vest.

I try not to drool at the planes of his body. I shake my head, using my hair to block his form. He is the last person I need to be finding sexy. Frowning down at my sopping clothes and pale skin that looks blue, I realize he's right. It seems I've forgotten my sword once more, so I take the scabbard off my hips. My numb fingers pull off my clothes, but I leave my underwear on. I don't care if they're wet. There is no way Killian will see me stark naked. It's like wearing a bikini. If anything, this covers more than most swimsuits these days.

A shuddering breath chatters my teeth as I lay out my clothes on the ground beside the fire in hopes they will dry too.

Killian sits by the fire, only in a pair of boxer briefs.

My gaze homes in on the flickering light as I settle in a few feet from him. I wrap my arms around my legs and pull them to my chest, placing my chin on my knees.

Killian's eyes trace over my legs, stopping on my upper thigh.

My muscles clench.

He's not appreciating my frail, bony body, but noticing the caved muscle with puckered skin covering it. A horrible reminder of my past. I used to make up stories. It was a werewolf attack and now I turn every full moon. I helped save a kid from getting hit by a bus thus earning me the key to the city. I survived skin cancer and they should feel rude for asking such a personal question about my scar. The survival part might be true, but nothing else from these false stories. Eventually, I stopped wearing shorts and skirts above my knee. The prying questions stopped, and so did my lies.

Thankfully, Killian doesn't ask about it. Every once in a while, he tenses, tilting his head to listen to what is happening beyond the cave, but after a few heartbeats he returns to his relaxed stance.

My chest aches and head pounds with the remnance of my curse and thoughts. If Shauna was here, I'd tell her I was having one of my heavy days. She'd let me curl up with my head in her lap and rub my back while watching trashy movies through the day. If it happened on a day she worked, she'd call in sick and order us delivery.

Tears silently fall as the tightness in my chest becomes so strong I rub at it with my frozen hand.

Maybe opening up to someone will help with the weight.

I open my mouth to say something to lift the heaviness, but my stomach flips with nerves and I close it. After a few minutes pass, finding the courage to say something, anything, I open my mouth again, but my vocal chords freeze in the last second.

Still nothing, not even a squeak.

Killian waits patiently. Every time I'm about to talk, I feel his intense gaze on me, but when I shut my mouth his attention reverts to the fire or listening to the outside world.

"My mother is a prisoner in the castle," his deep voice reverberates through me, echoing against the walls of the cave.

I lift my head and stare at him.

This time he doesn't meet my gaze.

I say nothing, wanting to return the same patience he's been showing me.

His body is rigid when he speaks, clearly as uncomfortable opening up as I am. "That's why I joined the competition. I've worked for the King for years trying to lessen her sentence, but she still has a better chance of dying in there before she's released. The wish is the only assurance I have of getting her out."

The air is musty in the cave.

I inch closer to the fire, outstretching my hands to thaw them faster.

Killian watches me do this. He closes his eyes and his face scrunches with concentration.

The fire doesn't get larger, but the heat from it radiates further outward, seeping into my chilled bones.

My body relaxes slightly and the pull of sleep hits my exhausted body.

I chew on my lip, worried my prying will cause him to shut down, but I work up the courage to ask the question on the tip of my tongue. "What happened?"

"She was the first to notice something was wrong with the land." A crease forms between his eyebrows. "My mother was the first to talk about the lack of sun, how the colors were dulling. Everyone blames the inconsistency of their magic on their feelings, but she knew better. She started to ask questions. Over time, other fae listened to what she had to say, but before she could figure out what was happening, they arrested her for treason." His jaw ticks with anger, no doubt spewing plenty of curses in his head towards the King.

Asking questions about the problem of the land shouldn't land someone in jail for the rest of their life, and fae live long lives. I wonder if that's what led to the problem between him and Shay.

"I'm sorry," I say, and I mean it. I worry my lip between my teeth as I think through the words I want to say aloud. A pit forms in my stomach when I first speak, but the words become easier and easier to say. "When I first heard the sound, it was only a thrum in my mind. An hour later, my dad received a call my aunt had died. A heart attack at forty-five despite being the epitome of health. I was six.

When I was eight, I was in the car with my family. The sound got so loud I blacked out. I woke up in the hospital with nothing but a leg wound. Shauna, my sister, told me our parents died." I pause, fingers tracing the bumpy scar on my thigh.

I take a shuddering breath before continuing, "It never got better from there. Every time I would hear the sound, even if it sounded different, death followed. Sometimes only a few days would pass before the next death occurred. I found myself hopeful when I would go months without it, hoping it was gone, something that was a weird coincidence I made up in my head. But it always came back. I'm… cursed. Even in this world, death has followed me to where I've caused it myself." My voice cracks.

Killian's face pinches together, eyes boring into me. His judgement is too much to bear, so I bury my face into my arms. I breathe through my nose, trying to control the sob that is threatening to escape. Admitting the truth isn't all it's cracked up to be.

"You aren't cursed," his deep voice soothes my nerves.

I squeeze my arms as tight as I can with my breath held.

"You are a banshee, Cara," he explains. "A *Beansidhe* predicts death. You are not cursed; you are fae."

Tears escape and dribble down my legs while ugly mucus-filled sniffles erupt from me. "But it's so dark. All I feel is the darkness that has surrounded my life. How am I supposed to live my entire life with this?"

I feel Killian's heat beside me before I hear him. His sandalwood scent masking the mildew of the air. "Look at me."

I don't move.

"I need you to look at me because I need you to hear what I have to say."

I raise my head to see his beautiful face illuminated by the fire, only a foot away.

His eyes search mine as he speaks. "I know darkness. I *am* darkness. I turn into someone's worst nightmare. But you… you're goodness. You're someone who understands the dark, who has walked in it, but it allows you to bring light into the world. You're someone who stands up for the weak and those who are hurt. You find strength where others would crumble."

"But… my powers," I sniffle.

He leans closer to me until our breath mingles. "Your powers may be about death, but you can use them to prevent heartache before it begins. To forewarn before the end has occurred. Nothing is set in stone until it has already passed." A lock of hair hangs in front of his face.

Tentatively, I reach forward and brush it aside.

He closes his eyes as I do, almost leaning into my touch.

"Why do you keep helping me?" I whisper, a nagging sensation that there's something he's not telling me.

His muscles tense, and his eyes snap open. He pulls away from me, stands, and is on the other side of the cave in a flash.

What the hell just happened? I thought we were finally starting to understand each other. Of course, I say something to ruin it. I shouldn't have pried. Just as useless as ever, good going Cara.

With a sigh, I place my head back on my arms.

Killian leans against the prickly rock wall, his hands pressed against the side of his head causing the muscles in his back to flex.

I focus on my bloodied hands now scabbing over, the cuts in my palm a reminder that I'm still alive.

"Well done, contestants!" King Harbinger's voice rings through the air. "Although some tactics were livelier than others."

A zip of energy moves through my spine, like the King was trying to direct the message to me, and dread washes over me. Only god knows how increasingly terrible the other trials will be.

"Those who have not already been removed from the arena will pass onto the next trial. The gates are now open to allow you to exit." The announcement goes quiet.

Killian is already pulling his clothes back on. "Get dressed."

With heavy limbs, I crawl across the stone floor to my clothes that have become more chilled since I took them off. My body shakes as I slide into them. I inhale through chattering teeth, imagining burrowing into my bed again.

This turned out to be a perfectly shitty day. I shouldn't have left my bed at all.

Killian closes his eyes and takes a breath, his back straightening with a confidence I hadn't realized he was missing until now.

"There you are," he whispers. With a snap of his fingers, we're dry.

A sigh of relief escapes my lips as my body sags when the shivers dissipate.

Killian steps over to me and offers me his hand. "Come, I want to take you somewhere."

I hesitate, eyeing him suspiciously. "I should get back. All I want is a bath and I'm sure Shay is waiting to give me an earful."

"Screw Shay," Killian states. "You need to get away from this place."

I twirl my hair around my finger. "I...I don't think I should."

"He doesn't own you, little rabbit."

I glare at him. "I know."

"Does he?"

"Fine," I acquiesce as I move closer to him.

He wraps his arms around me, pulling me tight against his chest.

My face heats at the embrace. "Is this really necessary?" I manage to mumble against his chest while my inside swirl like they're on a rollercoaster.

"Hold on, this'll be weird."

A vibration begins where his hands touch, and expands through the rest of my body. As it intensifies, my bones rattle together.

I squeeze my eyes shut when it becomes unbearable.

Killian's grip tightens when I go to pull away.

A yelp escapes me a second before we blip out of thin air.

TWENTY

O ur feet thud onto a stone pathway, sending jolts through my shins.

"Are you okay?" Killian's firm hand presses into my lower back.

I nod as I try to steady my breathing from the effects of our travel. Is that what Cadan goes through every single time he zaps away?

"Where are we?" My voice comes out stronger than I feel.

"Old *Rímor.*"

I blink at him in surprise before taking in the surrounding area.

We stand on a cobbled street. Fae walk along the sides, most in coats they wrap tightly around themselves to protect against the onslaught of rain.

A chill settles through the air with the setting sun.

No one is surprised by our arrival and everyone continues on their way. Buildings which are a combination of stores, townhomes, and apartments line the street, packed closely together to make the most of the limited space available.

A weight lifts off my shoulders, simply by being in a town and not trapped at the castle, trapped by the competition.

"Old *Rímor*? Is the castle nearby?" I ask.

"It's an hour on horseback. *Rímor* is a region, and this is the original settlement. Now it's nothing more than a fishing village." Killian takes my hand and steps up onto the sidewalk.

We walk down the street, hand in hand, and no one looks our way, too caught up in their own world.

My heart patters from the contact, and I worry he can hear it with his fae abilities. "You did what Cadan can do?" I don't have the right words to describe the zapping, but he seems to understand.

"In a way." He drops my hand as we turn a corner.

"Can all fae teleport?"

"It's called *taestial*. We traveled via magical currents existing within *Gon'an'rit*. Only stronger fae can manage it because their power can more directly connect to the raw energy of the land. But it takes a lot of practice and can be dangerous."

"Dangerous?" I slap him on the shoulder and shout, "And you took me on it?"

"I had faith you'd be fine."

"Well, that makes one of us." An idea pops in my head. "Wait, does this mean you can take me home?" My chest swells with hope.

"No. We are able to bind with the magic of our land only."

"Then how did Shay bring me here?"

"Certain fae have the right to travel between worlds via portals, but that's something both bestowed and taken by the King."

"Oh." My face downturns.

Halfway down a quieter street, we reach a doorway with a blue emblem of a crossed hammer and sword with the words *Blacksmith's Blacksmith* underneath.

I raise my eyebrow at Killian, the curve of my lips tilting up.

"Don't say anything about the name. Jameson hates that his last name coincides with his profession." Despite his warning, mirth reflects in his eyes.

"Why doesn't he change it?"

"It's a shop that's been in the family for fifteen hundred years."

My jaw drops. Here I am impressed my favorite pizza place has been around since 1971.

Upon entering, a blast of heat radiates over me. Within seconds, I'm sweating and the harsh scent of burnt material stings my nose. Perfect, this'll make my hair smell like campfire smoke for days.

We head further into the shop and the humidity makes it difficult to breathe.

A burly fae, who is built like a linebacker, swings a hammer at a glowing heap of metal. He looks up when we move closer, inclines his head to Killian, and returns to his work.

Each clash of metal is so loud I inadvertently jump each time.

"Nice to meet you, Jameson," I say under my breath, too intimidated to actually introduce myself.

Killian side eyes me, not having missed my comment. He drags me away until we are heading up an unlit stairwell in the back of the shop.

"Is this where you bring your victims before you." I make a slicing sound as I drag my finger across my throat.

A smirk traces his lips. "You think I'd keep saving you, only to kill you now?" Killian pushes forward into the dark.

I use the wall to help guide myself and try not to trip on the creaking steps. Falling right into Killian's backside is something I'd rather keep a fantasy. Definitely a situation I want to avoid in real life.

At the top of the steps we come to a door. Killian twists the knob and light blooms over us as it swings open into a small apartment.

The main area is small, a ten by ten foot area of a living room and kitchen. There's no space for a dining area. Off to the left is a doorway leading to a dark hallway. There's not much else. No decorations, limited seating. The bare bones to qualify as a place to live. It reminds me of my apartment back on Earth in many ways, but at least Shauna and I did better with decorations.

The stench of the sweat from below and heat from the fire permeates the air, but a cool breeze blows from an open window, bringing with it some fresh air.

A head pops up from a tattered couch in the center of the room. Big brown eyes widen until they seem to consume half the little boy's face with a giant smile below. "Killian!" His little voice hollers as he leaps up, runs around the couch, and launches himself into Killian's arms.

Killian laughs as he catches him, stepping further inside. He ruffles the little boy's hair before setting him on his feet.

What happened and who replaced the broody fae I know with a cyborg? I press my fingers to my lips, trying to hide my amusement.

"What're you doing here?" The little boy stands to Killian's waist and has to crane his head all the way back to peer up at him. "Is the game over? Did you win?"

Killian kneels onto one knee and smiles. A genuine smile that illuminates his entire face and has the floor disappearing from underneath me.

Holy fae, is he beautiful. I'm only used to his predatory smirk that makes me feel like I'm about to be dinner.

"Not yet, but today's trial was pretty hard." He gives a reassuring tussle of the boy's hair when his eyes go wide with worry at Killian's statement. "The next isn't for a few days, so I thought I'd come home for a visit."

I curb my reaction with a blink. He brought me to his home, and I'm meeting his family. Marcus's family lives an hour outside of Atlanta, and despite him seeing his family every few weeks, not once did he ever have me meet them. In fact, one time he kicked me out of his bed at the butt crack of dawn when he received a text from his mom that she was on her way over to take him out to breakfast. Not that I should be comparing Killian to Marcus or anything. Totally different situation. Boyfriend-type thing versus ally-competitors.

"Yay!" The little boy bounces on the balls of his feet. He stops when he finally notices me pressed against the wall beside the doorway. "Who's she?" He points at me.

Killian looks over his shoulder at me. "That's my friend, Cara."

Friend? A snort escapes me before I can help myself.

The little boy steps past Killian and puts his hand on his hips like a little Peter Pan. He tilts his head to the side and scrunches his nose while he scans my hair. "Are you from here? You don't smell right."

"That's rude, Hux." An older boy, who looks to be in his early teens, joins us from an open doorway.

"Sorry." The little boy stares at his feet as he presses his toes into the ground, his hands falling to his side.

"Go wash your hands. Dinner will be ready soon," the older boy says.

The little one rushes away into the area the other came from.

"I'm Jasper, Killian's brother." The fae strides over to me and holds out his hand. "Our youngest brother who you just met is Huxley."

"I go by Hux now!" I hear him cry from the other room.

"Sorry," Jasper raises his voice. "That's our brother, Hux!"

"Thank you!" Hux shouts.

"I'm Cara. Nice to meet you." I snigger at the brotherly exchange, which is joined by Killian's elusive grin. I grab his hand, my small hand disappearing within his long fingers.

"How're things?" Killian directs his question at Jasper.

"Good." He shrugs as he wanders over to sit on the tattered couch.

Killian gestures for me to follow and directs me to a small chair in the corner.

I sink into it, avoiding the small tears lining the cushion.

Another breeze wafts through the room, bringing in the scent of wet pavement. I wonder if that's what people mean when they say my magic smells like rain.

"How's Huxley's magic coming along?" Killian asks, taking the spot beside his brother.

They look similar. Same shaggy black hair, but Jasper's eyes are missing the golden hue, instead a dark brown. Acne covers his face, but with a broadening jawline anyone could tell he will be a handsome young man. His gangly limbs make him seem like a walking skeleton. If we were on Earth, people would no doubt ask if he plays basketball, but I don't think that's a thing here. I guess puberty's a pain no matter what realm you're from.

"Still getting the hang of it," Jasper answers. "He's a ball of energy and trying to get him to concentrate on anything for more than five minutes is hard."

"And how's school for you?" Killian leans his elbow on the back of the couch, propping the side of his head on his fist.

Jasper shrugs. "Fine."

Killian narrows his eyes and waits, clearly not buying what Jasper said.

He shifts in his seat, not meeting Killian's gaze until he bursts, "I could be doing better. It's hard. I needed to work to get some food this week."

Killian's face sours at the admission. "I should've come sooner. I'm sorry."

"No, no, it's fine. I spent some of the last money you bought on treats for me and Hux. It was dumb, and I know it's not meant for that. It won't happen again. You can trust me, I promise." His pleading eyes grow, adoration shining through coupled with need for acceptance.

Killian shakes his head. "You're a kid. You should be allowed to have treats. I'll be sure to leave more this time."

Jasper straightens in his seat, his jaw ticking in the same way Killian's does. "I'm not a kid. I can take care of us," he states firmly.

"That's not your responsibility."

"It shouldn't be yours either. If mom…"

Killian cuts him off with a glare. "This isn't her fault and I'm the oldest, plus the adult. You worry about school and helping Huxley. I'll take care of everything else."

The two of them compete in an unspoken staring contest. Killian's eyes are hard, waiting for his brother to acquiesce. Jasper's are rigid, forcing a maturity he is still trying to reach.

"Promise me," Killian breaks the silence, but his stone cold eyes never leave his brother.

Jasper is the first to look away. "Fine."

Killian claps him on the shoulder. "Next time, let me know. You don't need to work. You have ways to get a hold of me."

"Okay," Jasper concedes, hanging his head in disappointment.

Hux comes bounding into the living room, jumping onto the couch between his brothers. "Dinner!" He hollers. "Is there dessert too?" His saucer wide eyes search Killian with anticipation. It's clear Killian brings home special surprises for him when he visits.

"We'll see," Killian chuckles.

"Are you hungry?" Jasper directs the question to me.

Due to stealing the attention of the room, Hux glares at me and huffs with a cross of his arms.

I shake my head. "No, thank you."

Killian frowns at me with a worried crease forming on his forehead. "When was the last time you ate?"

It's hard to remember much of the last week. The times I was awake are foggy at best, but I'm not hungry, so I decide to lie. "This morning."

Jasper raises an eyebrow, his piercing gaze seeing right through me. He opens his mouth, and my muscles tighten when I realize he's about to out my lie, but Killian shakes his head at him.

"It's fine," he says. "I have something I want to show her."

My eyebrows shoot to my hairline. This wasn't what he wanted to show me?

"What?" Hux whines. "You aren't staying for dinner?" With his realization, he shoots me another glare like I am personally responsible for ruining his time with his brother. I mean, he isn't wrong, but it's not like I asked for this.

"I promise to bring you back a special treat," Killian bribes his baby brother.

Hux's face lights up. "Okay! Hurry back!" He leaps off the couch and runs off into the kitchen, leaving the three of us chuckling to ourselves.

Killian stands and I do the same.

I turn to Jasper. "It was nice meeting you."

Jasper smiles, "I'm sure we'll run into each other again soon."

"I'll be back in a bit," Killian says.

Once we are back down the stairs, I release a deep breath. Despite being in this boiling room again, I feel I can breathe easier. I was not expecting to meet his family and witnessing him with his siblings made my heart ache for my own. I'm grateful I wasn't forced to fake politeness through a meal. All I want right now is a bath and my bed.

Killian withdraws a wad of cash from who knows where and places it on the table in front of the blacksmith. They exchange some hushed words before the man nods, his meaty fingers grabbing the bundle of money and shoving it into his pockets.

"Let's go," Killian tells me before moving to leave the shop.

I shield my face from the sprinkling rain when we step outside. "Where're you taking me?"

"You'll see."

I groan as I trudge after him. Always so secretive, and I hate surprises. Even if I don't know about the surprise in advance, I still hate them. I don't enjoy the buildup over it, and I'm too curious of a person to not hold a grudge when I discover someone hid something from me.

It took Shauna years to learn not to surprise me. She did it a lot when our parents first died. She thought it would bring some happiness into my life, but when I wouldn't speak to her for hours, claiming she had lied to me, she eventually stopped. Afterwards, I started to receive a lot of "last minute gifts" instead.

We wind through the streets and I feel like I've been transported to an old Irish town. Not that I would actually know considering I had never left my home city until I was dragged to *Gon'an'rit*. But with the old stacked buildings, colored storefronts, and cobbled pathways, it's like I'm in the past. Actually, based on the things Shay has said, I wouldn't be surprised if the fae influenced the United Kingdom and other parts of Europe.

The street takes a sharp left to a huge hill.

Half way up I'm huffing and my legs burn. I rest my hands on my hips as I try to breathe through the stitch in my side.

"We're almost there," Killian announces.

"Thank god," I wheeze.

"Seems we need to add cardio to your practices," Killian notes, gliding across the steep path.

"I… got… this…" I'll say anything to get out of a cardio workout, but my heavy breathing between words isn't doing me any favors.

That's confirmed when Killian gives a concerned look over his shoulder and slows his pace.

I wave at him to keep moving. "I'm fine." I take a deep breath of the earthy wet-stone aroma of the city. First rains always have such a distinct smell, and even though there's been some form of rain the entire time I've been here, the smell never seems to fade.

At the top of the hill sits a quaint park. The street we're on turns into small pathways crisscrossing through the hillside.

A bundle of trees are at its peak, and benches dot the area along the way.

Of course, Killian heads for the crest of the hill.

If I ever make it home, I'm claiming I summited a mountain in the fae realm.

He strolls to a bench that's managed to stay dry from the boughs of a large tree above it. He makes himself comfortable on the seat, lounging like he only walked a single block and back.

I place my hands on my knees and take three deep breaths through my nose to lessen the panting in my lungs. Once I have myself under control, I finish my trek to the bench and plop down beside him. An annoyed comment is on the tip of my tongue, but it evaporates when I see the view.

The sun has set, but dusk allows me to still see across the entire city, the rolling hills, shadowed forests, and expanse of the ocean. If it weren't for the dappling of trees at our backs, I would have a 360 view of the area.

More and more lights of the town blink into existence as the sky continues to darken. They twinkle through the rain, reflecting off the wet rooftops which creates an enchanting quality to the old city.

It's quiet and calm and helps lighten my soul. It's as though I can breathe for the first time since I've arrived in this realm. The one thing missing is a clear night sky with stars to mirror the civilization below.

"This is my favorite place in this court." The reflecting light from the town below casts shadows on Killian's face, making his sharp edges more distinct. "Well, this and the forest, but this is a little easier to get to."

"It's beautiful," I whisper, afraid to disrupt the peacefulness. I relax against the cool bench with a sigh.

"My mother would bring us here for picnics every Sunday." His face softens at the memory. "I tried to keep up the tradition when she was," he pauses, "taken. Huxley was a baby, and I wanted him to have something from her. But it was hard on Jasper… and me. So, eventually, we came less and less."

My heart aches for him and his brothers, at the loss of their mother. Even though she isn't dead, I understand what it's like to grow up parentless. Appreciation fills me, masking my pain, with how he continues to open up to me. "Thank you for bringing me here."

"Even though you hated it every step of the way?" He smirks, a twinkle in his eye.

"I didn't hate it the entire time," I respond, hiding my mirth with a stoic stare.

"You were cursing me under your breath the entire way," he chuckles. "Don't like surprises, eh?"

My muscles stiffen. Had I said this out loud? Crap, I didn't even realize I was talking. I laugh awkwardly— *Whoops.*

"Okay, I have one more place to take you." He straightens from his slack position.

"We just got here," I pout. "Please tell me there are no more hills." I lean my head back against the bench, dead weighting at the thought of walking anymore.

"No more hills, promise." He leans closer to me and gives me a full smile.

My mind blanks as my heart thumps harder against my ribs. I imagine running my fingers along the curve of his jaw, tracing it until I comb my fingers into his silky hair. The crisp air hits my lungs when I suck in a sharp breath through my mouth.

His eyes wander to my lips, face becoming serious.

Will he kiss me? Do I want him to kiss me? I glance at his full lips. I definitely wouldn't say no to a kiss. I bet they're soft, like how I've seen him be today. Or maybe it'd be dominating like how he's been in the past.

My trance is broken when he draws back with a cough and moves to get up.

My face flushes, hoping I wasn't obvious with what was crossing my mind. Oh man, I bet I was totally obvious. What if I had been staring at his mouth? I swear I merely glimpsed at it, but then I zoned out. What if he coughed because he felt uncomfortable? My face burns and it takes all of my willpower not to bury my face in my hands.

I stand, casting my eyes back across the view, hyper focusing on it so I don't look at him. Yes, pretty lights. Lots of lights and buildings and people. Oh, look, that roof looks red. Yes, a very interesting red roof.

I feel his heated gaze lingering on me, but I don't relax until I hear him walking away.

Stepping away from under the protection of the tree, I follow him back to town.

TWENTY-ONE

Deeper in town, I'm inundated with a busy street. Groups of children run together, two little girls and one boy holding streamers above their heads at the front. A mother calls after them to slow down and apologizes to us as she moves past us. A group of men raise their glasses in merriment under the awning outside of a bustling bar. A short line exits the door of a bakery filling the air with caramelized fruit, chocolate, and baked bread when we pass it. It's lively and wholesome and exactly how I would've imagined a fae realm village.

At the end of the block, a red awning covers wicker chairs and small tables of a corner shop.

Killian opens the door for me to enter it. His magic trickles along my body, drying my clothes as I step inside.

The shop reminds me of pictures I've seen of Paris, with an assortment of baked items in a glass case, artwork lining the walls, hanging lights, and a welcoming, bright atmosphere.

I inhale the aroma of coffee. My eyes close and a small moan escapes me.

Killian leans over my shoulder, causing the inside of my chest to tickle. "We did my favorite thing, so I figured we could do yours."

I jerk around, eyes wide with surprise. "How did you know?"

The trace of a smile touches his lips. "From the sounds that come out of your mouth every time coffee's around."

I gape at him, a little confused until I remember the time we went to the kitchens. He must've noticed my reaction then. Pink tinges my cheeks. I really need to get my coffee addiction under control.

"Inside or outside?" A fae waiter with violet eyes, green skin, and curly brown hair asks.

I try not to stare while I try to discern their heritage. "Inside," I request. The coziness of nestling in a coffee shop was my weekly routine on Earth, and there's nothing that would settle my soul more than that right now.

Per Killian's request, we are taken to a corner table in the back. He pulls out the chair on the far side of the table so his back is against the wall and he can face the room. It's something I've seen Shay do multiple times too. I wonder if it's a coincidence or something they picked up from each other.

I take the seat across from him. As we sit in companionable silence, I think back to the coffee I received in my room with the note about being my lifesaver. "Was it you who sent me coffee?"

A knowing glint sparks in his eyes.

I lean back in shock at a loss for words. I guess it hadn't been Mrs. Hennessee or Marley who sent it. He's helped me from the beginning with the competition, even going as far to help me with my training with Shay despite those two having issues.

"You say you work for the King," I recall, watching his face closely in case anything slips.

"Correct."

"Is that why you helped train me?"

"Yes." His lips downturn. I'm unsure if he's unhappy about training me, working with Shay, or admitting the truth. "Shay had no intention of getting my help, but when the King learned his son was seeking someone to train you, he ordered me to do it."

"Is that why you've helped me in other ways?" I ask to try to understand him and the situation better.

"No."

So, he's helped me under obligation with the King, but nothing else? What about now? He didn't need to send me coffee, share his past, or bring me to Old *Rímor*.

The server arrives at our table, placing a cappuccino in front of Killian. "Would you like your usual dessert?"

Killian nods. "And whatever the little rabbit would like."

I scowl at him for calling me that around others. Maybe I was giving him too much credit for being kind.

I grin at the server. "Coffee. Extra cream. Biggest mug you have, please."

"Anything to eat?"

I shake my head.

"She'll have what I'm having," Killian interjects.

"Very well, sir." The waiter finishes scribbling on his notepad and departs from our table.

"Excuse you. I'm not some brainless woman. I can order for myself." I glower at him as I fold my arms in defiance. What is this, the 1950s?

"But you *weren't* ordering for yourself." His stoic expression remains unchanged as his arms cross too.

"Well, I'm not hungry." In this inopportune moment, my stomach makes itself known with a croak.

He raises his eyebrow at me and a half smile appears that practically shouts *I told you so.*

"I don't feel hungry," I grumble.

"You need to eat," he states.

"I told you I ate this morning."

"Even if that was true, which it's not, morning was twelve hours ago. Either way, you need to eat." He scans the restaurant behind me before landing back on me. I can see in his face there is no room for debate.

"Why're you doing this?"

"Doing what?" He leans back into his chair when he realizes I'm no longer going to fight him on the food.

"Helping me in the trial, take me to your house, take me to the lookout, and now the coffee shop."

He takes a deep breath, his eyes searching mine. His lips press into a hard line.

How can someone simultaneously be so open and closed off?

"I don't understand," I prod. "Help me understand."

"There're reasons." He sits up straighter in his chair, and I hear the waiter walking over with a tray of items. With his diverting attention, it's obvious the moment is lost to learn more.

The server places my mug of coffee in front of me, which is large enough it could be a soup bowl.

I snag it with a grin, and scorch my tongue when I take a delectable sip. Worth it.

Next, he places a cobbler in front of each of us. My mouth waters at the sugar coated crumble with purple juice seeping at the edges.

"Thank you," Killian tells the fae.

"Let me know if I can get you anything else." He gives a slight bow and walks away.

Killian joins me in drinking his coffee, taking a sip of the foam before placing the cup back in its saucer.

"Oh." I blink in realization. "You didn't need to wait for me."

He shrugs, lifting his spoon and dipping it into the dessert. Steam erupts from the broken crust. He closes his eyes with his first bite, relishing in the taste. A dribble of berry liquid sits on his bottom lip, and his tongue sweeps across it. His hooded gaze meets mine.

My eyes drop to my cobbler, trying to ignore the blush I know shows on my cheeks. I scoop a bite of cobbler and shove it into my mouth. A burst of blueberry, blackberry, and raspberry blends with the sugary crust. It warms my belly and I bite back a moan from how delicious it is. I dive back in for another bite, then another, and another.

Before I know it, my spoon is scraping the bowl dry and I'm considering using my fingers to get the remnants. I think this is the first time my coffee has been left forgotten off to the side.

Killian watches me with an amused smile.

Embarrassed, I push the empty dish to the side of the table. I dab at the corners of my mouth with my napkin as though I'm a proper lady and didn't just eat like a rabid dog.

He picks up his half eaten cobbler and places it in front of me.

I glance between him and the dessert, and shrug. His loss. I don't need to be told twice.

He settles into his chair, cappuccino cup in hand, as I finish off the meal.

"Seems I was more hungry than I realized," I casually chuckle. I swipe my thumb across my lips, wiping away any crumbs or juice, and lick it off my finger.

Killian's eyes trace the movement. "Seems so."

Crap, I should've used my napkin. "I, um, er...thanks for the food," I sheepishly say. Great, bumbling Cara is back. My favorite version of myself. I give an internal eye roll.

"Feeling better?" He asks with a tilt of his head. Based on the serious way he looks at me, I know he's inquiring more than about my hunger.

Actually, this is the most alive I've felt in weeks. It's the longest time I've gone without the burden of Cadan or this messed up situation weighing on my mind. I don't know how or when, but somehow Killian found a way to ease the darkness I've been carrying.

"Yes," I whisper.

"That's good." His eyes drift to my hair.

I purse my lips in annoyance. "Why does everyone keep looking at my hair? I know, I need to brush it, and probably wash it. But seriously, I can feel the judgement. So, stop it."

His forehead creases. "Do you not know?" He takes in my confused face. "Part of it's gone white."

"What?" I scream.

I spring from the table, the chair scraping along the floor, and run to a small hallway across from our table where the restroom sign hangs above it. I throw open a door and enter a single person bathroom smelling of apple cinnamon. I pause in front of the mirror. The person staring back at me isn't one I recognize. I'm gaunt and dark circles loom under my eyes. No wonder Killian insisted that I eat.

Partway back on the right side of my head is a huge chunk of stark white hair.

My mouth hangs wide open. My reflection brings a hand up to touch the area. Grabbing a chunk between my fingers, I follow it down until I can pull it in front of my face.

White. Completely white.

It looks like Yin and Yang with my all black hair and a streak of white. What the hell? Is that why Shay had asked about my hair? Damn. Have I really not looked in a mirror at all recently?

Someone knocks on the door.

"One minute!" I shout as I frantically move back the layers of hair to ensure there's no hidden white anywhere else.

"Are you okay?" Killian's gravelly voice responds.

Tears sting my eyes. Yeah, I'm perfect. Just one more thing to add to my messed up list.

"Cara?" he asks, knocking again.

I grab the sides of the sink, taking deep breaths to get myself under control. I will not cry. This is fine. I'm fine.

Killian's patience must be running out because the door handle twists and the door opens, letting in the sounds of the cafe into the small room.

"Ladies room," I note in hopes he will leave.

"Actually, all bathrooms in the fae realm are single stalled and gender neutral," he says from behind me as he moves inside.

"Then single person only." I still haven't looked up. My raspy voice makes it clear I'm holding back my anguish. I don't want to be around anyone right now. I don't want to be here at all. Squeezing the sides of the sink, I wait for my emotions to settle. I need to collect myself before I fall apart in front of him. Again.

"What do you need from me?" He asks with concern coating his voice.

I force myself to meet his eyes in the mirror.

He stands a foot behind me, hands flexing at his side.

I let out a shuddering breath. "It's fine. I'm fine," I repeat my mantra out loud to him. Hopefully it convinces him, because it's not doing much for me.

He says nothing.

"What do you think it's from?" I choke.

He grimaces, looking to the floor as he takes a step away.

I turn around. "No. Don't do that. Tell me why this happened to my hair." I am tired of fae secrets. I'm tired of pulling teeth to get answers. He is not getting out of this.

"I don't know for sure," he hesitates.

"But you have an idea," I accuse. I step closer to him and place a hand on his chest, drawing his attention back to me.

His eyes roam over my face before landing on my hair. He reaches forward, taking a strand of it between his thumb and forefinger. "I believe it's from your banshee powers. It showed up after the wit trial."

My hair hasn't turned white when I've heard the sound before. My eyes widen. "My hair turned white because I killed people?"

"It's just a guess. Your powers shouldn't kill people in the first place."

I hug myself. Not only do I have to live with what I did, but I'll have a physical reminder of it. "Freaking cursed."

His knuckle presses under my chin to lift my head to look at him. "I will repeat this a thousand times if I must. You aren't cursed."

I pull away from him. "Let's go. Nothing I can do about it now, so might as well finish my coffee."

His indiscernible face takes me in like I'm a puzzle he's trying to solve. Heaving a sigh, he relinquishes and leaves the restroom.

We head back to our table with me stalking behind in his shadow. He goes to exit the hallway, but stops in his tracks, causing me to run straight into his back.

"What the heck?" I gripe as I peer around him.

Shay reclines in a seat at our table. One leg propped on the corner of it, lounging without a care in the world. His eyes narrow the moment he sees me.

"What're you doing here?" Killian asks as he strides over, continuing to block me from Shay.

"I should be the one asking that." He leans to the left to see me. "What the hell happened?"

"You don't have to answer him." Killian's harsh voice cuts in.

Shay stands, coming face to face with Killian. Shay's a few inches taller, but where he is all broad muscle, Killian is lithe.

"You need to back off." Shay's spittle flies at Killian's face.

Killian's eyes darken as a rumbling growl emits from his chest. "She wouldn't be in this mess if it wasn't for you."

"You're right, she'd be injured or dead." Shay's fists squeeze.

"Just because she's physically intact doesn't mean she's okay," Killian hisses. "Why don't you get your head out of your ass for once?"

"I've been preoccupied with keeping her safe from fae like you. After," Shay pauses, his Adam's apple bobs when he swallows, "Roisin—"

"Don't say her name!" Killian pulls his fist back and clocks Shay across the face.

I jump at the crack, color draining from my face, but Shay doesn't miss a beat.

"I can say her name whenever the damn well I please!" He lobs a right hook.

Killian goes to back up, but hits me, allowing Shay to land his punch.

I stumble backwards, not only from the force of Killian but the punch Shay landed on him.

Killian grabs his jaw, spinning on Shay with murder in his eyes.

Other patrons stop to watch their scuffle.

Crap, I need to stop this.

I jump in between them before it can go any further. "Stop!" I hold out my hands to both of them, but Killian's already lunging at Shay ready to strike.

Alarm flashes across his face, but there's no way to stop his momentum.

A thick arm wraps around my midsection, swinging me out of the way as Killian flies past us.

Shay places me back on my feet.

I step away from him. Adrenaline causes my legs to shake, but I lock my knees in hopes no one notices. I look at Killian's stricken face. "Stop." I turn to Shay. "Both of you."

Shay's eyes don't leave Killian, his body rigid, but he doesn't make another move.

I turn back to Killian. "Thank you for your help in the trial and... everything else, but I should be getting back anyway. Let's go," I tell Shay.

The two grown men stare at one another, waiting for the other to make a move.

"Move it!" I holler at Shay.

His body shifts before he glances down at me. "Fine." He grabs under my arm and starts hauling me away.

"Don't touch her like that!" Killian storms after us.

I look over my shoulder and shake my head at him. *Leave it,* I mouth.

He halts in the cafe's doorway, and what looks like hurt crosses his face before it erases into a stern facade.

Shay ushers me to the palomino from the barn moseying in the street. A small yelp escapes me when he grabs me around the waist and hauls me into the saddle.

He swings behind me, grabbing the reins on either side. I shift my weight, trying to create room from the bulk of him. The stirrups are too long to fit my feet into, despite Shay leaving them open for me. I decide not to say anything, instead gripping the mane of the horse and squeezing with my thighs to keep me in place. I open my mouth to thank Killian again, but Shay kick's the horse's side.

The horse gallops away, the movement matching my heart beating my throat.

Shay uses an arm to pull me closer to him, ridding the space I created.

"I'm fine," I squeak, trying to shift away but almost tumbling off the horse to do so.

"Stop." He shoves me back into his body, which steadies me. "I can't have you falling off and getting hurt," he growls.

"Yes, can't have your precious proxy getting hurt before the next trial." Frustration laces my voice.

He doesn't respond, steering the horse in silence.

An hour later, back at the castle, Shay deposits me to my room and follows me inside before shutting the door.

I turn to demand he leaves, but he speaks before I get a chance.

"Are you okay?" His eyes trace me, a hint of concern showing in his tight face.

"Yes, I'm fine." I roll my eyes. Why is he being so dramatic? "Um, can you yell at me tomorrow or whatever? I seriously need a bath."

"He didn't hurt you?" He paces back and forth in the room. "I should've watched more closely. I should've never allowed his help with training, let him get close to you," he mumbles to himself.

"Why're you being so weird?"

He rubs his hand over his face. "Don't worry about it."

"You're freaking me out." I sit on the edge of my bed.

"What happened at the trial?"

I shrug. "Stuff."

"That's not a good answer." His tone is sharper, more than usual.

I don't appreciate being talked to that way, especially when I didn't do anything wrong. "Maybe you need to ask better questions," I say.

Ah, the satisfaction of throwing his words back at him.

He huffs. "Well, you passed it. That's all that matters."

I collapse backwards onto my mattress, annoyed. "Of course it is."

"And after the trial, what happened?" Even though he stands a few feet away, he towers over me.

I prop myself on my elbows. "Killian took me to see Old *Rímor*."

"And?"

"That's all," I say. Shay doesn't need to know any details, and technically that's all Killian did.

He studies me. "Fine." He walks to the door and pauses. "By the way, my father requested dinner with us."

"What?" I hop up. "When?"

"Tomorrow night. I'll come get you. Try to be ready and try not to run away with Killian again. In fact, it'd be better if you avoided him."

I sigh, knowing I have no say about the dinner, but perturbed by his comment with Killian. "Why's it better?"

"Just trust me. He's not safe." He exits my room without further explanation.

Typical.

I groan as I head to the bathroom.

While the tub fills, I take my clothes off, piling them in the same spot on the floor where I had found them this morning. It's hard to believe that only this morning Shay came for me for the third trial. It already feels like it could've been days ago. I squirt a dollop of lavender soap into the water so it'll bubble. Entering the water, the heat seeps into my frozen limbs, and I sink into the hot liquid and close my eyes with a sigh.

I wonder if there's a way I can dye the white of my hair. Although, if it's related to my powers, I wouldn't be surprised if there's some stupid magic that makes it impossible. I don't even know if they have hair dye here in *Gon'an'rit*. Maybe there's a way I can convince Shay to get me hair dye from Earth.

Ugh. Why does Shay have to be such a pain? And what's with him and Killian anyway? There've been moments where they seem to tolerate one another, but there's clearly history between the two of them. Shay's a locked book, so I doubt I'll get answers out of him. Not that Killian is any better.

A headache forms as I mull over those two and their messy relationship.

Killian did open up a lot to me today. A smile crosses my lips at the thought of him. The only other person who could pull me from the darkness before was Shauna. It seems Killian understands it, same as me.

Remembering the pain on his face when I left with Shay pulls at my heart. I hope the progress we made today isn't backtracked because of it.

The water rises to my chin as I slouch further in.

A yawn drags from me. I need to get out before I fall asleep, but the warmth feels so good. I submerge myself underwater, holding my breath until my lungs ache. Once I feel I can't go another second, I sit up with a gasp.

I busy myself with rinsing my hair for the first time in over a week and dry off. Lacking the energy to put on any pajamas, I drag myself to the comfort of my bed.

Shay's tendency to barge into my room flits across the back of my mind, but I still can't be bothered to put on clothes.

I pull the comforter over me, cozying into the soft mattress, and for the first time in weeks I truly rest.

TWENTY-TWO

In the morning, after coffee of course, I grab a pair of jeans and a blouse from the closet. I relish in the comfort of familiar clothes.

I half expected a note from Killian this morning with my coffee, but no such thing happened. I wouldn't be surprised if Shay found him last night and scared him away.

However, Killian doesn't seem like the type who scares easily. If anything, he'd probably try to see me that much more just to piss off Shay.

I slip out of my room, shutting my door quietly. It's reminiscent of when I'd sneak out of my apartment to attend an early class, and Shauna was sleeping because she'd bartended late into the night.

I scan the hallway, but don't see anyone. Aside from the trial gatherings, the palace is a wasteland. Even those who serve King Harbinger I rarely see. A guard here or there, a little more after the attack, but they keep to themselves. The bustling street of Old *Rímor* is the liveliest I've seen in this realm.

Earlier, I had considered lounging in my room until Shay came to get me for dinner. But where was the fun in that? For the first time in weeks I had gotten a good night's sleep, and I wanted to know more about where I was staying. Worst case scenario, this castle is as boring as it seems, and I'll go visit the horses in the barn.

I tiptoe through the halls, as if my body knows I shouldn't be here. It's because I'm not meant to be here, not just in this castle but *Gon'an'rit* as a whole.

I force myself into a casual walk because in the end, this is my current residence and whether or not I feel I should be here, I am, and I need to accept that. Plus, I don't need to seem suspicious and have a guard misinterpret it, tackling me to the ground or tattling on me to the king. No need to make the dinner tonight any more awkward than it will be.

A shudder runs along my spine.

Everyone seems so enamored with the King, and who am I to judge? He has kept this realm strong and at peace for centuries. But there's something about him that doesn't sit well with me. Needless to say, I'm not excited for dinner. The less time I have to spend with the man, the better.

While traipsing through the halls, I come across closed doors, huge paintings, and open windows revealing the overcast day. No surprise there. I find it strange that the bleary weather hasn't changed since my arrival. I understand places like the United Kingdom or Pacific Northwest have long periods of rain and clouds, but from what Killian told me, it's not natural here and has been this way for years, not months.

Didn't he say his mom knew something that was happening in *Gon'an'rit?* He said she was well on her way to discovering something, but got imprisoned for treason before anything happened. What if something did happen? What if she did figure out what happened and that's why…

No. The problem was with the realm, not the King. Whatever she did or found must've not been very good.

But Killian believes in her, trusts her. Trusts she's not a bad person. He's been working for years to lessen her sentence. Maybe she knows of a way for me to get home or a loophole to my verbal contract with Shay too.

I can't put all my faith in winning the competition to get home, especially when considering recent events. I need a backup plan. Finding her couldn't be any more dangerous than whatever trials lay ahead of me.

She's in this castle somewhere. She must be. Where else would a King keep inmates? It couldn't hurt to ask, right? She's already imprisoned, so if she helps me it's not like she'd be in a worse position.

Okay, that's a little morbid. Not my most empathetic moment.

My fingers flex at my sides. I know it seems cruel, but no one needs to find out. And it's not like she's doing anything illegal by helping me. This is merely a backup plan if I lose, so it's not like I'm breaking my contract with Shay by getting out of the competition.

What if I get caught where she's locked up? That'd be terrible. But what do I have to lose? The trials are getting harder each time and the only reason I didn't lose the last one, or survive in the first place, was because of Killian.

There can only be one winner, and Killian is determined to win. I'm unsure how much longer I can trust him to help me in the competition, and I'm not sure if I can trust Shay at all. The life debt is what I owe him. He could change his mind on taking me home, even if I do win, for all I know.

It's in his mom's best interest for Killian to win too. If she helps me find an alternative way to get home, I can focus on helping Killian win instead of winning myself. At the end of the day, I have myself. It's up to me to find another way home, and this is a shot I've got to take.

In movies and books, they keep prisoners in towers or underground. But towers seem to be more for confining princesses, not those who have been arrested for treason. I'd bet my life there's a dungeon somewhere. Okay, well not my life... I snort to myself. I don't believe I'm making deductions based on Rapunzel, but it's not like I have anything else to go on.

I continue through the halls and anytime I find a stairwell, I take it downwards. The main entrance of the palace moves further away from me as I travel deeper into the anthill-like palace.

It's eerily quiet.

The echo of my footsteps is the only sound to break the silence. Eventually, I hum to myself to calm my nerves and seem more casual in case I come across someone.

I'm not doing anything wrong. I'm simply walking through the castle. Don't mind me, fae guards. Just a fae raised as a human who doesn't know any better. Completely and one hundred percent innocent.

If anyone sees me, I'll say I got lost on my way to the barn.

My pace quickens along with my song. I feel like a child about to turn the lights off in the basement. My heart slams against my ribs, and I fold my arms to keep it inside my chest. I keep peering over my shoulder, waiting for someone to jump out and say, "Caught ya!"

Up ahead, I spot a stone staircase winding deeper underground. Bingo!

There are still no guards, but that doesn't mean there won't be any at the bottom. I need to be careful.

Naivety will be my best excuse, I remind myself.

A door in front of me swings open and I scream at the top of my lungs as I jump back.

A blonde fae gasps as she nearly crashes into me.

My body shakes with adrenaline.

"Cara?"

My brain computes who is in front of me after a few seconds, "Hey Marley."

She holds a tray of finger sandwiches and rearranges the ones that slid. "What're you doing all the way down here?"

"I… umm…I…" Crap. Are you kidding me? I had my excuse perfectly plotted in my head, and now this?

"Are you lost?"

I nod.

A kind smile brightens her face. "Where were you headed?"

"Uh, to the horses?"

She tilts her head, her azul eyes roving over me. Her head turns to the side with her focus skipping to the stairwell before training back on me. "Yeah, you definitely took a wrong turn."

"Whoops." I laugh awkwardly.

"No worries. Follow me," she brightens with a flashing smile.

The warmth of her demeanor calms my nerves. I glance at the stairwell once more before sidling next to her to walk back the way I came.

A deflating sigh escapes me from losing my chance for some answers with the lower levels getting further and further behind me.

"You okay?" She glances at me with a concerned face.

"Just tired." Guilt twists through my stomach for lying to her.

She nods in complete understanding, which just makes me feel worse. "The competition is tough for fae raised here. I can only imagine how difficult it is for you," she says.

"How'd you know I wasn't from here?" I don't think that was something I told her.

She chuckles and I couldn't imagine a more melodic sound coming from another person. I wonder if angels are a kind of fae or not.

"News travels fast," she explains.

We walk in silence through the halls.

I keep glancing at her as a billion questions form on my tongue. Perhaps she knows something that would help me out.

"How do you like it here so far?" She breaks the tension.

"It's... different."

She raises an eyebrow at me.

"I don't know," I shrug. "I wish I could enjoy it more, but it's kind of hard when it isn't something I chose for myself."

She lets out a huff of irritation. "Damn that fae. I'm sorry Shay did this to you. He's been different ever since..." she trails off.

Silence permeates between the two of us. She doesn't finish her thought and I don't push, but I find myself thinking about Shay and Killian. She used to date Killian, and based on what she said she's familiar with Shay too. I think back to last night, how they both were on edge with each other, per usual, but it wasn't until a certain name was spoken that it got out of control. A name I've only heard once before in the kitchens.

"Who's Roisin?" I blurt. I mentally cross my fingers she will answer, unlike most fae I've gotten to know.

Of course, Cadan is excluded from this. A pang constricts my midsection thinking of him. I haven't tried to visit him in the infirmary, which is where I assume he is since he got hurt during the trials. I really don't deserve his friendship. Swallowing my guilt, I refocus on the fae beside me.

Her steps falter from my sudden question, causing her to come to a stop. Her head is downcast, staring at the tray she holds between her hands. A stray blonde hair falls into her face.

"I'm sorry. Forget it." My stomach twists as I realize I've overstepped. I really need to think before I speak.

She shakes her head. "No," her voice is shaky, "it's okay." A sad smile crosses her face, her eyes glistening with unshed tears. "I'm just not used to anyone talking about her so openly."

"We don't have to, it's fine," I wave it off.

"No. I think I'd… like to." She whisks away her tears with the back of her hand before they fall.

I stand there, barely breathing, waiting for her to continue.

"She was my best friend." Her voice is soft, and holds a pain she tries to hide.

"Oh," I say. Well, that's kind of a relief. I thought it was something bigger than that. It still doesn't explain the weirdness between Killian and Shay when she was brought up though.

"And Shay's sister," she adds.

"Oh," I elongate the word this time. That makes a lot more sense.

"And Killian's first and only love."

A stifled "Uh" slips out, an unformed word that's more of a clipped sound. I don't know how to process what she's telling me by this point. I know what I want to ask, but I don't dare as this is clearly a sore subject for her, for all of them.

Marley begins to walk again, slower this time, and I follow.

"We all grew up together, all best friends." She gazes into the distance as though looking into the past.

I stumble. "Wait, Shay and Killian were friends?" I try to hold back my holler of surprise.

A faint smile forms on her lips. "Yes, we all were. But eventually we got older, and me and Killian weren't royalty. So our parents chastised us and told us to distance ourselves because nothing good would come from a childhood friendship that shouldn't have existed in the first place. But we stayed close. The four of us were nearly inseparable." She laughs to herself. "One time our parents tried to forbid Killian and I from seeing Shay and Roisin, but that only had us sneaking away and avoiding our duties. I'd use any excuse to bring Roisin food and Killian would do sword work for hours on end with Shay."

"Sword work?" I mutter. Now it made sense why Killian was chosen to help train me.

She nods. "Yes, Killian was initially hired as a kid to help Shay practice his skills. He was the most gifted fae of our age range. The King never fully accepted Shay. He isn't a full *Druid* and the son of a maid. The King values power and strength. He hoped having Shay become a strong swordsman would balance his weak magic. But even though he became as good as Killian, if not better, his father still never accepted him."

Killian had mentioned Shay being a bastard, and the King admitted to being quiet about their relationship, but I never understood how the two connected before now.

Wait. Shay has weak magic? Well now I understand why Shay needed a proxy for the competition. If his magic is weak, he wouldn't have made it past the first round.

Marley continues her tale, cutting through my thoughts. "Roisin was a full royal and King Harbinger's favorite. When she died, it ruined all of us. It tore apart Shay and Killian, and put an even larger rift between father and son. And... I lost my best friend." She sniffles, and a stray tear glides down her smooth cheek.

"We don't need to keep talking about it," I whisper.

She dabs the corner of her eyes with her shoulders. "No, it's kind of nice to be able to talk about it. I think it's been harder to hold all of this back over the years."

"How'd she die? If you don't mind me asking," I timidly ask.

"There was a fire. She died trying to save the fae in the burning building. But I think there's more to it than that."

Killian's burn scars flash through my mind. Before I can think further on that, Marley adds to her tale.

"We were eighteen. No one talks about what happened. Shay avoided me and Killian at all costs, and Killian closed himself off to the world. For a time, Killian and I used one another to console the hole Roisin left in our hearts, but it wasn't enough for either of us. So, even we broke apart."

We round a corner.

"You being here is the most they've interacted since it all happened," she admits.

"What about Shay and Roisin's mothers?" I grimace to myself. I could at least learn to ask more delicately. But aside from knowing Shay's mom was a maid and Roisin's mom was the queen, I knew nothing. Also, I haven't seen either woman since I've arrived. One would think they'd be at the trials.

"They both died in childbirth. No one understands how or why. With the magic we possess, we are pretty sturdy with birth and have a good success rate. The King had it investigated, having lost his wife and the mother of his son within a year and a half of one another, but he never discovered the reason."

"That's terrible." I bite my lower lip. "Poor Shay."

Marley nods. "Him and Roisin were close. She was the only family he truly had. He lost his mother and his father didn't accept him, but his older sister loved him more than anything. And he loved her just as much, if not more. When he lost her, it broke him." She takes a deep breath. "It broke us all."

I play with the cuff of my sleeve. I was too quick to judge Shay. Granted, he didn't make it easy to get to know him, but at least I understood why now. He lost his family, just like me, but at least I still have Shauna. All he has is a father who doesn't accept him. Even his childhood friends he's pushed away. But why do that? He should've held onto them tighter, used them for his support system.

"Thanks for that. It feels like taboo to speak of it, but it's nice to open up about the past instead of ignoring its existence," Marley says with a sigh.

We move into a hall that's familiar.

She takes me to the side door, the one I've been using for weeks that leads to the path to take me to the barn.

"I appreciate you opening up. It's like a breath of fresh air. I haven't been around the most forthcoming fae since I've arrived," I say.

Her chiming laughter makes me smile as well. It's a bit of a shock after the solemn conversation. "I can imagine."

"Maybe next time you can tell me some fun childhood stories of you four? I'd love to have some dirt to use against them." A wicked smile forms on my lips.

"Oh yes." The gleam in her eye is just as mischievous. "I'd love that and boy do I have stories."

"I can't wait. And thanks, I know where I am now. I appreciate the help."

"No problem! Do you want a sandwich? I'm sure the guards won't notice if one is missing." She extends the tray to me.

I shake my head. "No, I'm okay, but thank you."

She leans in and my body goes rigid when she gives me a side hug. "Let me know if you ever need anything."

"Thanks," I murmur, my body easing to casually hug her back. Affection is not something I'm used to from others aside from my sister, and she's family.

Marley pulls away and gives me one last smile before turning to walk away.

A warmth pools in my chest. Maybe I have one more person I can call a friend in this place.

❧

"Where've you been?" A booming voice hits me as I open my bedroom door, causing me to jump.

Spinning around, I see Shay storming across the hall to me.

"It's been hours." He stops inches from me with his arms crossed. "Everything okay? Where were you?"

I tilt my head back to look up at him. "Aww, was widdle Shay scared?" I mock.

"I'm serious, Cara." He glares down at me, but worry tinges the hard lines of his face.

"I'm fine," I huff, turning to waltz into my room. "I just went for a walk."

He follows right on my heels. "Where? Were you with… him?" He growls.

I roll my eyes and shut the door behind us. "No. I went to say hi to the horses."

His shoulders relax, face softening. Crossing to my sitting area, he makes himself at home by reclining into my lounge chair, propping one foot on the armrest.

"You know, I can take care of myself. I am an adult."

"I never said you couldn't, kid," he quips.

I glare at the side of his face. Of course he'd follow up with that infuriating nickname. "Well, you sure don't act like it."

"You don't understand our world," he says explicitly like it excuses his actions.

"And whose fault is that?" I narrow my eyes.

"Touché." Leaning his head back on the other armrest, he stares at the ceiling. "Do you hate me?"

I pause at the random question and search his face.

His brows pinch and lips press into a thin line, but it seems to stem from a place of worry for my answer instead of his usual frustration. I have no idea where this question came from, but my answer is clearly important to him.

The problem is, I don't think I know the answer.

I move around the couch and push his leg out of the way so I can sit.

Slowly, almost reluctantly, he bends his head to look at me.

My hands twist in my lap. "I should. It's not like you haven't given me plenty of reasons." I think of my conversation with Marley. Despite his grumpiness, I now better understand him and the protective side that he's recently shown me. "But I don't," I sigh.

His shoulders relax at my admission. His lips part like he wants to say something, but he thinks better of it, resting his head back. "You should get ready. Dinner's soon."

"Any requests on what to wear for dinner, Prince Shay?" I emphasize his name and give a little bow after I stand.

He swings into a sitting position, running his hands through his hair. "Whatever you want."

"You're going to regret that," I grin.

A slow smile toys at the corner of his lips. "That's exactly what I'm hoping for."

I walk out of the bathroom twenty minutes later, and Shay's eyes bulge.

My black hair hangs limply to my waist, but at least it's brushed. I've gone hard with the eyeliner, even adding wings to the edge of my eyes, and found ruby red lipstick to add to my fierce makeup. Tight, black leather pants cling to me along with the corset from the night I went out with Shauna, a piece of home. It's funny how what I was once so nervous to wear now brings me a sense of peace. I wear my black training boots, which remind me of Doc Martens, and are clean of their usual caked-on mud.

"Oh," I feign surprise. "Is this not appropriate for dinner with our Holy King?" I bat my eyes innocently.

A devilish smile darkens his face. "My father will hate this."

"In that case, I think I did a perfect job," I grin.

"As do I." He holds out the crook of his elbow. "Shall we?"

"We shall." I place my hand into it and we both snicker to ourselves as we leave my room.

Shay leads me to a new area of the castle, one with many more guards and less windows. I assume this is the King's residential area.

"It's about time," King Harbinger booms as we enter a private dining area.

The table in the center is a long rectangle that can easily fit ten people, but instead holds three place settings on one end. The rest of the room is bare despite being a large space, devoid of any plants or paintings. It has cream colored walls, matching the outside of the castle, and chandeliers hanging from the ceiling to illuminate the stark space. There isn't a single window, giving it a darker feel despite the lights above. Guards stand by all the doors and in the corners too.

Well, found where all the guards have been.

As we approach, the King stands from his seat at the end of the table.

"Father." Shay gives a slight bow of his head.

King Harbinger pays his son no attention, instead his focus trains on me. He frowns as he scrutinizes my outfit.

Inwardly I gloat at his distaste, but outwardly I bow. "Thank you for inviting me to dinner."

"Yes, well, you could say I'm intrigued with how far you've made it in this competition." He signals for us to take our seats. "Although, the last trial didn't seem like it should've been favorable to you."

The three of us scoot into our places at the same time. The King sits at the head of the table, Shay to his right and me to his left. Once seated, he snaps his fingers and platters of food appear in front of us.

"Typically, I would have us served, but considering you two arrived late, I figured this would be faster," he states.

"I'm sorry, Father," Shay apologizes. His voice sounds truly regretful, but his stoic face does not replicate that emotion.

"As you should be." King Harbinger takes a swig of wine from his goblet.

"It's my fault," I interject. Shay doesn't need any more lack of love from this man. I have no problem taking the brunt of the King's wrath over this.

Shay's eyes soften at me.

The King scoffs. "Either way, it's unacceptable. Although, I'm not surprised. Although you are fae, you were raised with humans, and they have ghastly mannerisms." Again, his eyes trace my outfit with a frown as though proving his point.

"Yes, sir," I mumble. I've had little practice on how to act around parents. I lost mine so young, and I never met any of my ex's families. I tried to avoid them at all costs, and I wouldn't consider anyone from foster care a parent.

Using my fork and knife, I cut into the pie in front of me, and chunks of meat spill out. The brown gravy seeps out in little tendrils like the blood that ran from Scarface's eyes. I stab a chunk of meat, and try not to throw up. Having been face to face with death, something I caused, now has me thinking about the poor animal this came from. I have helped pigs, cows, chickens, and so many animals on the farms. Was it a quick death for them or was it long and painful? Would we even know? My lungs constrict until I can't breathe. When I finally manage a shuddering breath, I place the fork back on my plate.

"Is there something wrong with the meal?" The King asks with offense in his tone.

"Umm, I, uh." I groan in my head. Why do I always become tongue-tied in the most inopportune times? I don't want to offend him, but I don't know if I can put the chunk of meat into my mouth.

Shay must see my conflict because he pipes in. "Do we have a vegetable pie, father?"

I have no idea how Shay knows what is bothering me, but I am beyond grateful for it.

King Harbinger frowns, but obliges with a snap of his fingers. The plate in front of me disappears and is replaced with a fresh pie. "I hope you like mushrooms," he states, hinting how it's my only other option.

"I do, thank you." My eyes flit to Shay when I utter my appreciative words, hoping he knows I mean them more for him than his dad.

I try not to moan at the flakey crust of the pie with its buttery texture melting into the creamy filling.

"So, how do you two plan to win this?" The King nonchalantly asks.

I look to Shay, who stares at his plate, face as hard and emotionless as stone.

I decide to answer instead. "Well, Shay and Killian have been training me. They've taught me a lot. So, I'm sure we will figure something out together."

"Together?" King Harbinger's deep laughter bounces off the wall. "My dear, there can only be a single winner. And based on your last performance, I cannot say you've learned much from my son, if anything at all."

Shay's fist flexes around his fork. "She's a lot stronger than she looks," he mumbles.

"Speak up," the King chastises. "You may be weak in magic and many other areas, but you can at least hold your demeanor with more power. I hope to have passed on one trait to my son aside from this hair."

His nostrils flare at his father's comment, chest rising with each deep inhale.

My spoon pauses above my mashed potatoes, my glance bouncing between the two of them. I clear my throat. "Dinner is delicious."

After a moment's hesitation, the King snaps his attention to me. "Yes, I have the best cooks in the kingdom. I would expect nothing less."

"*Rímor* is really amazing. I'm impressed by how long it's been at peace. Your people seem very happy," I add. Compliments help, right? People love to hear others speaking highly of them.

His back straightens as pride lights up his face.

Check.

A rumbling chuckle comes from him. "*Rímor?* My dear girl, I have kept peace in all of *Gon'an'rit* for centuries. Only someone of true strength and power could have this amount of success." His face sours when it travels toward his son, the disappointment apparent.

"I'm sure someone hopes to be as fortuitous to rule the way you have one day," I say.

Shay's alarmed look shoots to me, an imperceptible head shake accompanying it.

King Harbinger pauses, looking between the two of us. He gently places his utensils down on his plate and steeples his hands in front of his face. "Ah, so that's what you have planned."

My eyes go wide as I fumble to backtrack my statement. "What? No! Oh, I didn't mean—"

"I'm not daft, girl!" The King shouts. "I have not been in this position for this long to be duped by a weak fae who is essentially human and my good-for-nothing son."

"I'm surprised you still admit to me being your son," Shay finally speaks up.

"Trust me, you weren't my first choice," the King shouts.

Shay's eyes shutter at the insinuation of his sister and the clear distaste his father holds for him.

My heart breaks at their broken relationship, at what it's like to lose family. But I can't imagine what it's like to have a parent actively not want me.

"I think we should be going." I stand. "Thank you for the dinner, but in the future do not feel it necessary to welcome me."

"I did not invite you to welcome you," the King sneers. "I want to know why Shamus joined this competition with you as a proxy. It seems I got my answer."

"Let's go," I tell Shay.

He stands with me and we make our way to the door.

"Only one can win!" The King calls to our backs. "Killian is not your ally, and neither is my son!"

We hustle back to my room, panting when we arrive.

Once my door is closed, Shay paces across the room, smothering his face with his hand.

"What's wrong?" I ask.

He mumbles to himself, but I can't comprehend a word.

I step in front of him, putting my hands on his chest to stop him. "What's going on?"

Once he looks at me, my stomach drops. His eyes are wide with fear.

"He knows," he breathes.

"Knows what?"

"What I plan to do with my wish."

"What do you plan to do?" My breathing quickens. Through all of this, not once has he told me why he's going through all this trouble to win the competition.

Instead of answering, his stricken eyes search my face, unsure if he can trust me. That's when it hits me.

"Wait, you actually want to overthrow him?" I screech.

His hand flies over my mouth. "Shh!"

I talk against his hand, freaking out, but only muted mumbles come out.

"Calm down," he says.

I continue to talk against his hand.

"Calm down and I'll explain," he hisses.

I fold my arms over my chest and wait.

He releases his hand from my mouth and when I say nothing, he talks. "I want to show him I'm not weak. I want him to see me as an equal, or at least a worthy son. I want to show him I can rule just as well as him. But... But... Crap! I was an idiot. Of course he wouldn't see it that way." His words trail off as he begins to pace again.

"You were going to win the competition and then use the wish to overthrow your dad, all for his love?"

"Well, when you put it like that, it sounds stupid!"

"That's because it is!" I throw my hands in the air.

"Now we have to win," Shay becomes more frantic, stepping closer to me with wild eyes.

"Any bright ideas on how to make that happen?"

His features narrow in determination. "You need to kill Killian."

TWENTY-THREE

My foot swings lazily over the side of the chaise lounge. Once again, I'm dressed in my comfort clothes— jeans, boots, and a green blouse. While I wait for Shay to collect me for the next trial, my mind reels over our conversation from last night.

"You need to kill Killian."

My stomach roils at the image of Shay's face. Hard, without mercy.

"You want me to what?"

"He's the strongest contender. If we have a chance of winning, you need to take him out."

"But he's been helping me."

"My father was right; it'll only last for so long. You need to get him before he turns on you."

I twirl my hair around my finger as I stare out the window into the dusky sky. Would Killian really turn on me? He's definitely prickly. Well, he can be a prick, but he has helped me time and time again.

Then again, not that I want to admit it, Shay is right. Only one of us can win. It has to be me if I ever want a chance of going home.

Now that the King thinks our plan is to overthrow him, the urgency to leave is much greater.

I shouldn't need to kill to win, though. There've been plenty of trials where competitors didn't move forward in the competition because of other reasons. Not enough power, going unconscious, and we were still gaining points too.

Guilt sweeps through me as I think of Cadan. I have yet to visit him, and no one has mentioned him waking from his coma. Avoidance is my specialty, but it's revealing I'm not as kind of a person as I thought.

Killian was mistaken when he called me good. He mentioned my darkness too. That part he was right about. Nonetheless, I don't think I can kill him.

Shay hadn't discussed any semantics with me. After his declaration, he told me he needed to take care of some things and left. Hopefully, he forgot about his whole asinine plan. He made sure to inform me before leaving, the next trial is today. Typical Shay, dropping things in my lap and then leaving to attend to some unknown duties.

A knock sounds at my door.

Finally!

I jump off the couch and scurry to the door.

Shay stands on the other side. "Let's go." He holds a bundled cloak under his arm.

"Hello to you too." I provoke, following him down the hall. "I have had a rather boring day, but good. Thanks for asking. I think my favorite part of our interactions is how welcoming you've been through all of this."

He stares down at me, unbothered.

I let out a huff and we continue walking in silence.

I roll my eyes when we waltz up to the recognizable wooden doors. "You know when the trials are in the throne room, you can tell me to meet you here. I know where it is by this point. I don't need a babysitter."

Before we enter, Shay grabs my hand and pulls me to the side. He looks around, using his large frame to cover our conversation from those who go inside. "You remember what I said?"

I pale.

Crap, I'd hoped he'd forgotten, or at least would've given me more time. My stomach drops when he reveals a dagger from the bundle of cloth. He slips it into his waistband and I let out a sigh of relief.

With a swoop of his arms, he unfurls the cloak, billowing it over my shoulders. He fastens it at my collarbone, grabs the knife, and attaches it to my side. After situating the cloak, he gives a curt nod when he's satisfied it covers the weapon.

I gulp down my anxiety, staring at him with wide eyes.

He leans forward and murmurs, "Whenever you get the chance, use it. The sooner the better. Before he takes you out. You can't harm him outside of a trial or there's consequences, but during a trial there are very little rules by this point in the competition."

"I don't think I can do this." My throat rasps. I wish I had my turquoise water bottle from home to put moisture back into my dry mouth.

He frowns, placing a steadying hand on my shoulder. "We need to win this, Cara. Both of us. Do what you need to win."

"I...can't," I choke.

His imposing figure dominates over me as he folds his arms. "We had one last agreement, one last deal from the questions you asked me."

My windpipe closes when I realize what's about to happen.

"For my final request, as deemed by our last deal, you will kill Killian in the competition."

He says it with finality.

My stupor is broken when there's a zip of magic through my body, enacting the deed. I'm not totally sure what would happen if I don't abide by it. I remember the pain from before when I didn't obey, but could it get worse? I don't even know if I have a choice, but either way nothing good is going to come of this.

I don't respond, I can barely think as I'm distracted by how my right hip, where the dagger sits, feels heavier than my left.

With a nod, Shay turns to leave.

I wrap the cloak tighter around me, fearful of someone seeing the weapon.

Upon entering the throne room, I see a line of people in the front of the room, including Killian.

His amber eyes meet mine when I walk up, and my face falls to the ground.

Shay breaks away from me to stand with the rest of the crowd.

I continue on until I am in line, on the opposite end of Killian. I am the last to arrive— the tenth contender. Once I'm situated in line, hugging my cloak closer despite the warmth emitted by the crowd, King Harbinger appears in a flash.

The crowd gasps and gives applause. Many chant his name.

The King waves to his supporters and strides forward. He inclines his head at every contestant; each of us return the greeting with a bow.

"Today we will test the virtue of Courage, which is typically tested by facing your biggest fear," he announces.

The crowd cheers.

I peer over to Shay, but his menacing gaze homes in on his father.

Sweeping my hair out of my face, I turn back, waiting for the instructions for the next trial.

King Harbinger smirks as he traces along the ten of us, landing on me at the far left. Once he speaks, it's like a message to me directly. "I have decided to mix up this trial a little this year."

Sparks fly from his hands when he throws them up, a true showman, which causes the crowd to go wild. He continues, "In our truth trial, we learned one of the contestant's biggest fear is himself." His eyes sweep over to Killian. A haunting smile spreads his lip. "Therefore, his trial will be to perform the fear trial on the other nine competitors."

The crowd whispers to each other. This is not anything that has been done in the past.

The three fae council, who sit at the same table, watch the king with blank faces giving no indication whether they agree with this or not.

"He cannot give any help to anyone, and he must make their deepest fears come to life." His attention drifts back to me.

I clench the sides of the cloak to stop my hands from shaking. I only got a taste of Killian's nightmarish powers before and it was crippling. How was I supposed to pass an entire trial?

The King is doing this on purpose. He's trying to prove what he claimed last night, what Shay claims now. He's forcing Killian and I to become enemies in these games sooner rather than later.

I take a steadying breath to calm my nerves. I don't dare to look at Killian, worried about what I'll see. The dagger heats at my side, reminding me of Shay's mission. No, of my mission. Will the magic force me to do it today? Is there a way I can prevent it?

"Come forth, Killian Mactíre," King Harbinger announces. "As the second to last trial, may you all face your fears with courage."

The crowd repeats, "May you face your fears with courage."

His mention of the second to last trial was a warning. To face something that cannot physically harm you should theoretically be easier than combat, but my gut tells me this will be the hardest trial yet.

I wish Cadan was here to tell me what to expect. To use his unfiltered view of the world, to show me the truth instead of the deception and hidden messages of the fae.

Killian glides up the stairs with his head held high until he's beside the King on the dais. His face is a mask, giving away no emotion. His composed features make him look deadly, and I'm left wondering how many times the King has used his abilities before.

The lights flicker above us.

The King glances at the ceiling with a glare, snaps his fingers, and the lights steady. He leans over and murmurs to Killian, who nods in response. The King moves to stand on the side of the stage, not to his throne, as they announce the first contestant.

"Teagan O'Hanley."

A confident fae steps forward with her brown eyes trained on Killian. Her dark hair is braided down her back, and she steps forward like she owns the room. Her light brown arms are toned, a clear warrior. She faces Killian, lips in a grim line and eyes steady.

"Begin," King Harbinger instructs.

Black clouds form around Killian, oozing out of his pores. It grows until it slithers around their legs, moving up and spreading into a large circle to surround them.

Everyone watches intently, but there's nothing to see but black smoke.

King Harbinger's eyes shift though, seeing something the rest of us cannot. A smile tugs on the corner of his lips as a low grunt erupts from the dark mist.

I listen more closely, but only hear my bated breath.

A growl erupts from the ball of darkness, followed by a random scuffling sound.

Through the corner of my eye I peer over to King Harbinger, whose face scowls at the dark mist, eyes dilating with a flare of his nostrils.

An instant later the mist dissipates.

Killian stands in the same spot, unfazed by whatever occurred.

Teagan kneels on the ground, head hanging. With a huff she stands, sweat beads on her forehead. She descends the stairs and joins us back in line.

"Pass," the King projects. "Next."

I glance at the fae council who glower at the King. He's not even waiting to hear their scores. They don't speak up, they don't provide a score. Instead they whisper amongst themselves and write something down on a scroll.

"Cole Barrett," the announcer calls.

A wiry old man steps forward. His white hair curls at the tips of his pointy ears. He moves with ease up the stairs, and the wrinkles around his eyes become more prominent when he smiles at Killian.

Killian doesn't react, his face void of emotion. Again, the black smoke pours from him, surrounding them both within seconds.

The crowd's hushed breathing fills the silence. After a couple of minutes, a cry echoes around us.

A few fae jump at the sudden sound, but the corner of King Harbinger's lips rise.

No one else notices but me.

Another gurgling cry, but it's cut short. The dark mist disappears, revealing the old man lying on the ground, unmoving.

Killian's jaw ticks as he stares at the wall. He doesn't move, but his chest heaves a little more than before. His eyes are dark, not even a touch of gold, and black wisps cling to him, darkening his form. Not fully absorbing back into him.

I itch to go to them when no one makes a move, but before I can King Harbinger flicks his finger and three guards move forward. They lift the old fae's limp body off the ground and exit the room.

The King nods to the announcer to continue.

Another four fae go through the trial, each time being encompassed in Killian's dark fog. They all scream at one point or another, some more than others.

Each time my stomach twists at the horrific noises.

One of the fae passes the trial, another is found unconscious like the old man, when the third fae is revealed he's crying in a fetal position, and the last runs from the room in terror.

No one stops him.

Killian's form gets darker and darker with the pass of each trial, his magic coalescing with his body. He shows no emotion, unmoving like a statue except for his shaking fists.

I long for the smile he had around his younger brothers, to lift the heaviness from him like he did me. My fingertips brush the cool steel on my hip and my breath hitches. I rub my fingers against my pant leg, wiping away the feel of cold steel, wishing I could wipe away the deal as easily.

"Cara Winters," the crisp voice of the announcer echoes and I stiffen as fear washes through me.

TWENTY-FOUR

My shaking legs carry me forward. My hand sweeps across the dagger at my hip when I stop in front of Killian. I ignore the pulse of magic in my arm urging me to grab it.

Killian's energy sucks the oxygen from the air. The darkness around him feels inky, thicker than I'd imagined. His eyes turn a darker shade of black as his hands clench at his sides. The black penetrates further around the two of us.

I hold my breath when it swoops near me, closing my eyes on instinct. It takes me a moment before I realize my hand is gripping the handle of the dagger under my cloak. I peel my hand away. My eyes pry open to see we are in a dome.

The dark cloud surrounds us, but inside is empty.

The mist continues to curl from Killian, solidifying the barrier.

He glances at me before looking back over my head. For a heartbeat a pained expression crosses his stern features. He presses his lips in a hard line as he flexes his fingers.

"Killian," I whisper.

With each contestant, he's gotten more consumed by his magic.

My heart pulls in my chest, urging me to help him. I take a step forward, and the magic drags my hand back to the blade. I step back to my original position and the need dims.

We are both on our own, just as Shay and the King said.

King Harbinger's piercing gaze pierces the back of my head. His magic sifts inside despite Killian blocking everything else out.

The hair on my arms rises from his unwanted presence.

"I can't help you," Killian mutters, almost imperceptibly.

Again, the desire to go to him arises, to help him, but I don't dare risk it with Shay's final deal pressing on me.

His brows pinch together, a drop of sweat trails down the side of his face while he holds back his magic, trying to give me a moment to collect myself.

I know what's coming; I've seen it before. I'll be ready this time.

Killian begins to transform. His eyes turn into a depthless black, his muscles thicken, and wavy dark hair becomes a disheveled white-blonde.

Tears spring to my eyes as I look at Cadan's familiar face.

His eyes train on me, piercing my soul. "Why did you do it, Cara?"

"I'm sorry," I gasp, unable to contain the words or my welling tears. I know it's not him. He would never hold eye contact with me for so long, but the guilt I feel still overwhelms me.

"I thought we were friends, but I should've known," he claims, hurt crossing his features. "You don't care about me. You don't even care about yourself."

A sob heaves from my chest. He's not wrong. I want to say he is, but I have done nothing to show him I care for others, and a soul wrenching need to leave this life is something I've battled many times in my past.

An agonizing sound strangles from him, filled with a pain matching what I feel inside. "You did this," he hisses before he transforms.

Within seconds, Shauna is before me, her bright green eyes boring into me. Where they'd usually be kind with a hint of mischief is replaced with anger and blame.

I take a step forward and the magic has the dagger half way out of its perch before I snap back.

This isn't Shauna; I know this. It's Killian.

"Why'd you leave me?" Shauna reaches for me with a trembling hand.

I step back, trying to keep my distance, replacing the dagger at my side.

"I... I didn't want to," my voice shakes.

"You left me. First you kill our parents, then you abandon me." She draws her hand back into a fist against her chest with a scowl taking over her soft features.

Unwanted tears spill over. This isn't real. This isn't real. This isn't real.

"Worst of all, you're so selfish you want to take yourself from me forever. You gave up on me, on yourself. You're selfish."

"I'm... sorry." My body shakes as I continue to weep. I need this to stop. It's too much. How do I beat this trial? Do I face my fears until it stops or is there a way to win against this torment?

My sister's body morphs until she no longer stands before me, and in her place is the wounded dog from the alley.

Sadness fills his amber eyes as he lowers his head and whines. Blood drips from his wounds onto the ground; a small puddle forms within seconds. He curls into a ball, but never stops watching me.

A tingle in my chest forms, driving me forward without thought. My hand reaches for the dagger. I have no control. In my mind, I try to fight the pull of magic, to will my hand away, but it's no use. I urge my legs to backtrack, to put distance between us, but I've covered half the distance and my legs keep taking me closer. The grip is warm in my palm as I slide the blade out, keeping it hidden under my cloak.

The dog growls, the hackles of its black mane rising.

It knows. He knows. But I can't stop.

I take another step forward, readying the dagger. My eyes train on the dog's lower chest, envisioning where the heart beats beneath.

I want to scream, to tell Killian to run, but I can't. The magic stops me, holding me under the power of its will.

The dog moves onto its legs, bending into a crouch to get ready to pounce. His fangs bare when he snarls.

Before I can make it any further, he launches himself into the air.

Instinctively, the blade comes in front of me, tip pointed out to protect me, but I shut my eyes and cringe away.

I can't watch.

The feather light touch of his tail brushes the side of my cheek.

I open my eyes from surprise and see him soaring over my right shoulder, missing the blade by mere inches.

As I turn, he lands on a monstrous black entity. A featureless black creature that's twelve feet tall, thick, and semi-formless. Killian's black smoke now mimics a person, but cannot fully form one.

The dog disappears into the darkness of the creature.

It roars and throws Killian, who is now back to his usual form, out of its body.

Killian hits the ground on his side with a thud I feel in my feet.

The dagger in my hand is forgotten as I race over to him. Bending atop him, I check to see if he's okay.

His eyes are dark, bottomless, but he's awake.

"Get back." His voice is so deep and growly, I strain to understand the words.

I fall backwards as he gets up. My eyes widen in terror as he spreads his fingers and black spikes form in his palms.

With a thrust of his hands, he shoots them at the creature.

The thing absorbs them, unaffected.

"Killian," my voice is weak, "what's going on?"

"It's too strong." His voice sounds more beast than man.

I stand and face the creature with him.

The blade in my hand pulses, and the need to stab Killian in his back begins to override my train of thought. I pull my hand back, and as I swing it down, I use every ounce of mental strength for a last little whip of my wrist, and let it go.

To my relief, it soars past Killian and lands into the abdomen of the monster. It sinks in, but soon the glint of the blade emerges from the center of its chest. More and more of the weapon reveals itself, but now the sharp tip faces us.

With a roar, the beast throws his arms to the side, thrusting his chest forward, and the dagger shoots back at me.

Killian wraps his arm around my waist, hauling me out of the way. He hisses in my ear as the blade sinks into his shoulder. With one hand he reaches back and pulls it out.

The bloody weapon clatters to the ground.

Pressed against him, I can feel the immense heat radiating off Killian. His body is feverish, more than feverish, almost like he's on fire. A warning of second degree burns flashes across my mind, but he lets me go.

I fall to the ground from his sudden lack of support, my knees cracking against the stone.

The creature roars, and, in doing so, dark tendrils pull from Killian into the body of the beast.

Killian cries in agony as the black dome thins.

The crowd becomes more and more visible, and with each passing second the monster absorbs Killian's magic, the larger he becomes.

The orb dissolves completely, and Killian drops to the ground.

The monster now stands twenty feet tall and when it roars, the building shakes.

I lean forward to cover Killian's body with my own as bits of debris fall from the ceiling.

Screams erupt all around us. People flee the room, not waiting to die like the last attack in this room.

Teagan pulls a blade from who knows where and steps forward. The remaining contestants in the room follow her lead and reveal their own hidden weapons.

The beast closes the space between them in three steps. His bulky hand swipes at one fae who swings his long sword, but instead of being thrown across the room, he's absorbed into the monster.

His cry cuts off when his head goes under the darkness. He doesn't come back out.

Teagan dodges the other arm swinging in her direction. With a low spin, she swipes at the beast's left leg, but her blade moves right through the black fog.

The monster's fist careens down on her, but she rolls out of the way at the last second.

Everyone moves away now, some faster than others, as they realize fighting is futile.

Shay appears at my side. "We need to go, kid."

"But Killian," I say, still hovering above him to protect his still form.

"Leave him. It's his evil magic that's doing this," he responds, pulling at my arm and away from Killian.

I fight against his strength by digging into the ground. "But he's passed out. This isn't him. I'm not leaving without him!" I yank my arm out of his grip and crawl back over to Killian. I loop my hands under his arms and drag his deadweight across the ground. My teeth clench with each pull, but every holler of his beast pushes me forward.

Shay doesn't leave my side, watching the creature to figure his next move, but he doesn't help me with Killian either. If Shay would use his brute strength, we could get away much quicker.

I can't expect Shay to save Kilian's life, especially when he's ordered me to kill him. So, I ignore the strain of my muscles when I give another pull.

King Harbinger steps forward, squaring off with the demon.

The featureless form turns toward him and takes a realm quaking step.

The King throws his arms open wide, magic crackling in his hands. Lightning continues to build around him as the magic thickens in the air.

A few fae fall to the floor from the power building in the room. A light rain starts to fall from the ceiling.

Shay winces beside me and lands onto one knee beside me.

This is the true power of the King of *Rímor* who has ruled for centuries. This is what the fae realm both admires and fears, how he has kept the peace, and why no one has tried to win his place.

"Be gone!" King Harbinger's voice radiates through the air, piercing my ears, as his magic crackles and arcs across the space to the beast.

The second it hits the monster, Killian's body retracts. His back goes rigid, arms locking at his side like he's being electrocuted.

The monster roars, fighting the King's magic.

King Harbinger hollers and throws more magic at it by taking a step forward to brace himself.

More fae fall at the suffocating power.

I feel woozy as the magic courses across my body.

Killian's body begins to convulse, his eyes snap open, rolling into the back of his head until white replaces the dark irises.

They're killing him.

"Stop!" I scream, but the magic saps the sound before it reaches the King. I pull Killian into my lap, hugging him to my chest, as he continues to shake in my arms.

Gurgling sounds rise from his throat like he's drowning from the power.

Wetness covers my cheeks. I try to scream, try to use my powers, but the King's power sucks everything from the room like a vacuum.

The monster shrinks, but the King continues to pour his magic into it. Finally, the beast evaporates from the room and the King's electrical power along with it.

King Harbinger's shoulder sag when he releases his magic. He wheezes in a breath before looking to the soldiers that still stand. "Take care of this," he rasps, and disappears a second later.

The lights above us flicker again.

I hold Killian's motionless body against my own. I'm terrified to let him go, of what I'll find if I check for a pulse. Please, please do not let him wind up like Cadan, or worse.

Shay scoots closer to me. "We—"

I look to him with tears brimming my eyes. "Shay." My voice sounds broken.

He pauses, mouth still open. His eyes drift to the person he once considered a friend before landing back on my agonized face. He slowly stands, grabs Killian's arm, pulling him into a sitting position, and hunches to prop Killian's stomach against his shoulder. He stands with a grunt; Killian's lifeless form hanging over his shoulder.

I stay on the cold ground, trying to find the strength to stand.

"Let's go," he grunts.

"Where?" My throat aches. It hurts to speak.

"The infirmary." Shay turns and walks toward the open door, stepping over fae lying unconscious on the ground. Not dead. Thankfully.

I scurry after him, leaving the dagger and nightmares behind.

TWENTY-FIVE

L ight footsteps patter across the floor, waking me from my slumber.

I lift my head from my folded arms where I was resting on the side of Killian's bed.

The nurse quietly checks his vitals, writes a few notes on the chart at the end of the bed, and walks away.

I scoot over and snag the chart to read what she wrote. I don't understand the jargon or numbers, but I can tell that nothing's changed. With a sigh, I replace it and return to my seat.

His face is calm as he sleeps, but pale. He hasn't woken since Shay and I arrived yesterday. The doctors injected him with some various liquids, but little changed. They patched his shoulder, where my blade hit him.

I choke on my guilt as I remember my feet feeling stuck to the ground as the knife flew toward me, how his powerful arms banded around me, pulling me out of the line of fire, but he wasn't quick enough for himself. It hadn't been my doing, but it was my weapon originally meant for him, and he got hurt protecting me. Always protecting me, and I still don't understand why.

They told me not to worry, that he lost a lot of his magic and his body is recuperating. To give him a few days of rest and he'd awaken from the coma his body put him in. The doctors say it's a natural sleep that happens during these times, but I saw how he reacted to King Harbinger's magic. It wasn't natural. I can't help but wonder if he's in this state because of the King. Not that I dare voice these concerns to his loyal subjects.

Before he left me yesterday afternoon, Shay told me how fae can die if they lose all their magic. How it's as much a part of their life force as their heart beating or brain signals to the body.

The doctor said his magic was very low, but there was enough in him that he should pull through.

Originally, I was nauseous with worry to where I didn't even eat when Marley visited with muffins.

Should pull through wasn't confidence inducing, but then I'd realized the only good thing about my banshee powers. If he were going to die, I'd know.

It's the reason I haven't left his side. I can't foretell when anyone in the world is going to die, deaths occur all the time. My mind would burst from constant ringing. Which means, I need to be within a certain vicinity of them to foretell their death. If I left Killian and he took a turn for the worse, I may not know. This way, if his condition changes, I'll be aware immediately and can hopefully get him help in time.

His chest steadily rises and falls.

I match the pace.

His face seems peaceful, quiet, not filled with his usual tension and whatever weight he carries. I finally understand how someone can seem younger when their stress is gone.

A current ripples in my chest as I stare at him, and my unease builds with it. I fear it's the magic and it'll force me to kill him when he's defenseless. Thankfully, I left the knife in the throne room.

The main thing to help calm my nerves is that Shay said I can't harm him outside of a trial.

Relaxing back into my chair, I rub the temples of my throbbing head. My stomach aches, reminding me I haven't eaten or had water in a day.

Sighing, I get up, deciding to stretch my sore muscles and for distraction. The adrenaline rush along with the all-consuming power of King Harbinger from yesterday and spending the last eighteen hours in a chair has not been kind to my body.

My breath catches when I reach the corner at the end of the ward. I can't see the bed since a curtain wraps around it, but I know who's inside. I turn away from it, walking toward the front doors of the room. I worry my lip between my teeth as I pace in front of the doors.

I can do this. I have to do this. Yesterday's trial was a stark reminder of what a terrible friend I've been.

Finally finding the courage, I head to the back of the room, my eyes never leaving the white cloth. I reach my hand out and pause an inch away from it. I sip air between my teeth, and tears threaten to break free. Rolling my shoulders, I close the distance, and pull back the curtain.

Cadan's lifeless form lies on the hospital bed. His eyes are closed, his hair disheveled as always. In any other circumstance, I would assume he's simply sleeping.

I watch him as I move to the side of his bed. My bottom lip trembles. I pull the side chair closer to his bed and sit down.

I watch him for a few minutes. His pallor is better than Killian's, more his natural paleness compared to Killian's darker skin tone being unnaturally light. Carefully, I reach out to touch the back of his hand but stop.

He's avoidant with physical contact, minus brief moments between us. It doesn't feel right to initiate it, but there's a growing need to make sure he's truly okay.

My finger grazes the back of his hand. A quick gesture, ensuring he's real and alive.

It's warm. Not cold or clammy or overheating with a fever like someone would expect from someone sick in a hospital.

My hands drop into my lap and I lean forward. "I'm so sorry, Cadan," I whisper.

Killian said I'm not cursed, but with both of them in a coma in the same room, I can't help but feel the burden. At least, Killian's condition isn't my fault, but Cadan is a different story.

A tear slips out. "I never meant to hurt you."

I have no idea if he can hear me, but all I crave is to hear his timber voice chime in with some explanation of the situation. I've always been driven by my emotions, or my need to escape them, but Cadan has a way to calm me. His views, descriptions, ways of viewing the world, it's something I cherish about him.

A nurse pops her head from around the white curtain. "You shouldn't be back here," she says.

"Oh," I sit back. "Sorry, I'm worried. I…" I don't know what to say. I'm the cause of this? It's my fault he's here? Instead I settle on, "I want to know how he's doing."

The nurse steps forward, staring down at Cadan. "He's doing fine. We have seen little change over the last week."

I inhale sharply through my nose. Has he stopped getting better?

"No." The nurse reaches toward me, noticing the panic in my face, and rubs my cold arm supportively. "That's a good thing. It means he's finishing healing. The swelling went down in his brain a week ago, and his vitals have stabilized. We're waiting on him to wake up now."

"Do you know what's wrong?" I mumble. These were answers I should've gotten weeks ago and was too much of a coward to come here to get them. No wonder Cadan was the first to appear to me in yesterday's trial.

"Not fully. There was swelling of the brain, which caused bleeding from his ears and loss of consciousness. The brain is difficult to understand and there is a lot we don't know. All we can do is give him time to heal himself. If he's to wake up, he should do it soon."

"If?" I swallow the lump forming in my throat.

She gives me a sad smile. "Again, the brain is a mystery to both us and humans. Best to give him rest, but feel free to stay a few minutes longer if you want."

"Thanks," I tell the nurse before she leaves.

It's this moment I decide I will not leave *Gon'an'rit* until Cadan is better, to find out exactly what I am, and to learn to control my powers.

I stand and lean over Cadan, bringing my lips to his ear. "I promise I will do everything I can to bring you back. It's a deal." With the magic words, an electric pulse hums through my body.

I replace the white fabric curtain to give him his privacy and return to Killian's bedside. As I settle in and close my eyes to nap, a throat clears. I tilt my head further back, opening one eye to see who it is.

Shay stares down at me with a small basket hanging off his folded arms.

I would've laughed in most other circumstances, imagining his hulking self in a little red cape going to his grandmother's house with the dainty little basket hanging from his arm.

"You haven't left." It's not a question, but I shake my head anyway.

"I ran into Marley. She told me to bring this to you." He places the basket in my lap. It's filled with a muffin and a bottle of water.

I unscrew the lid and drink half the bottle within seconds. Next, I unwrap the bottom of the muffin and barely chew as I scarf it down. I lick my fingers clean and finish the rest of the water.

"Thanks," I say with a sigh as I place the basket on the ground.

Shay pulls up a chair beside mine. "Did you even taste it?" He grunts.

I shrug.

"The next trial's tomorrow."

My back goes rigid, shooting him a horrified look. "What? Already? But... but... what about the contestants? What about Killian?"

He pinches the bridge of his nose. "Always with the questions."

"Shay," I grind with annoyance. I don't have time for his games.

He sighs. "I don't know, Cara. It's my dad's will. All I know is you passed. So did Teagan and the other fae who took the test. The fae who ran from Killian's magic lost their trial. My father said if they cannot handle that, there is no way they would've passed the test of their own greatest fears."

"What about the fae who attacked the thing and was... absorbed?" To say aloud what happened to him is difficult.

"He was never recovered. Absorbed, killed, who knows what, by the magic."

"Did Killian pass?" I shoot a worried look at the still fae.

"If he doesn't awaken before the next trial, he won't," Shay states.

"What?" I white-knuckle the armrest. "That's not fair!"

"It's 100% fair. This is a competition." Shay shoots me a firm look.

"But it wasn't Killian's fault. Your father made him use his magic. Your father put him in that position, over and over again. He essentially did the trial multiple times instead of once like the rest of us, he should get an automatic pass."

"I don't know what to tell you. If he can't compete, he loses his spot. It doesn't matter how it came about. I thought you'd be happy. If he loses his spot, you don't have to kill him."

I gape at him. How could he say something like that so casually?

"Anyway, it is his fault for losing control of his magic." Shay picks imaginary dirt from under his nails.

As someone who has no control over their own magic, I feel personally affronted. "It's not that simple," I spit. "He was being pushed to his limit. It's not his fault."

"You're so quick to defend him, but he almost killed you." His tone is stern with his reminder.

"He didn't almost kill me! He saved me!"

"From where I was standing, it looked like you were stuck in an impenetrable dome with a monster three times your size that wanted to kill you. A monster made from *his* magic. The only reason it didn't was because the thing absorbed the magic of the dome and became distracted by the others in the room."

"That's... that's not what happened," I say, but my voice sounds weak, even to my ears.

"Either way, tomorrow is the last trial. Wisdom. I think my dad wants to hurry up and be done with this competition." His face hardens when he looks at me. "This'll be the most dangerous and most important trial. You need to win this."

"What if I don't compete?" I muse.

"Don't even joke about that. I haven't come this far just to lose," Shay growls.

For him to lose? Are you kidding me? I'm the one who keeps risking my life and sanity at his bidding, but it's him who has come this far? I open my mouth to give him a piece of my mind, when a raspy voice breaks my concentration.

"Who's losing what?"

I startle halfway out of my chair.

Killian's amber eyes peek between his slitted eyelids, moving between the two of us.

"You're... you're okay," I mutter.

"Shh." Killian closes his eyes, face contorting with pain. "Not so loud."

Shay snorts. "She barely spoke."

"Oh god," Killian groans. "Your terrible voice is even worse. If Cara's scream doesn't make my ears bleed, the sound of you will." He covers his ears with a partial truth of the pain he feels, but the small tilt of his lips shows his humor is still intact.

Shay rolls his eyes. "I'll find you later," he directs at me, and departs.

Once he's gone, Killian lowers his hands from his ears, turning his head to look at me. He reaches up a shaking hand and wipes away a tear I didn't realize was there.

My heart hammers against my ribs. "I'm sorry," I use my quietest whisper.

"It's not your fault, little rabbit."

"What happened?" I ask.

He scowls at my question, annoyed with an answer he doesn't seem to have. "I lost control, or my magic became unstable. I don't know…" he trails off, lowering his hand from my face.

I reach to grab it, and he watches with slight surprise in his eyes. "It's not your fault either," I say.

He sighs. "That's never happened before."

A burning question tugs at my tongue until I give in. "Why do you keep helping me?"

His eyes bore into me for a few breaths, "I owe you. A life for a life."

I burst into laughter, covering my mouth with a shocked expression.

He raises an eyebrow.

"Sorry, it's just, after everything you've done to help me, I'm pretty sure I owe you by now."

He shakes his head.

I have no idea why he thinks he owes me, but if he did, he's paid me back five times over by now.

"I need to figure out my magic before the next trial," he grumbles as he stares at the ceiling in thought.

"About that," I swallow. "The next trial is tomorrow."

"Shit," he hisses. "He's doing this on purpose."

"Who?"

"King Harbinger."

It is suspicious the King had Killian run the last trial, then have the next trial immediately after. This gives him no recovery time. The other trials had days or weeks between them.

"Why do you think he's doing this?"

"I don't know." His brows furrow.

"Will you be able to compete tomorrow?" My hands curl in my lap. I want to offer my help, but I'm unsure what I could do. It was the last trial and only one of us could win. There was, also, the small problem of needing to keep my distance so I don't kill him myself.

"I'll have to be ready, but so do you. You should get rest," he says.

"I'm fine."

His eyes trace over my face. "You have black circles under your eyes, have you slept?"

"Yeah, kind of." I squirm in my chair under his penetrating gaze.

"I need rest too." Worry crosses his face again, but he doesn't express what plagues him.

"Oh, okay." I don't want to push him. The patience of waiting for the other to open up is something we established, and I want to respect it. Whatever he's thinking, he wants to do it alone. "Well, good luck."

He frowns at me, which has me pausing in my seat.

The awkwardness builds between us. In the end we are enemies, and tomorrow we will learn who will win.

We both realize our moment as allies is a thing of the past.

My stomach clenches as I think of my deal with Shay. Please do not let it come to that.

I stand, but before I can leave, Killian gently grabs my wrist.

"Be careful tomorrow." His eyes are sharp with concern.

"You too." It might be the last time I speak to him before we are on opposing sides, and I can't think of anything more to say, so I leave.

TWENTY-SIX

My stomach heaves, expelling a dribble of stomach acid. Considering this is my third time being so nervous to where I'm getting sick, there isn't much left in my stomach.

I lean my forehead against the crook in my arm and breathe through my nose. The sour smell from the toilet hits me and I nearly retch again. With shaking hands, I pull the toilet handle, flushing away the contents. I lie down, my cheek against the cool stone floor, and close my eyes. The feel of it helps settle my stomach.

I don't think I can do this. All night I've been wracking my brain about how to win, how to help Killian, or a loophole for the contract with Shay and the competition. Add in the fear of magic taking over, forcing me to murder Killian, and the exhaustion from the past two days catching up with me, I've been a total mess.

I wasn't even able to drink my coffee this morning when it appeared on my desk. I still tried because I'm so tired from not sleeping last night, but it immediately came back up.

I have yet to find a solution. I'm so close to finishing, I'm one of four candidates who made it to the last task. To my surprise, I actually have a chance of winning and going home. But I made a promise to Cadan and sealed it in magic. So going home will happen later than I'd like anyways, and the thought of participating in one more dreadful trial is making me sick.

My stomach rolls at the dread of telling Shay I want to forfeit. With my life debt intact and his decision to have me murder Killian, I don't even know if it's an option, but I have to try. Despite getting butterflies at telling Shay this and how he will react, it still is the only idea I've run in my head that settles my mind instead of ratcheting it.

I drag myself off the ground and rinse my mouth with water. Cool water splashes over my face, which helps me wake up. My pale features stare back at me in the mirror. I've never been the epitome of health with my pale color and limp hair, but I look especially ghastly right now. I throw my hair into a messy bun.

After leaving the bathroom, I open the glass doors to the balcony, allowing the grey light of the sky that matches my mood to filter across me. It's raining harder today than in previous weeks, but I ignore it as I step outside.

My clothes soak through within seconds, but it feels good against my skin, the rain cleansing everything that's happened. As I lean against the railing, my eyes roam the rolling hills, wondering how much of this world I have yet to see. I wonder if the fairies from the ball live in trees in the forests, or if leprechauns are found at the end of rainbows. Although, sunlight is needed for there to be rainbows. So if not there, where would they be? Or are they even real?

This damn palace has been my prison from day one, except for the brief trip with Killian. My priority after today is to help Cadan, but perhaps there's a chance to do some exploring before finding a way home.

I have no doubt Shay will not help me get home if I don't win. Even if I stay in the trial, when I think of Teagan or Killian that's what I imagine a victor to look like, not me. I'm on my own, even Killian's my competition now. No one can help me but myself.

This is when the inkling to prove myself ignites, to show I can win this, but I don't know if I'm trying to prove myself to others or to myself. In the end, forfeiting is the safest and best option for everyone.

Killian is safe now, and if I go there today, there's a good chance he won't be. I can't risk it.

I need to focus on my next steps, on a way to help Cadan, and I'm assuming Shay won't assist with that either. The reason he's bothered himself with me for this long is because I'm his proxy. Once that is gone, he has no need for me. Perhaps I could talk with Marley or Killian about what to do.

Once the trial is complete, will Killian stick around? Will he still help me? He has his family he needs to care for. It was obvious how much it tore him apart to be away from them, and if he wins and gets his mother out of jail, they might need to leave so she isn't a target. At a minimum, he'd need to be there to support her. I can only imagine the trauma the woman will have to work past.

No, he's here to win the competition. I can't rely on him either.

I groan loudly, wanting to scream out my frustration, but I don't dare. My emotions are all over the place and I don't know if I'll accidentally trigger my curse, I mean magic.

A throat clears behind me.

With a squeal, I spin, slipping on the wet stone. I fall. Squeezing my eyes shut, I wait to hit the hard railing.

Strong hands grab the sides of my arms and lift me off the ground to place me back on my two feet.

Shay's somber face stares down at me.

"Thanks," I mumble. I could use this as another reason I shouldn't continue in the competition. I can't even turn around without threatening mine or someone else's life.

He steps up beside me, placing his hands on the railing, and looking across the green vista the way I was doing moments ago.

I lean my back against the rail and cross one leg over the other.

"Are you ready to go?" His deep voice rumbles.

"I," I hesitate. Best to spit it out before I lose courage. "I want to quit the competition."

He doesn't react, doesn't move; I don't even think he's breathing.

Finally, he exhales, turning to prop himself against the rail with the cross of his arms. "You owe me. You have to do this."

"Don't you think I've done enough?" My throat sticks together, and I take a shaking breath to reopen it. "I've risked my life time and time again. This isn't worth it."

"It doesn't matter if you find it worth it, you owe me a life debt and this is how you will repay it." There's an edge to his voice.

"Well, I refuse. Have me do something else."

"Kill Killian."

I blanch. "Besides that!"

He turns and glowers at me, his frame enlarging until his shadow casts over me. "Those are the two tasks that would be sufficient for me saving your life."

"I didn't ask you to do that!"

"You'd rather die?"

I don't answer, which has Shay's eye widening.

"You've got to be kidding me," he spews, anger lacing his voice.

"You don't know me. You don't know my life or what I've been through." Tears spring to my eyes and I curse them in my mind. I'm really freaking tired of crying. "You know nothing about me, nor have you tried. All you care about is winning for your father or getting revenge on Killian for your sister. Can you not see past your own self-interest?" I shout.

"Everything I do is for a reason." His body is rigid, each word seething through clenched teeth with his barely controlled temper.

"Why do you hate him so much?" I cry. "He lost her too, you know." I didn't even know her, but the pain I envision for them clenches my heart.

"He's the reason she's dead."

"What?" I blink at him in shock, my anger deflating.

"Killian's mother created a cult. They were investigating the magical instability of *Gon'an'rit* and my sister joined it. Killian and his mother convinced her to ally with this group of lunatics." He heaves a sigh, finding the courage to continue. "There was a meeting of the leaders of the different courts. It was supposed to be top secret, but Roisin told Killian's mother. Her and her followers staged a coup. They claimed it was for the good of the realm. They set off bombs in the building, and the parts that didn't get blown to pieces, they lit on fire.

Roisin was there, was a part of it. She gave them inside access to the meeting, and because of it she died in the fire. Killian was there. He walked away with a few scars, but my sister lost her life. She'd still be here if it wasn't for him, if she hadn't learned of his mother's group through him. My father is the one person I have left." His voice is thick with emotion. His eyes close, unable to handle the admission of what happened to his beloved sister.

I hug myself at the horrible story. No wonder Killian's mom got imprisoned. The King blamed her for Roisin's death, but it's hard for me to envision Killian purposefully trying to hurt his childhood love, especially with how Marley described it.

"Did you ever try talking to him about it?" I whisper.

Shay's eyes snap open, fire burning within them, which cause my hairs to stand on end. "I don't need to hear from his lips how he let my sister die, how he brought someone he loved to her death. He deserves the same, if not worse."

My heart aches for Shay's loss, for the family he craves, but it doesn't feel right. The story doesn't add up. "I'm sorry, Shay, for what happened. But I still can't do it."

"You have to."

"I don't. I have gone along with this long enough, but I don't care what happens to me if I break this contract. I'm not afraid of dying, but I will not live as your puppet any longer."

Shay's stony face surveys me, devoid of the emotions that were there seconds ago.

I face him head on, cocking my hip with my arms folded. "I'm not doing it. It's over. Move on."

"Cara." His eyes search mine. "You have to go."

"No. I. Don't!" I holler, taking a step closer. Meeting his chest with my face, I lean my head back to glare at him.

"You don't understand." He rubs the scruff on his chin.

"Then for once, why don't you try explaining something to me without me needing to pry it out of you? Let me guess, if I don't go, the contract will kill me. Again, dying is not what I fear."

"I won't let it kill you," he sighs. "I'll release you from it before I allow that."

"You could've released me from it the entire time?" I want to throat punch him.

"It is my debt to claim, so I can claim it how I see fit."

"Then claim it already!"

"Cara, you have to do this last trial," his voice booms.

"Why?" I shriek.

"The last trial is the same, every single time. It is the trial of Wisdom. You will be asked a series of questions, of scenarios, and how you answer will bring you closer to your goal."

I roll my eyes. "Aside from the first test, I'm pretty sure this is the easiest one. I don't understand why it's necessary I compete when I just told you I quit."

He searches my face, his mouth opening and closing as though trying to search for the right words. "There's a catch."

"Okaaaay."

"There's a distraction technique. With each question you get wrong, the person you care about most in this world gets closer to death," he finishes.

The tension in my body eases with a laugh. "Well, thank goodness Shauna's on Earth."

Shay says nothing.

"She's on Earth, right?" I pause, the humor dissipating from my body.

Still no response. Instead his face looks apologetic.

"She's... here?" My mind whirls at the possibility of my sister being here, but my stomach clenches at what Shay is telling me. "She'll be hurt if I don't go?" My eyes plead for him to tell me it's not true.

He's silent for a moment before telling me my worst nightmare. "She'll die."

I grab the banister for support as I fight the need to crumple to the ground. Oh god, Shauna is here, and in danger, all because of me. The only way to save her is to do the trial. "If I don't win?" I wheeze.

"You can still save her."

Relief barely registers past my fear. My hands tremble as I clench them into fists.

Shay is right, I have to compete.

TWENTY-SEVEN

I scan the arena as I walk toward the stage where the King sits on a throne and the council lines the same table to the right. My sister is nowhere in sight and my stomach clenches at what they've done with her.

The area has been transformed again. The forest and creek are gone, instead a large pond resides to the left of the large stage. The stands are lower than during the battle trial, and the crowd huddles in the seats closest to the King, leaving the back half of the arena empty.

There are less fae here than I would've expected, especially with this being the last trial. I assume a majority of the crowd is here to support family or friends, and with most of the fae out of the competition there is no reason to stick around. They don't want or care to know who wins the wish if it's not who they were rooting for. Sore losers, in my opinion.

There are four circles on the ground, lined in a row to face the King. Teagan takes the second from the right. The fourth fae, whose name I haven't memorized, takes the other middle circle to the left of Teagan.

I take the circle on the furthest left, closest to the dark lake. As I step in, I smile at the male fae beside me.

He shoots me a scathing look. Scars cover his face and wisps of brown hair escape the hood protecting him from the rain.

I open my mouth to offer my name, competitors don't have to be destined to be enemies, but am interrupted before I speak.

"Switch places with me."

Over my shoulder, Killian stares down at me. There's some color back in his complexion, but he doesn't hold himself with his usual power that seems it'll explode out of him at any moment.

"What?" I squint up into his serious face.

"Switch places with me." He points to the circle at the other end, on the far side of Teagan.

"Why?"

"Please, just do as I ask."

"Fine," I huff.

Weirdo.

I stalk out of my circle, but stop short when Killian hobbles into it. Thank goodness this test isn't about physical ability. I'm equally thankful I don't have a dagger on me.

Before we left, Shay tried to give me another dagger. In fact, he wouldn't let me leave until I took it. But somehow, after we separated at the entrance, the blade seemed to slip into a row of bushes. How in the world could that have possibly happened? I smirk to myself.

Once I enter the circle on the far side, the four rings light up a pale blue. The magic shoots from the ground into the sky, encasing us in its glow. I expect it to dim, but it doesn't. Tentatively, I reach my hand forward.

"I wouldn't do that if I were you," Teagan hisses under her breath.

I drop my hand, taking a half step back before I remember I'm surrounded by the shield. I wonder at her warning, at the magic circling me.

King Harbinger has a lingering smile on his lips as he watches me, waiting to see what I'll do.

My fists ball at my side, and I hold his stare until his shoulders shake lightly with a chuckle before he looks away.

Cara one, King zero.

The King clears his throat, his magic amplifying the sound, which causes the stadium to quiet.

"May the blessing of light be on you," he speaks lazily.

"Light without and light within," everyone choruses.

This time, I press my lips into a hard line. I don't know what King Harbinger has up his sleeve, but I don't trust him and I will put up even mild defiance. If I could, I'd walk up there right now and demand he return my sister to me. If only it was that simple. I need to play the game, his game. I need to play to get her back; it is the only way. Shay had admitted as much.

"Welcome to the final trial of the *Naim* Competition," King Harbinger announces.

The crowd cheers.

"The last trial is Wisdom. Each contestant will be faced with three scenarios. Each answer will get them closer to their success, but each failure leads them to losing the person they care most for in this world." The King looks at me. "Or any."

He snaps his fingers, a cruel smile forming on his lips, and a couple feet above the lake four cages appear. Inside each one is a person.

Teagan hisses between her teeth, but I'm too distracted by a wailing little boy to see why.

In a cage furthest from the stage, Hux holds the bars, pressing his face between them, crying for help. His face is beet red and when he sees Killian in the line, he reaches out for him. Hiccupping sobs break his pleas, and when his big brother doesn't come to help him, he cries harder.

My hand presses against my chest, the pain there from my own heart breaking in two. Slowly, I lean forward a little to check on Killian.

His usual amber eyes are jet black as he stares at Hux. His jaw ticks and his fists are white with rage. He doesn't take his eyes off his brother, as though with the will of his mind he can get him out.

In the cage beside Hux is a wrinkled, elderly woman who hunches over her cane. Her eyes land on the male fae on the other side of Teagan and she gives him a curt nod.

The third cage holds a woman with curly brown hair. Her fierce gaze is locked on Teagan and I watch as her lips form the words *I love you. You got this.*

My eyes tear away, feeling like I'm trespassing on an intimate moment. Finally at the end of the line in a cage closest to the stage, I see her.

Her hair is shorter, and she's lost weight. She searches the surrounding area with giant, bright green eyes. Her mouth hangs open in shock as she rattles the bars of the cage. The second she spots me, she gasps, her hands dropping to her sides, stepping away until her back presses against the far side of the cage.

Instinctually, I step forward, reaching for her. My hand meets the barrier, and a bolt of electricity zaps through my body. It sears my nerve endings and a faint cry escapes me before I release myself from its hold. A ragged breath wheezes into my aching lungs.

Shauna has herself pressed back against the front bars, fear coating her face as she watches me. Her lips are moving, but the blood pounding in my ears makes it hard to hear her.

"First up," King Harbinger interjects, clearly satisfied with his reveal. "Cara Winters."

My body goes rigid. Shay didn't tell me much. All I know is Shauna's life is at stake and it's up to me to save her. I don't care if I win by this point, just as long as I can get Shauna out of this.

"You're on a sinking ship," the King starts.

My eyes bat in surprise. Riddles? Isn't that repetitive of wit?

He continues, "An accident forces everyone to abandon ship. As people line up for lifeboats, you realize there's three boats with different sets of people. Do you choose to join the boat composed of families with young children, the boat of seniors who obviously could use your help, or the boat of young, strong people, with whom you might have a better chance of survival?"

Not a riddle, a dilemma. It's obvious right away there is no perfect answer, but I have to give one. I shouldn't choose the last boat, too selfish. Although, this trial is about Wisdom, so it would be wisest for my life to choose that boat. However, these are virtues of the fae, and the virtuous thing would be to help others.

I look to the four people in cages, my stomach in knots. Hux continues to cry, the elderly woman's cane shakes as she puts more of her weight on it. The cages are big enough to sit in. I don't understand why she wouldn't sit down instead of struggling to stand. She could use the bars to support herself when getting up and down.

Teagan's person's face is stoic, not giving away any thoughts or emotions. My heart lurches at Shauna, the way she stands with confidence while suspiciously watching the world around her.

"The...the boat of elderly," I announce as my gaze moves back to the old woman. I would be most useful there. The boat with the families has adults to help the kids.

"Incorrect," the King bellows.

"What?" I cry out. How can there be a wrong or right choice in this circumstance? Will they not even allow me to explain my reasoning?

"In *Gon'an'rit*, we value a life to be lived more than one that already has been. Protecting children and the lives they have yet to live should take priority."

"That seems rather cold," I retort.

The crowd doesn't hear me, but I know the other contestants do by the snap of their heads, and the deathly glare the King gives me says he did too.

Without breaking eye contact, he snaps his finger.

This time it's me who looks away first when there's a splash of water followed by a shriek— Shauna's shriek.

Her cage has lowered, submerging her to her knees in the water. She stares at her feet in shock before grabbing the bars and shaking them until she screams through her clenched teeth. Her cage is the closest to the stage, the closest to me, and to the King, whose eyes twinkle while he observes her.

He doesn't miss a beat, moving onto the next scenario. "A moving train has lost its brakes and is coming to a fork in the tracks. You can pull a lever to decide whether it goes left or right. On one side," he eyes my sister, "is a dear family member. One the other are five strangers. Who do you choose to save?"

Another question for me? I guess we aren't taking turns. I gulp at the lump of panic of what will happen if I get it wrong. I close my eyes, but my sister's angered shouts pierce the air as she continues to batter at the cage with Hux's sniffles in the background.

If Killian got his first question wrong, the water would be to Hux's chest. Does this mean he has fewer chances to save him? Will they drown if they go under the water? Would they actually kill these people simply because they don't agree with our answers? Rage simmers inside me until my hands shake at my side.

"Family," I whisper, pulled by those in front of me. I don't know if it is the answer the King is looking for, but I know the fae honor the virtue of Truth, and saving my family member is my truth, even if it's incorrect.

I know my answer is wrong when the King snaps, causing a gasp to rip from Shauna's throat.

The water is to her chest now. Her hands grab the side of the cage like a lifeline. One more incorrect answer and she'll be under. She may be able to swim up and keep breathing if the whole thing doesn't submerge in the water.

My stomach plummets when a ringing develops in my head.

No.

I stare at Shauna in horror, tears pooling in my eyes. Oh god, please no.

"You're a monster," I seethe to the King.

The sound increases in my head, causing me to flinch. My muscles are tight from the agony over everything that has happened. Taken into another realm, learning I'm not who I thought, joining this competition, almost dying, killing; this wasn't okay. But I was always okay at the thought of risking my own life. It mattered so little to me until this point. But for the people I care about get hurt repeatedly, to risk losing my sister, the only family I have left. This is too much.

The pain increases in my skull, the tension in my body builds until I can't handle it any longer.

My fingers wind into my hair along my scalp, balling it into my clenched fists, and I release a blood-curdling scream. Screw this competition, screw this world, screw the king. I scream and scream, praying I'm not hurting Shauna or any other innocent, but I'm fearful she'll die if I do nothing and this drives me. I scream for so long I bend at my waist to release every bit of air from my lungs.

I place my hands on my knees, taking a ragged breath through my nose. I'm nervous to look up, to see who I hurt.

The ringing still resounds through my skull, and part of me fears I'm the one behind it.

Peering through the black strands of my hair, I can see Teagan's standing form beside me. She's not on the ground, which is a good sign. I stand upright, and King Harbinger's cocky smirk greets me, completely untouched by my powers.

The crowd murmurs amongst themselves at my odd reaction. Everyone is unharmed, I'm simultaneously relieved and pissed.

"Moving on," the King acts as though nothing big has happened.

I'm not a threat, not to him, and he's proving that not only to me, but to all the fae. He is the strongest fae who has ever ruled, and he's reminding us all.

"You and someone you care deeply about are in a competition," mirth fills his eyes, "and only one of you can win. You either must kill him... Sorry, I mean must kill them, and take the victory for yourself, or allow them to win when they kill you."

I fight my need to eyeball Killian, to see his reaction, to feel the comfort of his gaze. This is merely a question, not a threat. I want to remind myself of this, but I don't dare turn his way.

The King knows more than I realized. Not that I should've expected anything less. I wipe away the wrinkles of my shirt to calm myself, trying to think through this situation. What is the correct answer? I try to envision the answer he wants from me to pass, but again there is only one answer that feels correct to me, one path I would follow.

"I'd forfeit my life."

The King leans forward, eyes blazing as he flashes a big smile. "Wrong."

Shauna's eyes are wide in terror.

The buzzing reverberates through my head, causing it to become almost unbearable. Tears leak from my eyes when I realize the truth. I'm about to cause my sister's death.

Her eyes find mine. "I love you," she shouts.

I barely hear it with the rising sound in my head. All I want to do is squeeze my eyes shut, to throw myself into the barrier around me, and end this before I see my sister die. But I don't. I need to face what I've done.

King Harbinger raises his hand, readying to snap, when an explosion erupts on stage. He flies backwards.

I duck with the massive boom.

The barrier protects me from the blast the same way it protected everyone from my scream. The blue magic flickers out as the screams begin.

Half the stage is blown to pieces along with part of the stands. A body is on the ground ten feet away from me. Fae run for their lives with a few disappearing in thin air.

Men in dark cloaks, the same ones from the throne room attack, swarm the area.

"Get my son!" King Harbinger shouts to some of his guards as he pries his bleeding body off the ground. A gash on his head oozes blood down his face, making him look that much more terrifying. He takes a step, but grabs his side where more blood drips between his fingers. He looks between his wound and his people. With another step, he lifts his left hand, magic crackling between his fingers, and he lobs the orb at the closest hooded figure.

The figure dodges, running toward the king as he reforms another magic sphere.

King Harbinger winces when he takes a step back, the magic he was forming in his hand sparking out. With a frown, his gaze sweeps one last time over the panicking crowd before he phases and disappears.

Coward.

The side of the stage that exploded is the area closest to the cages, closest to Killian.

The cages were blasted from their spots. The one with Teagan's person is submerged in the lake, only the flat metal top is visible on the water.

Teagan is already racing to the water, throwing away the heavy sword off her hip as she dives into the water.

My stomach leaps into my throat as Killian drags himself to Hux's cage lying on the ground fifteen feet from the lake. Hux's wails have stopped and his limp form is in a ball on the grass beside the cage.

Shauna's cage is tipped on its side, half on the shore and half in the water.

My legs carry me forward, picking up pace until I'm running to where she is. I fall to the ground beside the cage. Her eyes are closed, legs in the lapping water. Her arm rests at an odd angle and her pant leg is soaked in blood.

I pull at the metal, but nothing happens. I search for a door, a latch, a lock, anything. But there's nothing.

"Shauna! Wake up, Shauna!" I call her in panic, but receive no response.

My heart jack rabbits as I frantically reach to her through the cage. Pressing myself against the bars until the metal digs into my shoulder, I can just reach her hand. I grab it and drag her closer to me, trying not to retch when her other arm falls to the side unnaturally. I press two fingers against her wrist, and relief washes through me when I feel her pulse.

"Killian!" Hux's tiny voice shouts. I look over the cage as he sits up and throws his little arms around his brother's shoulders.

Killian kneels on the grass, hugging his brother with one arm. He pulls away and talks quickly to his little brother.

Hux's face is set in determination as he nods. He continues to listen before nodding again and turning to run to the woods.

Killian searches the area, his dark eyes tracing over everything until they land on me. He must see how terrified I am because he doesn't hesitate before heading my way, eating up the distance in seconds.

"Move," he says as he stands beside me.

I scoot back on my knees, giving him space.

He presses his hands on the bar. His inky magic slithers over the bars until there's a click and the bars closest to us disappear.

I launch myself into the cage and shake Shauna.

Killian places a hand on my shoulder for me to stop. He bends down, scooping Shauna into his arms, careful of her bad arm, and moves her to an area of grass further away from the lake where he places her down gently.

I lean over her, searching her face, my anxiety stabbing at me until I'm trembling.

Shauna's green eyes peek out as she comes to. She coughs a few times, her good hand moving to her ribs. "What happened?" She croaks.

I burst into tears, throwing myself on top of her to hug her.

She returns it, pulling me closer with her one hand. "I thought you were dead," her choked voice says.

"I thought you were going to die." My throat closes with all my emotions.

"Where are we?"

I pull back, eyes roaming over my sister who's here, with me, now. "It's a long story."

"You two need to get out of here," Killian rumbles from the side. He continues to watch our surroundings, but his body is rigid, fighting to stay by our side instead of joining the fray.

"I need to find Shay," I say.

"Forget him," Killian snaps. "The competition is over. Your deal is done."

I pay him no attention, focusing on my sister. "Can you stand?"

"I think so," Shauna sits up slowly.

I help her to her feet, but she favors the leg coated in blood. I try to ignore her arm as it hangs lower than the other, limp at her side.

A hooded figure races toward us. Killian faces him as I step in front of my sister to block her from his view.

Right now, I wish I hadn't ditched my dagger, but I have full faith in Killian's combat skills. It's only one man.

"Sir!" The figure calls to Killian, slowing to a walk as he gets closer. "We've secured the premise. Your route is clear."

I blink at Killian.

"Good," he tells the attacker. "Start relieving men. The King was hurt and fled. He shouldn't be a problem. Leave enough men to make our presence known and keep everyone at bay until we're cleared."

The man nods.

"You know the sign," Killian adds.

The hooded fae runs off in the direction he came, calling to others hidden by their dark cloaks.

"This… this was your doing?" I choke out.

Killian turns, his amber eyes momentarily showing sorrow before hardening into determination. "I'm sorry. Take your sister and go to the woods. It'll be safest there."

He was in charge of this? Was he in charge of the last attack too? I gasp when something clicks in my brain.

"You knew the bomb was going to go off! That's why you switched places with me, so I wasn't in the circle closest to it!"

He frowns, but makes no attempt to contradict me. "Go, little rabbit."

The bomb was directly next to Shauna's cage. She's hurt because of him. He created a coup, and for what? Dozens of fae are dead.

I reach my hand back and slap him across the face. My hand stings from the impact.

A pink handprint develops on his cheek. When he looks at me, there is no apology, no remorse, but he still says words I don't think he truly means. "I'm sorry."

I want to slap him again. Scratch that— punch him. My right fist balls, and I'm ready to lodge a blow, but his dark magic consumes his body.

I step back, bumping into Shauna, afraid of what he'll do.

The mist shrinks, taking him with it, until a shaggy, dark haired dog with amber eyes stands in his place. The dog from the alley.

He gives me one last mournful look, and dashes away toward the castle, leaving me to blink after him in shock.

A few hundred yards away, Marley races to us. Her eyes catch on Killian, but she continues past him to us.

A memory of Killian in the hospital echoes through my head. *I owe you. A life for a life.*

TWENTY-EIGHT

"Cara!" Marley's panic-stricken face enters my peripheral. "Are you okay? Where's Killian going?"

"Forget him," I sneer. Anger envelops my pain from his betrayal. "What're you doing here?" I ask, focusing on her.

She looks panic stricken with her wide blue eyes, her cheeks tinged pink from running, and her usual pristine hair is disheveled, otherwise she looks untouched. "I was in the far stands when the bomb went off. I came to help you." She takes in the state of my sister, eyes landing on her arm. "It looks dislocated."

"It feels dislocated," my sister grumbles.

"I need you to take my sister. Go to the woods and wait there." Killian sent Hux in that direction and he told me that's where it would be safest. I may be angry, but I still trust his word, at least when it comes to keeping his family safe.

"What about you?" Marley raises her eyebrow.

"I need to find Shay," I explain.

"There is absolutely no way in hell we are separating when I've just gotten you back," Shauna interjects, stepping closer to me.

I place my hand on her good shoulder. "Shauna," I sigh. "Long story short, we are not on Earth but in the fae realm. I'm a banshee and there was an attack on the King. There's a chance he may blame it on my friend because the King thinks we mean to overthrow him." My heart races, remembering King Harbinger telling the guards to retrieve his son.

Marley gasps. "Shay."

I nod at her. "Please, I need to know my sister is safe from everyone. When I find him, I'll find you. Stay hidden, but if you are in a part of the woods where you can still see the arena, we will meet up."

"Okay." She steps closer to my sister who takes a step back.

"Yeah, I'm pretty sure I'm in shock because you made it seem like we're surrounded by a bunch of fairies," Shauna softly chuckles.

"Shaun, I know you're in shock. But please do this for me," I plead.

Her eyes narrow into slits and lips purse.

I'm 99% sure she's going to deny this and force herself to stay with me.

She sways on her feet, causing both Marley and I to reach out and steady her. Crap, she's really not doing well.

Marley sees the worry on my face. "I can set her shoulder and stop the bleeding. I used to do it all the time for Killian and Shay when we were kids."

"Thanks." I lean forward, giving my sister a light hug. "I love you. I'll find you soon."

"Oh, hell no!" She calls, reaching to grab my wrist when I pull back, but I dash out of the way.

Refusing to second guess myself or allow her to change my mind, I run toward the castle. I sprint past fae, including a handful of the ones in cloaks, and the guards who fight them, but no one bothers me or tries to attack.

Where would the King take Shay? Would he put him in the dungeons? I don't even know where Shay's room is, so I can't check his quarters. In fact, I've learned very little about who Shay is as a person. The most I've learned was from Marley, not him. Months with him, mostly with him infuriating me, but I have learned little to nothing about him. I may be in this situation because of Shay, but I now know about his history. And now knowing Killian was behind all of this gives me more faith in Shay's too. I was so blinded with my life debt, I didn't give him a chance.

Inside the castle, my shoes squeak on the ground as I round a corner. My lungs burn. I find a set of stairs and take them two at a time.

I should've listened to him and killed Killian when I had the chance. He hurt Roisin, innocent fae, and my sister. The emptiness in the pit of my stomach is distracting.

Shay's tactics of using me as a proxy may not have been the best, but he never set out to hurt anyone, and him forcing me to murder Killian was for my protection. I see that now.

I move into a part of the palace I've been once before— the King's personal wing. This is the one place I can think King Harbinger would bring Shay. To his own quarters. Where else would he feel the safest hiding while he interrogates his son?

There are fewer guards than normal. I assume they're busy with the attackers.

I pause at the opening to the dining area. This was where Shay took me to in this area of the castle. Honestly, I'm surprised I found my way at all. I didn't realize I had a layout of the palace in my head until I was racing through the halls, knowing where to turn to move away from the throne room, from the kitchens, and to the part that held the King. And hopefully Shay.

I breathe deeply, my lungs burning, and press my fingers into my side where there's a cramp. Where do I go from here?

Urgency twitches my muscles to take action, but I can't blindly run around, especially with Shay on the line.

I search in both directions of the hall, looking to my left and then my right. I listen for a clue, for a sound to tell me a direction, but there's nothing except my harsh breathing and pounding heart.

Think, Cara, think.

If I turn right, it will take me closer to the kitchens. That would be good for access to food, but it's also closer to the front of the castle. With the King's powers, he doesn't need to be closer to food.

The left takes me deeper into the castle, an area I don't know as well, but deep underneath, under the ground, lies the dungeons. I would worry being closer to prisoners, worry about them sneaking out and seeking revenge, but the King relishes in his display of power. Living above those he's imprisoned, showing his prowess aligns more with the King I know.

I walk down the left hallway, not inching along as time is of the essence, but I go slowly enough to help keep my steps quiet.

The area is bland, similar to the dining area. There are no windows or openings, and a lot less doors. It was designed for limited entry and exit, rising hundreds of feet in the air, for protection.

Surprise flickers through me the more I traipse deeper down the hall. I still have yet to come across a single guard. I know they're busy, but I still expected more. I round a corner and a sizzle of magic tickles across my skin with rising goosebumps.

A burnt taste of raw power forms on the tip of my tongue. I take three more steps, and the power grows, vibrating my bones. There's no doubt in my mind it's King Harbinger.

The power multiplies as I tiptoe forward until my teeth clench and hands fist from the raw magic flowing over me.

No wonder there are no guards around here. Each step becomes more painful. I stop in front of a closed door where a blue light emanates from the crack on the bottom. As I reach my hand out, a crackle of lightning shocks me.

I don't know what I'll find behind the door and nerves slither through my stomach like worms in a pile of dirt. Fear presses on me to turn and run, but determination keeps my feet planted.

I didn't come this far to leave Shay behind. We've been partners through all of this, and he needs me.

I take a deep breath, holding it as I twist the handle and push the door open.

Magic blasts through me, causing me to take a couple steps back, and I grit my teeth as I push against it.

King Harbinger looks up from where he stands in the middle of the room, magic of various colors radiating off of him. His wounds have healed, even the blood that covered him before has evaporated. He holds his hands over Shay, who lies on the ground.

Shay's eyes are open, anger and pain simmering in them as he stares at his father, but he can't move.

My hand covers my mouth as a gasp slips out. The King is hurting him, and I've seen this before. The magic around the King grows stronger, flowing from Shay to him.

He's sapping Shay's magic, his life force, like he did to Killian during the courage trial. I need to get to them. If he absorbs all of Shay's magic, he'll die.

I widen my stance, bracing myself as I shove myself against the invisible barrier. My teeth chatter together from the raw power.

King Harbinger's laugh booms through the air. "You think you can go against the strongest fae in the realm?"

"Stop, you're going to kill him!" I scream.

Shay's color drains from him and his eyes droop for a moment.

"I am his King. I am his father. What is his, is mine!" He shouts, the power from him rising.

I cover my eyes as the colors surrounding him grow brighter.

"No one can take my reign. No one can best me at my own game!"

Shay's hard form slumps further into the ground, weakening.

I move closer to Shay, to the King, but each time I take a step, electricity pierces up my feet and through the rest of my body. This is only the remnants of the power between those two, I can only imagine what Shay is going through. The pain lacerating every cell in my body has dark spots pulsing in my vision, pushing me closer to unconsciousness. A high pitched ring forms in my mind.

Oh no.

Shay's going to die, or me, or both of us. Either way, this is bad.

The ringing increases.

I need to do something. Now. Before it's too late.

I sip oxygen into my lungs, bracing myself against the power in the air. After I've taken in as much as I can, I give a little prayer. *Please don't kill Shay.*

And I scream.

My eyes close as I let every emotion consume me. My fear for Shay. My anger at Killian. My worry for my sister. I allow myself to loathe what my life has become, but embrace who I am.

I am strong. I am fae. I am *Beansidhe.*

I scream until my throat hurts and with each passing second, the sound diminishes and magic wanes until it extinguishes with light static electricity tickling my skin.

I open my eyes to see the King face down on the ground beside Shay.

After a staggering breath, I shuffle over to Shay. Please let him be alive.

I press my fingers to his throat, and a stunned sob-laugh escapes me when his pulse beats against my fingertips. I did it. I didn't kill him.

His hands flex against the stone, lying flat against it as he presses himself onto his knees. His head hangs against his panting chest.

"Shay," I whisper.

"Why'd you come?" His stricken face rises. It's pale, and the usual fierceness in his eyes is dull.

"It was the right thing to do."

"You owe me nothing." He grimaces, hanging his head once more in defeat.

"I owe you my life. Isn't that the whole reason you brought me here?" I tilt my head and smile, trying to lighten the mood.

"Consider it repaid." He lifts a leg and rises onto his shaking feet. His body rocks from side to side and when he's about to teeter over.

I wrap my arm around his waist, allowing him to lean against me. The weight of him almost topples us both, but I lock my knees to brace my stance from the added burden.

"We need to go." I grip Shay, moving us to the door. I stop, "What should we do about him?" I look over my left shoulder at King Harbinger's still crumpled form. His back slowly rises and falls, even breaths to indicate life. I used my powers and didn't kill anyone.

"Leave him," Shay states.

"Are you sure? He's not dead."

He shakes his head. "Let's go."

"Okay, I have Marley and my sister waiting in the woods for us." I help guide him into a staggering walk. He has a slight limp, still weak from his loss of power. With how much was radiating off the King, I'm surprised he didn't pass out.

"We can't leave yet." His voice is stern and holding no room for debate.

My eyebrows shoot to my hairline. "What? Why?"

"We need to get Cadan."

My feet stop working and I stare up at him with my mouth hanging open. I forgot about him. Again. Even after my promise to not leave until he got better. The diversion of my sister and worry for Shay completely distracted me from my other friend.

I push my bitterness aside, instead focusing on my appreciation for Shay for thinking of him. It's unexpected, especially from him, but if there's anything I've learned, it's how there's a lot more to this man than I realized.

"King Harbinger, my father," the admission of their relation comes out strained, "has been stealing magic. I don't know why or for how long, but I have a bad feeling that's why Cadan hasn't woken yet. He received a high score on his Power trial. I wouldn't be surprised if my father saw this as an opportunity."

My stunned expression blanks my face as I search for what to say. Instead, a single word strains out. "Okay."

I allow Shay to lead us, unsure how to get to the infirmary from this part of the castle. We move faster than I would've anticipated, but I can tell Shay is pushing himself by his labored breathing.

Shock still clings to my mind. I've never seen Shay look out for anyone but himself. Not only is he going out of his way to help someone, it's someone I care for, a person I have a connection to, not him.

Anger at myself resurfaces. Worst. Friend. Ever. Even if I hadn't made a deal to Cadan's sleeping form, I would be staying until he's better, now more than ever. Regret may be my driving force right now, but that's the least I deserve.

Shay's weight presses further on my side.

I grunt, moving my arm to wrap more firmly around his midsection, adjusting his position so I can help him.

"Um, Shay?" I bite my lip. "How're we going to get Cadan out?"

Shay can't walk by himself, and I can't carry both him and Cadan. I don't even think I could carry only Cadan. I can barely assist Shay with walking, and there's no way Shay can do it.

We round a corner, both of us mulling over our predicament for a solution, and we nearly bump into Killian.

A frail woman, nothing but dark skin draped over bones, long wavy black hair, and brown eyes stands to his right. The resemblance is unmistakable. It's his mother.

His eyes flick between Shay and me, eyebrows stitching together in concern.

My lips press into a grimace, clenching my jaw until it hurts. I want to scratch that worried look right off his face. How dare he fret about us after everything he's done. I shoot daggers at him, wishing my powers could manifest real ones.

"Do you need help?" Killian inquires.

"Yes."

"No."

Shay and I speak at the same time.

"Absolutely not," I emphasize, giving Shay a stern look for him to stay quiet.

"We need someone to carry Cadan," Shay murmurs to me.

My arms tremble as anger courses through my body. This is the last person I want helping us. I don't even know if he would help us. And of all people, how could Shay trust him right now? If we ran into a guard, he'd probably throw Cadan's body at them so him and his mother could escape.

"Let me help." Killian's piercing gaze pours over me.

I bite my inside cheek, wanting to scream. This isn't fair. Why'd we have to run into him, of all people? Isn't there another way? I wrack my brain, but I can't find any other solution. The hospital beds aren't on wheels.

"Fine," I bite out.

Killian's eyes flash with hope. Stabbing them with a dagger sounds good to me right about now.

"Don't think for a single second I trust you. There is nothing, *nothing*," I say, "that will change this."

Shay shifts against me and I ignore the surprised look he gives me.

"Let's go," Shay breaks the awkward silence, taking a step forward, and forcing us past Killian and his mother.

TWENTY-NINE

N o one is in the ward when we enter. Killian and his mother follow closely behind us as we shuffle to the back of the room. We haven't spoken a single word to one another.

Shay shoves the curtain to the side, revealing Cadan peacefully asleep on his bed.

His chest rises and falls steadily. There doesn't seem to be any changes since yesterday, but at least he's not worse. The idea of King Harbinger sucking away Cadan's powers, keeping him in this coma, allowing him to lose his chance to win the *Naim* Competition, makes me want to march back to the room and kick him in his disgusting face.

We move aside as Killian steps forward. He pulls Cadan into a sitting position before hauling him into a fireman's carry. He moves swiftly, the weight and height of Cadan having little impact on him despite his weakened state from the last trial.

We head back the way we came, finding a set of stairs leading us to a side entrance. Once outside, the ringing in my head picks back up as we hurry to the tree line.

Killian leads the way with his mother close behind him. Shay and I bring up the rear. We don't tell him where to go since his brothers are hiding in a similar area.

Again, we pass cloaked figures and guardsmen. Every time a guard heads for us, one of the hooded attackers intervenes, distracting the guard, which ends with the guard falling from unconsciousness or death.

I cringe at the throbbing in my head, my powers growing with each new body added to the ground. A pit forms in my stomach as I glare at the back of Killian's head. I don't care if he helps us or grovels at my feet; he is the cause of this. I don't care if it was to save his mother. All he needed to do was win the trials. No one needed to die. Part of me wants to ask why, wants to understand, but no reasoning is worth all these deaths.

Once we make it to the forest, Shay unwraps his arms from my shoulders and leans against a tree. Killian lowers Cadan's limp form to the ground.

I look at Shay. "We still have no way to carry him."

"We need my horse," he comments.

Oh, his palomino. Both him and Cadan could ride it. If needed, him and my sister could take turns.

I nod in agreement. "Okay, I'll sneak back—"

"No," Killian interjects.

"You aren't a part of this." I don't dare look at him. I don't know whether I'll cry or scream or punch him, but nothing good will come of it.

"I've got it," he says.

Shay watches him over my shoulder and gives a nod.

I don't feel Killian's presence leave, and eventually my curiosity gets the best of me and I turn my head.

He stands with his eyes closed, his dark eyebrows knot with concentration. After a couple moments, his shoulders relax and his eyes snap open. "It's done."

What the… what's done?

"Let's find the others while we wait," Shay adds.

We decide as a group Killian and I should split up, leaving Cadan, Shay, and his mother to rest in hiding while we search the tree line. I insisted we go in opposite directions, refusing to be alone with him, and to my surprise he agreed.

After five minutes of trekking, I hear a rustle. Unsure if it's friend or foe, I halt and plant my feet deeper into the soft ground, bringing my hands in front so I'm prepared to flee or fight.

A head of blonde hair pokes out from behind some bushes.

"You're okay!" Marley stands up, relief washing over her face. She reaches into the bushes and helps my sister to her feet.

Her arm is bandaged against her body using part of Marley's dress, while another strip wraps around her thigh to staunch the bleeding.

Within seconds, we're in each other's arms. Shauna's here. She's safe. I start to cry.

"I'm so sorry. I'm so sorry you got dragged into this," I snot into her shoulder.

She rubs my back with her hand, her voice choking with her own tears. "I can't believe you're alive. I waited for weeks before I… I'm sorry I gave up on you."

Finally, we pull apart, our eyes puffy and red, and when we see each other's faces we laugh. Gross, mucusy, hiccupping cackles that make us seem so insane Marley shifts uncomfortably, which causes us to laugh harder.

Our laughter dies off, and as the weight of everything settles on us we become solemn.

"We should join the others," I say.

"Show us the way." Marley motions for me to lead them.

By the time we return, Killian is already back with his brothers, who are in a group hug with their mother. Hux sobs into her chest and Jasper's bottom lip trembles as he tries to act like a young man.

"It's okay, my sweet boys, I'm here," she whispers to them, causing Jasper to release all the emotions he was holding back. Despite towering over his mother, he curls himself around her. Her arms encircle them both, tears lining her own eyes.

Killian watches them, leaning against a tree four feet away.

When we step into the small clearing, he straightens, his eyes finding mine.

I help Shauna sit down next to Shay and she glances at Cadan's body.

A soft whinnying sound comes from a distance. I turn to see the palomino trotting over a green knoll, headed straight for us. It enters the woods where we stand, and Shay pushes himself off the tree to meet her part way.

The horse drops its head against Shay, who leans his forehead against the horse as he pets down her neck. I see his lips move, soothing his horse.

Shay turns to me. "Your life debt is complete. I will take you and your sister home."

"Do you have enough energy to take them safely?" Killian steps forward.

I glare at him. "I don't need your help or your worry."

Shay still responds to him. "Yes. I'll have enough to get there and back. Beithíoch will take me to where I need to go." He gestures to his horse.

"You should go to *Tuatha*," Killian suggests.

Shay nods his agreement. "But first?" He raises an eyebrow at me, waiting for me to leap at the chance to go home.

Home. He's offering to take both me and my sister home. I can put all of this behind me, but my throat closes. I want nothing more than to do exactly that, pretend this was nothing but a horrible fever dream, but I can't.

"I can't." I peer at Cadan. "I made a promise to someone and I won't, I can't, leave until I fulfill it."

"I'll take care of him," Shay offers as he leans his weight against his horse, who happily supports him.

I shake my head. "I made a deal. It's not that I only won't leave, but I can't," I emphasize.

"What?" Killian stalks over to me, fury lighting his face. "What deal did you make?"

His sandalwood scent envelops me and I take a steadying breath. Something I once found intoxicating is now infuriating.

Shay stands a little more attentive, eyebrows drawn to his hairline.

"I promised I wouldn't leave until I found a way to wake him up."

"Are you stupid?" Killian yells. "You made a magical deal for someone who could've died! What would you've done then?"

I shrug. "He was stable, and I didn't know there was a traitor in my life that'd be risking my life and those I care about." The last part I say with a leveling glare at him.

He flinches at my reference, but doesn't back down. "You do not understand this world, little rabbit. Making deals without understanding the magic behind it can lead to fates worse than death."

"I don't need or want your advice." I fold my arms while I bite my cheek, hoping he didn't hear the pain in my voice.

"Little rabbit," he begins.

"Stop calling me that! You lost the right to call me that." Courage builds inside of me to ask for the truth. "Was any of it real?"

He doesn't speak, which drives me further into fury.

"Was it?" I shout at him. "Or was it only because you owe me? A life for a life."

He frowns at my use of his words. His amber eyes burn through me. Eyes that perfectly match the wounded dog from the alley. During the trial of courage, it wasn't him *manifesting* as the dog, it *was* him. It was him all along and he never told me. He hid it from me, along with everything else.

"You helped because of a life debt, because I saved your life in the alley. Tell me I'm wrong."

He doesn't deny my claim, his dark face searching my angry one.

My heart breaks a little more. I had wished I was wrong, held out hope that he'd deny everything, tell me what we had was real. That he cared for me and that's why he helped me. Or he did it out of the goodness of his heart. But he won't. All he's done is warn me about him, this realm, his darkness. Shay did too, even the King. I ignored it all, thinking I saw good in him, but it was all due to some stupid fae debt he believed he owed me.

"Go," I whisper, looking away to hide the pain in my face.

He takes a step forward, but I hold up my hand to stop him.

"Just go."

This time he backs away, drifting to his family. "Come on," his gravelly voice tells them.

I don't watch as the four of them walk away.

Shay's calm voice breaks the silence. "Cadan will wake, now that we got him away from my father. You saved him by getting him away from the castle. My horse will watch him as I take you two home."

"I can watch over him too," Marley adds from the side where she and my sister sit, having watched everything unfold.

I shake my head. "I'm not leaving. I want to help Cadan, and I want to learn to control my powers. I can't safely do that from Earth. Take my sister home."

"Oh, hell no! I am not going home without you!" Shauna stands, limping closer to me. "It's always been you and me. If you stay, I stay."

"It's not safe."

"I don't care. We are not being separated again." She holds her head higher, the stubbornness I share with her seeping out.

My bottom lip trembles. "Are you sure?"

"Positive."

I lean to hug her, breathing in her citrus scented shampoo. "I love you."

"You and me, forever." She squeezes before letting go.

We turn to Shay, our green eyes a mirrored determination, hers bright and mine murky.

"Alright, but it's a long journey. Let's get Cadan on the horse."

It takes Marley and myself a while to get Cadan on the horse, and in the end Shay helps us with an annoyed grunt. He claims he has more energy now, *Gon'an'rit* already replenishing his life force. So, we assist my sister onto the horse behind Cadan.

Initially, Shauna refused, saying she could walk with the rest of us, but Marley's worry about her leg wound bleeding was enough to convince my sister's hardheaded self to use the horse.

She makes eyes at Marley when the fae isn't looking, and I can't help but chuckle to myself. Leave it to my sister to still have one thing on her mind through all of this.

Shay begins to trudge through the woods, still with a slight limp, followed by me and Marley, and in the rear is the horse with Shauna and Cadan. The trees help to block the rain that has become a torrential downpour.

"At least I'm not in heels this time," I murmur.

Shay's shoulders give a subtle shake and I hear a low rumble come from him.

Wow, laughter, a rare sight to behold. He must be weaker than I thought. I snigger to myself, but decide not to poke fun at him, not after what he's been through.

Despite everything, my soul feels almost complete, being surrounded by those who've slowly become my inner circle, having my sister with me once more. Still, in replacement of a tingling sensation is a small hollowness gnawing at my insides.

"What now?" I ask.

"We find a way to stop my father."

A dog howls in the distance.

WHISPER OF DARKNESS

SNEAK PEAK

Chapter 1

Dawn is approaching. The scent of dewy grass tickles my nose. My paws press into the cold ground as I race through the trees. Early morning birds chirp to each other from the treetops, out of harm's way.

It's been too long since I've stretched my legs for a night. There's something exhilarating about being out while the rest of the world sleeps. It's as though I share a secret with the moon and the stars; not that I've seen them in a while.

Another droplet of water finds a path through the canopy, and lands on my snout. I chuff at the abrupt contact. My black fur, which matches my hair, keeps me warm, but what I wouldn't give to bask in the morning glow of the sun after a run. Since clouds have masked the sky for the last fourteen months, I don't believe that will occur anytime soon.

My pace slows as I reach the edge of the *Fiáian* forest. With a deep breath through my snout, I allow my powers to leak from my pores. An inky mist thickens around me, darkness envelops my mind and body. Awareness of the people in the neighboring town appears in my head. More specifically, their fears.

A man whose greatest fear is losing his wife. A little boy afraid of a *Sluagh* stealing his soul. His older sister beside him fears losing her beauty, while an elderly couple fear losing their outdoor cafe if this weather persists any longer. A woman fears falling off a cliff at the edge of the town, and another fears drowning. Even in their sleep, I feel it all.

I wince when heat fills my chest from someone who is closer to me than the rest. It seems to be a young man a couple hills over, coming back from a hunting trip.

His fear is being burned alive.

I fight against the drive to go to him, unleash his fear upon him. Sweat beads on my brow as I push the need deep into my mind. Instead, I concentrate on the swelling black cloud until it consumes me.

Within seconds, I transform myself. Two legs, two arms, ten fingers and toes. Deeply inhaling, I pull my power back into my body, swallowing the darkness as though I can bury it away where it can't touch anyone. But it always touches me.

Continue reading Losing The Light Banshee's Curse Book 0 For FREE by signing up for Kristen Braddock's monthly newsletter!

Killian can turn into a person's worst nightmare and it haunts him. With his two best friends and beloved mate, the darkness within him stays at bay. But there's a problem in the fae realm, one that his mother found, and it's leading to civil unrest. With a secret uprising in the works, he could lose everything he holds dear.

Learn about the day everything changed for Killian and Shay in this prequel novelette to the Banshee's Curse series.

Beyond The Mist
Banshee's Curse Book 2

Cara is magic-bound by her promise to Cadan, keeping her in the fae realm. On the run from the power hungry King, Cara and her friends search for a way to stop him and bring back balance to *Gon'an'rit*. Still hurt by a recent betrayal and confused by her heritage, Cara struggles to find her place within her evolving life.

Perfect for fans of fated mates, enemies to lovers, complicated & diverse characters, slow burn romance, and Celtic folklore.

10% of author profits will be donated to Foundations of Divergent Minds Org.

GLOSSARY

Beansidhe: Commonly known as a banshee. A predictor of death and can cause unconsciousness with their scream

Brownie: also known as a *brùnaidh* or *gruagach*. A household sprite known to come out at night to clean dwellings

Druid: High-ranking fae who are often in positions of power, such as leaders or legal authorities. Very strong powers and are often recognized for their red hair.

Dryad: A forest nymph, whose powers are connected directly with the natural world, especially with the forest and trees (specifically Oak trees).

Fae: Magical race of beings native to *Gon'an'rit*

Fáidh: Also known as a seer, sage, prophet or wise man. Able to see pieces of the future, especially in regards to specific individuals, and their powers drive them to inform the person of what they saw.

Fenian: A Court in the Southern area of *Gon'an'rit*. Known for their virtue of wisdom and a society that does not assign gender at birth.

Gon'an'rit: The name of the fae realm, broken into four Courts.

Korrigan: A water sprite that can see the truth within the past, present, and future.

Naim Competition: Also known as the Wish Competition. Every 7 years, fae from all over Gon'an'rit compete in a set of trials that represent the Virtues of the realm. The winner wins a single wish that is granted by the King and the magic of the realm.

Púca: Can be bringers of good or bad, and have black or white fur. They are known shapeshifters, including taking the form of dogs, birds, horses, goats, cats, and hares. They have the ability to see someone's worst fear and use their shapeshifting abilities to have it manifest before the person.

Rímor: Also known as the court of the kings. The strongest and ruling Court in Western Gon'an'rit, known for its value of Power.

Sluagh: Also known as a host of the dead. A solitary, beastly fae that feast on souls. The only known way to kill one is to weaken it into a transparent state before it can devour more souls and replenish its state.

Spriggan: A fairy often found at old ruins or guarding treasure, said to have gigantic strength and the ability to swell to an enormous size. Often associated with bad dispositions.

Tuatha: The Eastern Court of *Gon'an'rit*, with their values in Courage and Strength. Has the largest high fae army in all of the fae realm.

Ulster: The Northern Court of *Gon'an'rit*. A court known for its Truth and Wit, and the most secluded of all the courts.

Dear Reader

Thank you for coming on this journey with me. I understand some of my characters may not be what you'd typically expect from a fantasy novel. For example, Cara is not always the 'hero' as she battles with her mental health, but I hope you came to love them nonetheless.

I started writing for me, but I continue writing for you. Without your support, excitement, and kind words, I would become lost. So, thank you.

If you enjoyed Whisper of Darkness, please feel free to leave a review. This is the best way to support an indie author outside of initially purchasing and reading the book. I endorse this for any author you love because reviews are what help garner attention and can help make or break an author's success. I'd greatly appreciate it if you do so on Amazon and Goodreads.

Finally, remember it's never too soon to embrace your life, to be the person you want to be, and to take steps toward a better future.

-KB

Stay Up To Date

Keep up with new releases, special offers, giveaways, and exclusive content through any of the following:

Join my monthly newsletter (and get a free novellete):
https://www.kristenbraddock.com/newsletter-1

Join my Facebook Group:
https://www.facebook.com/Kristen-Braddock-Books-533014020945418/

Follow me on Instagram
https://www.instagram.com/kristenbraddockauthor/

ACKNOWLEDGEMENTS

First and foremost, I want to thank my husband, Rudy. Your support for my dreams and everything I've wanted to pursue over the years means the world to me. Not once have you balked at an idea or questioned what I want to accomplish. My love and appreciation of you is endless.

Next, I want to thank my family. Thank you to my sister for being the first to celebrate my successes. Thank you to my dad who helped me write stories as a kid into the wee hours of the morning when my hand got tired. Thank you to my mom for believing I had the imagination to become a published author since I was little.

A huge shout out to my beta, editing, and critique-partner team— Jess Grimes, Becky James, Claerie Kavanaugh, Francesca Ryde, Pearl Amistoso, Caroline Jones, and Jennifer Perry. Chinelo Anyadiegwu, my sensitivity reader for Cadan, you are a God(dess) and I have no words with how invaluable your insight and feedback was. Thank you a thousand times over. This novel, this series, is stronger and more developed because of all of you. Both myself and my readers are grateful for all your help.

Finally, a huge thanks to you, my reader. Thank you for reading this book, and thank you for reading into the acknowledgement section. Without you, I could only go so far.

About the Author

Characters and their worlds have inundated Kristen's mind since she was a kid. Traveling to far off places and having words on a piece of paper transform into entire scenes pulling at her emotions is an obsession.

Her goal as a fantasy author isn't solely to relish in her imagination, but to bring representation to this genre. She wants stories with characters who are diverse inside and out. Their differences are not the focal point of the narrative, but rather a natural part of their being. Due to this, you will often not only find characters of varying ethnicities, but also of the LGBTQ+ community, who battle diseases, are neurodiverse, and plenty of other areas that make us all so different from each other. These are not their defining qualities. It's simply a part of who they are.

When Kristen isn't cooped up on her computer or curled up with a book, she is often outdoors-- traveling, hiking, snorkeling, diving, camping, etc.

Currently, she resides in California with her husband and fur babies (two dogs and a cat).

WHISPER OF DARKNESS

www.ingramcontent.com/pod-product-compliance
Lightning Source LLC
Chambersburg PA
CBHW031610100726
47898CB00006B/1727